9/14/00
Dear Lisa,
Thanks for
support on fe
for your close *Other* ...
these years. Spread Love,
the word to others.
Gretchen

Those Who Trespass
Against Us

Gretchen Cook-Anderson

Writers Club Press
San Jose New York Lincoln Shanghai

Those Who Trespass Against Us

All Rights Reserved © 2000 by Gretchen R. Cook-Anderson

No part of this book may be reproduced or transmitted in any form or by any means, graphic, electronic, or mechanical, including photocopying, recording, taping, or by any information storage or retrieval system, without the permission in writing from the publisher.

Published by Writers Club Press
an imprint of iUniverse.com, Inc.

For information address:
iUniverse.com, Inc.
620 North 48th Street
Suite 201
Lincoln, NE 68504-3467
www.iuniverse.com

ISBN: 0-595-09659-X

Printed in the United States of America

Dedication

This book is dedicated to my parents, Freddie and Rachel Strickland Cook, and was penned in loving memory of my grandparents, Simon and Willie Mae Strickland, and to the late Ronald H. Brown, who brought definition, dignity and statesmanship to the Secretary's post at the Department of Commerce.

Epigraph

Trust
Confidence or firm belief in the honesty, dependability or
power of someone or something.
American Heritage Dictionary

Acknowledgements

I would like to thank my very good friend, sister-of-the-heart, and inspirer, Sharon Shahid, whose words of wisdom and encouragement re-lit the fires of days when the words would not come as smoothly as I wished. I thank TaRessa Stovall for her you-can-do-it-girl attitude and follow up phone calls to check up on my progress on this manuscript. I thank Dawn Florence for her friendship—and the long, expensive long distance phone calls we have spent talking about this manuscript. And…to my husband Thomas-thanks for your love, supportive hugs and enthusiasm. And, finally, to my mother, Rachel, my "soul's inspiration", who has always believed in my ability to do best at whatever I tried, and who has lived her life with an enviable degree of goodness, forgiveness and sincerity.

Introduction

The anger in the eyes behind the knitted mask flashed at Janet as the man moved closer to the row of teller windows. Nothing but hate stared back at her. The barrel of his sawed-off shotgun darted wildly in the air in a random manner, the gunman's pointer and middle fingers fidgeting nervously around its trigger.

"Bitch, you deaf? I said, get the fuck away from that window!" he shouted in Janet Polasky's direction. She hesitantly moved backward, careful not to trip over her purse that laid strewn on the floor, kicked over in desperation by her colleague Vanessa Ruiz.

Janet felt the blood rush to her head and the tips of her fingers go numb from instant fear. She tried to shake the sense of impending doom that had taken her over the moment she noticed the young, strawberry-blond woman reach hesitantly in an oversized bag hanging from her shoulder.

Janet tried to calm herself, praying that the intruders would not hear the loud thumping of her heart, racing so quickly as to make the rising nausea uncontrollable.

"If you fucking move, you'll be fucking dead, now get the hell out of my way!" shouted the blond, stepping behind the teller window to snatch at the crisp bills visible in the open drawers.

The high Northern California afternoon sun radiated through the narrow, elevated windows of the bank, bouncing off the camouflaged interlopers' shimmering gun metal. The four gunmen moved through the bank with speed, warning customers to remain still and silent, threatening to plow down anyone who dared to challenge their authority.

Janet stared at the small silent alarm button under her window while pulling frantically at the sleeve of her polyester button-down blouse. Her eyes drifted over to peer at Russell Williams, the branch guard on duty. Russell, still armed, stood with his hands held above his head as ordered. He returned her look, signaling with the wink of his left eye and movement of his brow that she should carefully move to push the button. Janet blinked her eyes in acknowledgement.

Her gaze fell to the calendar on the right panel of her window. *June 6, 1972*, just two days away from her twenty-third birthday. She tried to steady her hands, afraid that her shakiness might cause her to misjudge the location of the button. She was jolted by a menacing voice.

"You fucking pigs! All of you…part of the goddam problem in this country, working these slave jobs for slave wages," yelled the one who was obviously the leader—tall and black and wearing a black collared shirt, jeans and boots.

"All of you should be working to further the cause of the people! These presidents are gonna fuel our cause, the *people's* cause. Fuck all of y'all. Cowards. Shameful cowards…Hey, man," he cried out from behind his mask. "Move a goddam inch and I'll have the pleasure of shooting the daylights out of you! My queen, take that guard's gun. *Now*!"

The strawberry blond began to move toward Russell Williams, one hand reaching toward his holster, the other firmly gripped around the trigger of her .44 magnum. Janet's thoughts swung wildly to the plans she had for her birthday.

Her husband Dan had said he was going to take her out to see "The Godfather" followed by dinner at Elardo's, the cozy little restaurant in Orinda near her hair salon. She just loved Marlon Brando. He reminded her of an Italian version of her own father. Dan had already surprised her with a new lava lamp, glowing with alternating currents of orange and blue and yellow. She loved it. And she loved him. He was so good to her. Now all she prayed for was the chance to see his face again, to feel his arms around her, his voice soothing her, safe from the maddening commotion taking place before her.

Janet prayed that the God to whom she had not always been faithful would keep her from harm, would just come to her defense this once. She would do anything, promise anything to Him if he would just let her reach that button without being seen. "Oh God, please help us!" she whispered softly, feeling a wisp of air escape her lips.

Without thinking further, as if another second would leave her paralyzed, Janet deftly crept toward the button at the same moment that Russell reached for his holstered .38. The masked black man spun around, his trigger finger in motion.

A shot rang out. The bullet slammed into Russell's upper chest. Russell's large body slumped over the branch manager's desk, while the now-limp body of the strawberry-blond fell in slow motion to the black-and-white-tiled floor.

The leader of the armed group ran to the panting woman, at once aware that his shot had reached its destination only after penetrating her neck first. "Anthony! I'm shot. I'm…shot, Anthony. Uhh…God, I'm shottttt…" she said, trembling, as the redness of her blood emerged from her lips and ran along her jawline, staining her burnished-blond hair. "Don't let the pigs get me, kill me here, just do it baby…Anthony, please…" she begged, pulling at his shirt.

The armed man released the dying woman and ran furiously toward Janet, his rifle's barrel pointed directly at her face. "*You!* If you hadn't moved, none of this would have happened! You just killed my wife, bitch!" the gunman screamed at Janet. Her forehead tingled with fear, her knees felt as if they would give way if she didn't grab for something to steady her legs. Janet reached for the coathanger to her left—just to keep standing.

The impact of the bullet knocked her through the air causing her shoulders to slam against the back wall of the branch. Janet sank to the floor, grabbing at her chest. She wiped at the stickiness that dampened her blouse—her auburn hair—the red torrent that pooled below on the black-and-white squared tiles, seeping below the crack between the floor and the wall.

"I...I...I...didn't mean to...I...Oh, God, help me. O-u—r father...who art in hea...ven...hallowed be thy name," panted Janet, groping for the silver cross charm around her neck. The gunman rushed back over to the flailing blond, her body convulsing. Another gunshot rang in Janet's ears as she struggled to retain her senses. She could hear the voice of Vanessa Ruiz in the foreground, gasping. "He killed his own wife. He'll kill *all of us*. Ohhhh, ohhh," she sobbed uncontrollably.

The gunman yelled for the remaining two intruders to flee the branch with their money-filled back packs. He paused and looked down at the dead blond. "Y'all mothafuckas! This shit didn't *hafta* go down this way," wailed the leader, his voice shaking slightly as he backed his way out of the rear door of the bank. "People don't listen. The power is on *our* side. She died for *us* mothafuckas. The black man is risin' up! The power...is on...*our* side."

Vanessa Ruiz ran to Janet's side, lifting Janet's head into her lap. "Janet," she whispered. "Janet, we're going to get you some help. You're going to be fine, Janet...Janet, stay with me, *look at me!*"

Janet's breath became labored as a rush of hot, bloody fluid rose like vomit and gurgled in her throat. "Thy kingdom come, thy will be done...on earth as it...uhh, uhhh...is in heaven," Janet held her hand up to see the blood dripping from her fingers. She looked up at Vanessa, her hand falling onto Vanessa's arm.

Her birthday, she had to be there for her birthday.... She was going to move the new lava lamp over to the dining room table where her friends could see it better during her party.... her new blouse, how would she get this stain out...her hair was getting so...sticky...oh, the pain, something was...

"Give us this…day, our…daily…bread, and for…give us, our tres…passes," Janet gasped, staring at Vanessa. Vanessa mouthed words she couldn't hear, her movements were jerky, fuzzy. The light from the sun was blinding her. Too bright. "…as we, forgive those…who…uhh, uhh, ohh, tress…pas-sssssssss…against, usssss…"

"Janet! Janet!" shrieked Vanessa, shaking Janet's arms. "Did someone call an ambulance?! Janet! Talk to me, look at me! *Janet! No! Janet!*"

1

Over 20 years later, December 18

Rachel hung up the phone and sighed. For the third time in half an hour some nut had called the office and panted ominously for several seconds, saying nothing. It frustrated the hell out of her, broke her concentration, already shaky at best, and was beginning to frighten her a little, exactly the instinctive reaction she knew motivated the creep on the other end. *Some people have nothing better to do than get on my nerves,* she thought. Rachel took a quick look up at the clock on the wall to her right. *Damn, 7:45.*

Her desk was a mess. Files and policy briefings uncharacteristically littered her work space. It had been a tough day. She looked out the window of her corner cubicle. A cold winter draft blew flakes of chipped paint off the window sill onto Rachel's desk as she turned up the brightness on her desk lamp. Her window overlooked the horseshoe-shaped driveway of the Rayburn Building, the austere white edifice where many of the nation's Members of Congress drafted the laws that governed the country, battled across party lines and relentlessly campaigned for reelection.

Darkness had fallen over the city hours ago and the Rayburn horseshoe, usually crammed with taxicabs and black sedans picking up and dropping off a parade of political elites, was nearly empty except for a few security guards sharing mugs of coffee by the front door. Capitol Hill appeared to be, oddly enough, nearly deserted this Monday evening before Christmas, despite the ongoing budget battle, furloughed government workers and the rampant rumors of campaign corruption leaking from the Speaker's office. Aside from Rachel, the office was empty and uncomfortably quiet, absent the familiar everyday chatter, ringing phones, the whirring of the copier and the hum of laser printers. Persy Pritchard and Chuck Marinelli had left just half an hour earlier, having slaved over Medicaid budget figures since early morning. Only on the rare occasion in the past four years had she stayed late alone. Rachel glanced over her shoulder into the murkiness that was the rest of the office. Except for her lamp and the light in the supply closet, the lights had all been extinguished one by one as the Congressman's staffers had departed for home.

Seeking relief from the stuffiness of the overheated building, Rachel Mooreshelton reached up and lifted the rickety, flaking window frame a couple of inches, letting in a chilly draft. Cool air helped her to think. She needed all the help she could get tonight to formulate arousing, smooth-flowing thoughts that would help redefine Georgia Congressman Raymond Jackson, Jr.'s position and that of the Black Caucus on key issues in the coming election year.

She hated the fact that he'd put all the weight on her, a 26-year old legislative assistant with a gift for word weaving, to script a speech that would get pulses racing, emotions fueled and minds thinking. The black electorate needed a match lit, he'd told her, needed to know that these were desperate times. The recent aftermath of conservative Republicans' takeover of Congress and its agenda made her feel she had to craft nothing less than the blueprint for the second coming of the Civil Rights Movement! It was a hell of a lot of pressure, but she also knew that the Congressman needed her and had every confidence in her abilities. She'd pulled it off before. And that's what life on Capitol Hill was all about. Pressure and politics.

Beltway politics weeded out thousands every year who just couldn't take it, Type A eager beavers poised to save the world, but who lacked enough "bitch" or "balls" in their repertoire of policy hocus-pocus, or the thick armor of a strong sense of humor to survive. Rachel had never had much in the way of "bitch" nor "balls", but up to now, had made it by mostly on strong conviction and rugged loyalty to Congressman Jackson. Now, she needed all that plus a little inspiration. A press conference had been scheduled for tomorrow at two p.m. with other members of the Caucus, and her words had to be just right…The delicate features of her face, two shades darker than wet sand, went taut. The tangle of metaphor, church sermon, and hard statistic, racing through Rachel's mind, had to encompass the essence of Congressman Raymond Jackson, Jr.'s vision and the growing needs of his predominantly black constituency.

The phone rang again, just as Rachel's thumb and index fingers tapped the computer keys of her Packard Bell. She hesitated for several moments, wary of yet another encounter with the voiceless breathing that had sent a creepy tickle up her arms. Often the Congressman would call late into the evening requesting changes to a speech or some piece of bill language. But especially tonight before a major meet with the press, he could be phoning her from the swank Washington Hilton across town where he was attending one of several annual awards banquets, honoring the who's who of Washington's black elite. Rachel impatiently grabbed the handset.

"Hello, Congressman Jackson's office," she mumbled tentatively. The voice on the other end brought a relieved, dimpled smile to her face.

"Hey girl," she giggled, hearing the funny nasal voice of her girlfriend Dawn.

"Why so tense, Miss Politics?"

"…I sound tense because I'm still at work at eight at night while you're home chillin' on your couch watching Law & Order! No, but really, I've got a miracle of a speech to write, oh, by the time the sun comes up tomorrow, and some nut keeps calling the office breathing like a mad animal."

"You know you should know better than to be there by yourself this late. You gonna be okay?"

"Yeah, the door's locked. I'll be fine. Look, if I was afraid to stay late, I wouldn't still be working on the Hill."

"Rach, guess who I saw looking cute on prime time last Thursday?"

"You caught me on CNN last week, huh. Yeah, well, one of the perks of the job. I got to sit in in Persy's place. They needed enough black faces on the panel to make sure a debate on affirmative action would be *balanced*. But did I look good? Um hmm, right answer, right answer." After a few minutes of animated laughter, Rachel's watch told her she needed to get back to the speech.

"Yeah, yeah, yeah. I've gotta go back to staring at this computer screen," she said emphatically.

"Wait a minute. Don't even *think* you're gonna get away that easily without telling me about this mystery man of yours," purred Dawn. "Everybody knows you've been sneakin' around with *somebody*. Give up the goods."

"Um hmm. I haven't been hiding anybody from you, girl. Please," Rachel said working to change the subject quickly. "Look, I have *really* got to go. Enjoy the Monday night line-up for me."

"I'm not finished with you yet Miss Rachel. You're gonna spill the beans on this man sooner or later. And you *know* this!"

"Okay, whatever," Rachel smirked, a wide grin on her face. "Goodnight!"

With her mood lightened, Rachel hung up the phone and zoomed back in on the sentence she needed to finish in the second paragraph. The phone rang again.

"Dawn! I thought I told—" The silent anonymous caller breathed heavily. Rachel could feel her temperature rise.

"Look, you either say something or stop calling here!" she said, her voice rising. "I don't have time for this, and I won't be picking up again, so you might as well stop!" She waited seconds for anything but the spooky breathing on the open line. That was it. She'd had it.

"It's all over for him, you know." Rachel was jarred by the voice, someone's attempt at a crude disguise. The caller repeated the message.

"Who is this? What are you talking about? I'll call security. I swear, I'll call security!" Rachel slammed the phone down with the force of an axe fall. *I don't need this shit tonight,* she thought. She rubbed her temples with the middle fingers of both hands and attempted to shove the disturbing call into the back reaches of her consciousness. She needed to be focused, unperturbed, composed.

A nearly inaudible buzz could be heard from the glow of her lamp, which illuminated tiny specks of dust build-up on her computer monitor, keyboard and the surface of the walnut-paneled desk where she sat. The rythmic swivel of her ergonomic office chair squeaked out faint noises as she rocked gently. The cool draft that blew under the crack in the window resonated like air being sucked through a straw. All else was silent.

*   *   *

HALF AN HOUR LATER, Rachel rose lazily from her chair and stretched, her movements pulling awkwardly at her short, form-fitting gray wool skirt and cream-colored button-down blouse. It had become apparent to her that she'd be pulling a late-nighter on this one. She took a quick glance at the words leaping at her from the computer screen. Rachel's mind roamed, a mish mash of policies, campaign rhetoric and soundbites swooshed around in her head, forming no coherent pattern of thought that she could bring to life. She was tired and stuck, drawing a blank of major proportions. This hadn't always been a problem.

When her suede, high-heeled shoes first ascended the white, marble steps of the Rayburn Building for her first day on the job, a rush of anticipation and a sturdy idealism had fueled her pace. It wasn't long, however, before some of the surly realities of lawmaking began to chip away at her textbook ideas on just how a bill became a law. Public displays of cronyism, nepotism, and vote buying on the Hill, all done with a slap on the back or a hand shake, across racial and party lines, had begun to make her grow increasingly sour on political life. The hell if she knew what forces had driven the southern Congressman's unremitting political hunger all these years...

Many of Rachel's upwardly mobile girlfriends had seriously doubted the common sense that the Congressman admired in her. *A government job? Girlfriend, are you crazy? You're not going to make any money, and politicians are full of shit,* they had told her. And no doubt, her salary left a lot to be desired. A sixty-thou-a-year corporate paycheck, or stock-optioned Internet start-up job was something all the long nights at the office would never earn her. Money like that was about as rare on the Hill as partisan consensus on abortion rights.

Rachel had turned down acceptances to a dozen top-name law schools and shut her ears to Henry Mooreshelton's angry declaration that his daughter had lost the good mind God gave her and had wasted all the money he'd put into her Ivy-League education. In her opinion, there were enough lawyers of color out there already without her joining the bunch. In her opinion, more brothers and sisters needed to be on the inside *making* the laws.

As a Congressional aide, she would not get her own cushy office, with a big desk and a potted plant since the trappings of the Congressman's office weren't exactly oozing with largesse, by any account. And there were no bonuses, no fat commissions and no company-paid vacations for putting out constituent fires. But then money wasn't really the pot of gold she was chasing after anyway. She had chosen to do what she loved.

Restlessly, Rachel stared up and out into the darkness at the shadowed portrait of Congressman Jackson on the far wall in the central room of the office, so large and striking as to grasp the attention of even the casual visitor to the office. There was no denying the man was a heavyweight.

Rachel's boss had served nine terms thus far, was Ranking Member on the powerful Appropriations Committee, had been the chairman of the Congressional Black Caucus for the past two years, a position that granted him high visibility as the voice of the 40-odd black members of Congress, and had the ear of the President on all "minority issues key to the national interest." In fact, in the current Administration, Jackson had served as President Gray's advisor on matters that had wreaked havoc on race relations in the country over the past year, wresting that position from others among the African-American leadership who felt more worthy.

Rachel's bladder tugged at her without warning, pulling her out of her thoughts as abruptly as a child tugging at its mother's shirttail. Still standing from her stretch, but exhausted and fidgety, she headed out into the outer office toward the small staff restroom to the right near the main entrance to the Congressman's office.

Rachel walked into a tiny, two-stall restroom with an unlabeled door, serving both the male and female staff of the office. During regular office hours, Rachel would usually just knock and wait to hear whether a male or female voice answered from inside before she entered, and it was the same custom everyone else in the office usually followed to avoid any provocation that might invite nasty sexual harassment charges. Rachel emerged from the stall and casually scrutinized her image in the small mirror above the cracked marble sink.

Everything about the Baltimore native said, "African American, and proud of it." The long, conservatively-styled, medium-width braids. The delicate roundness of her lips. The high, royal cheekbones. The deep, midnight eyes complemented by lengthy lashes that, like a ranch hand's lasso, were apt to rope in any man who made her mouth water. She'd been told by admirers for years that she strongly favored actress Angela Bassett, a serious compliment coming from the brothers. Everything about her exuded a beautiful blackness that the covers of *Ebony* and *Jet* would eat up, except the absence of a boyfriend of fine, ebony stock…*Ack!*

Something hit the floor with a rude thud outside the restroom, jerked Rachel from her thoughts and sent her rushing to the closed door, engulfed in sudden alarm at the faint sound of footsteps rushing out into the corridor beyond the American flag standing at attention outside the Congressman's office. Uneasiness still nagged at her from the vivid and disquieting memory of the evening's crank calls. As she opened the door, though, she suddenly felt her uneasiness begin to quell. It probably was just a member of the staff who had probably just returned for something left behind.

*   *   *

WITH HER PULSE STILL POUNDING, Rachel peered into the reception room of the office. It appeared exactly as she had left it. She walked at a clipped pace to the main entrance to the office and checked to find the lock still on. Her heart's throbbing slowed a notch. She knew it was strict practice and courtesy for the last few staffers on their way home to lock the door behind them to secure the few who were forced to stay late, despite the presence of well-trained Hill security guards who regularly patrolled the outer corridors.

On the surface, nothing appeared to have been moved either. Darkness in the remainder of the five-room office still swathed the place in a dusky stillness as if Rachel were standing in dense fog rising off a quiet river. Feeling slightly more at ease, Rachel walked in padded, shoeless feet straight ahead and down the short hallway that led to the Congressman's and Persy Pritchard's offices. Inside Persy's office something seemed amiss.

Persy, damn, that's what happens when you're always in such a rush, Rachel reasoned. *It must have been Persy.* She ducked into the immaculately organized office to turn off what she thought was the chief of staff's radio alarm clock. But she flipped his desk lamp on to find a microcassette recorder running a tape, the volume so low that she would never have heard it had there been any noise in the now-silent office. Assuming the tape to be of a press conference or C-SPAN interview on the current budget battle, Rachel turned the volume up to hear if the contents might be anything she could use for her speech.

"....*bank teller, guard and armed female intruder were gunned down today in a botched robbery at California Federal in Oakland. Twenty-three year old teller Janet Polasky of San Leandro, 36-year old security guard Russell Williams of South Oakland and an unidentified white female intruder were pronounced dead on arrival this afternoon at Alameda County Hospital. Witnesses at the scene, including Vanessa Ruiz of Berkeley, attribute the crime to the Oakland-based Black Panther Party, claiming that the unknown assailants, all black males except for the slain woman robber, repeatedly shouted nationalist slogans similar to those of the militant group. Law enforcement officials, including the FBI, are reportedly already seeking information about a young black male, identified as Anthony Ford in connection with the murder-robbery. Marty Rich is at the scene to give us....*"

Rachel lowered the volume, wondering why Persy would be listening to a news report about a bank robbery in California. Rachel always prided herself on being relatively well-read, especially on the history of her own people. But she'd never heard of any story about the Black Panthers being involved in bank robberies. It didn't fit the controversial former organization's style, the way they pumped up media attention. She fast-forwarded hurriedly and pressed play once again.

"...*in other news today, President Nixon charged that—*" the tape halted, clicked and began its automatic-rewind-and-playback.

Rachel put the recorder back on Persy's desk wondering why he would want to listen to news from over twenty years ago, from the *Nixon Administration. Well, she thought, he's probably just doing some research on a policy matter for Jackson, digging up some old audio. There's probably some interesting stuff on here though...from the 70's or something, maybe even some music she could groove to...ooh, maybe some Marvin Gaye...*

Persy had mentioned to her before he had left the office that evening that he was taking off tomorrow to do some Christmas shopping and could be contacted on his pager. She lifted the cassette from the recorder and slipped it in the right pocket of her charcoal gray, wool-and-cashmere blend skirt and tip-toed back toward her cubicle as if this act would somehow be detected. She would listen to it at home tonight and put it back tomorrow during lunch. Hell, Persy had removed things from her desk before without asking. *Big deal.*

On her way out of Persy's office, Rachel halted her stride after feeling something snag her stockinged left foot. She bent down and picked up what appeared to be the corner edge of an old photo. A few inches to her right lay two more pieces of what seemed to be the same photo, a faded color photo. She casually shoved the pieces together on the carpet to see if they connected. Two of the pieces fit together, but the third was apparently missing its mates. All that was visible in the two photo fragments was an urban roadway, and a street sign so far in the background as to be unreadable. The third piece showed three sets of legs, men's legs Rachel figured, two with red leather shoes, with platform heels, the third pair, in the middle, she couldn't quite make out.

Rachel smiled to herself at the sight of those funky shoes. *Persy must be getting rid of his old pictures from the 'old school' 1970's. He probably looked horrible with an eight-inch Afro, butterfly-collared button-down and platforms,* Rachel mused.

She righted the overturned trash can, realizing that Persy must have kicked it over when he'd just returned for whatever. But, Persy'd never even know she had found these fragments, and it would be a trip to show them to Phyllis. Despite the love-hate working relationship between her and Phyllis, they still managed to put their differences aside long enough to share office gossip. She grabbed the pieces of the photos and headed back toward the office she shared with three other aides.

Fully recovered from the crank call scare, Rachel grinned, feeling strangely exhilarated from her brief adventure through the office, as if she had carried off the crime of the century under the watchful eye of the Capitol Hill police. Of course, the past few minutes had amounted to nothing more than added procrastination on her part.

Rachel threw her newly-encountered finds into her shoulder bag, pushed her pad and chewed-down pencil aside, and pulled up the notes that she had drafted earlier. Settled, she sat in front of the black screen, mesmerized by the blinking green cursor. She was a worrier, and tonight, a distracted one at that.

Unresolved tangles in her life were keeping her from completing a full thought. The situation with her new, very *white* and very *Republican* boyfriend, Thad. The ticking time bomb of AIDS that was zapping her brother Yarrick's strength day by day. And the budget mess that was getting on everyone's nerves. On top of all that, D.C.'s Mayor Grace, a sly character whose slick grin and clammy handshake were the least of the traits Rachel despised, had visited the office no less than five times in the past month. A little much, even for His Majesty, despite the fact that Congressman Jackson sat on the House Subcommittee on the District of Columbia, which currently held the fate of the financially battered city in its hands. Even Persy Pritchard had seemed slightly off balance lately, downright nervous....

She was seriously out of her flow tonight. By tomorrow, she'd be a worrier without a job if she didn't get it together fast. A short nap, she decided would be exactly what she needed to kick her mind into gear. It had always helped her in school...She pushed aside the stale turkey sandwich she'd taken a few bites of earlier in the day, adjusted the braids that shaped her slender face, laid her keyboard on top of her computer monitor, crossed her arms before her, and peeped at her watch. *Hmm...Nine o'clock.*

"Okay," she said to herself. "Half an hour to snooze, just thirty more minutes of procrastination. Then I'm getting down to business. No more playing around." Having convinced herself that a half-hour nap would be harmless, she laid her head between her arms, shifted in the chair to shake the sleepy tingle in her right leg, and dozed off.

2

Just a few minutes shy of nine, Persy Pritchard wiped his moist palm against the side of his tuxedo pant leg. *Keep it together, man,* he coaxed himself. He joined in the applause as the Vice President of the United States, his jet black hair fashionably gelled, wound down his long-winded keynote address and, encircled by half a dozen Secret Service agents, departed the podium to a standing ovation,.

It was time for Persy to excuse himself from the unabashedly opu-lent, thousand-dollar-a-plate PPF dinner. Putting People First, a nationally renowned advocacy and legal aid organization was celebrat-ing its twenty-fifth year in the civil rights business, and all of Washington's shining stars had turned out for the exclusive fete. Persy quickly said his apologetic, premature good-byes to his front row table mates, a graying Mid-Western automotive manufacturer, honored that evening for his company's renewed commitment to affirmative action; a bespectacled, 72-year old Civil Rights heroine; and the aging president of one of the country's most famous historically black colleges.

"Persy, well if it isn't the man behind that telecom legislation that's been working in my favor. How has life been treating you, son?" Persy slowed his pace and turned around to see a squat, round, silver-haired white man, who had already managed to dig his fingers into Persy's arm. John Wayne McCormack was CEO of the nation's third largest long-distance telecommunications company. The year's huge battles over competition and service rates in the industry had been acrimo-nious. Persy and his boss were among the architects of legislation that would determine the way the industry made its money and which companies would make money in which markets. It was power they had used as leverage to score votes on other issues. "How's the movement on that amendment language my office sent over three weeks ago? Are we gonna push that through before next session? Things *are* moving in my favor, right?" the man asked, his grip getting tighter.

"John, hearing talks on telecom competition have been postponed until after the winter recess, but we're moving along. Any more progress on the new neighborhood rec center you guys are subsidizing over in Grant Park in center-city Atlanta?" In this business, it was always a game of you-scratch-my-back, I-scratch-yours. It was a dirty little necessary evil Persy had accepted years ago, and had used to the Congressman's and his constituency's benefit. The two men smiled knowing grins at one another. The older man winked, shook Persy's hand and stood close, his breath ripe with a few too many glasses of the evening's Chardonnay.

"Now Persy, you know we'll come through on that by summer. Construction starts in March. Soon as the weather breaks. So, does our bill have the Congressman's support?" Persy took steps to extricate himself from the man's point blank inquiry.

"Things look good. How about that? But we sure would like to see that rec center up and operational by June. Our children need a place to play, stay off the streets. John, as always, it's been a pleasure."

"You leaving us so early?" Persy began backing away from McCormack, whose chubby, diminutive frame made him look far less the image of a Fortune 500 CEO than an unemployed couch potato.

"Yes, we've got some busy days ahead to settle this budget battle. I'm afraid I haven't slept well from all the long hours. I'm bowing out early. If you'll excuse me." Persy gave the man a plastic smile as he had so many times that evening and turned away to leave.

He watched a towering, dark-brown figure with an equally imposing carriage make his way like a sleek panther through the thick crowd of cultured black corporate ladder-climbers, educators, politicos and other notables barely recognizable for famed deeds done long ago. Congressman Jackson charmed, grinned, hugged, kissed, and high-fived every other sequined and tuxedoed individual he passed. They knew he cared.

Ray Jackson, Jr. was, at once, admired and resented by many of his colleagues for the cozy political and personal relationships he had forged with not only the President but with other, old-line Democrats *and* Republicans. He was one of the few black Members who could float with ease and expert grace through both the black and white political worlds. Persy stood in awe, even after all these years of how, with just the right mix of compliment, pat on the back, and whispered persuasion, Jackson could win vote here, an amendment there—the game being somehow his to play.

The man was a master in the fine art of contact politics. As he schmoozed the "booshie" crowd, he knew every name, every problem and exactly what to say to make each person feel important. It was the sincerity that Persy knew was so real, the genuine concern that Ray Jackson felt for the people who had re-elected him term after term, that bothered him, that made him feel so bad about what he had to do.

Then he noticed *her*. The face that emerged from behind the Congressman caused Persy to clench his teeth. He tightly squeezed his program booklet and turned hurriedly to go. The last thing he needed was to be forced to confront Juditha Hurley again tonight.

"Persy, running home so soon?" asked the voice of a woman who'd made her way through the crowd with lightning speed. The PPF's executive director stood behind him, her very presence demanding attention, her intense hazel eyes awaiting a reply. "Now, Persy, you know we need to talk, and tonight is as good a time as any, I think. Why don't we take a walk, sweetheart?" As if he'd heard a dog whistle, silent to all but himself, Mayor Grace appeared at Persy's side, his guileful smile intact as always.

"Yes, Persy," he whispered, adjusting his kente-cloth bow-tie. "We have a little unfinished business about that budget request we need to have." There was no more that needed to be *discussed* about the mayor's inflated budget request. Persy knew exactly what they wanted from him. Those two had been sharing secrets for years, since their well-documented civil rights days. But some secrets weren't worth keeping. Some secrets needed to be told. They were the last two people he would be talking to, about *anything*.

Without anything in the way of the fanfare accorded the notables in the grand ballroom, Persy rushed anonymously past both Hurley and Grace, out of the gala event and into the open doors of a cab, still wiping his palms repeatedly against his pants. He knew they wouldn't follow, at least not then. They wouldn't dare make a scene in front of Washington's creme de la creme. And no one but Hurley or Grace would even miss him.

*   *   *

PERSY KNEW HE'D BEEN WALKING A dangerous tightrope for months now. He looked down at the pile of papers—bound, official-looking documents marked with the seal of more than one government agency, his own scribblings, a set of cassette tapes, recent news clippings from the *Post* and the *Times*, copies of bank statements, a few other press clips and three stamped, addressed envelopes—scattered on the rumpled bedspread of the queen-size bed in his apartment at 12th and N Streets near downtown. The address was his third in nine months, a result of the paranoia, warranted or not, that had begun to haunt his every waking moment. Beyond the closed doors of his latest apartment building, he-she hustlers solicited passing cars in the rough-edged, partially-gentrified neighborhood, shivering in rear-less tight jeans while showing off exposed hormone-induced breasts.

Like an Olympic runner on a stop watch, Persy had timed the movements to come, down to the very last moment. Had thought them
through and then re-thought them for weeks now. He had slept
uneasily, and had tossed and turned once his decision had been made.
Sweat stains spotted his pillow and sheets despite the arctic-like wind
outside the room's two narrow, curtained windows.

The glare of light from the small, half bath in the master suite of the
two-bedroom unit shone brightly onto the bed's mirrored headboard.
Persy halted his paper rustling long enough to stare at his reflection. His
eyes were tired and red. The lack of a good night's rest was almost too
apparent. He reached up and with the fingers of his right hand, gently
patted the dark-shaded patches underneath his eyes, now a hue darker
than his excema-blotched skin, the color of day-old coffee with just a
dab of cream. Lately, he'd begun to look older than his thirty-three
years. His hair was usually kept cut meticulously low to his scalp. He
had a well-shaped head; the low cut fit it perfectly. Since his college days
at Morgan State, Persy had always thought that the shape of his head
was one of the best features of his otherwise uninspiring appearance. As
a tall, lanky young man with an over-sized eagle beak of a nose, paper
thin lips, round, slightly bulging eyes and bad skin, he knew that his
calling in life did not include seducing women. But intelligence inherited from both of his working-class parents, an inbred respectfulness
toward women that so many of the sisters held out for in a man worth
marrying, and a better-than-average paying job as Congressman Ray
Jackson, Jr.'s chief of staff had helped him to compensate for what he
lacked in looks.

On this night, Persy ran his fingers over a rough, kinky black tuft of
hair that had become unsightly. Even the staff had been riding him
about his need to take a quick emergency trip to the barbershop. But
other, more compelling things had been consuming his thoughts. His
appearance was inconsequential compared to the shocking information

he'd uncovered slowly and painstakingly over the past two years. The whole terrible truth of it, of more than he'd bargained for.

He hated what he knew he had to do. He hated like hell that his life had become so complicated, so secretive. He hadn't had a date in over nine months for fear that a curious young woman might ask too many questions about the stacks of government documents, old photographs as well as newer ones and other questionable items assembled neatly on his wicker kitchen table and tucked under the top cushions of his kente-embroidered couch. He had no desire to hide these things. He'd spent too long categorizing them and placing them in the appropriate piles. Dating had become an inconvenience, and sex a memory he wished like hell he could revive.

Persy carefully and quietly deposited certain papers into certain envelopes, double-checked the postage, licked his well-watered tongue over the flaps and rubbed his hands over them three times to ensure that his saliva had stuck well. His home was quiet, not even a radio to help calm his fragile nerves. In fact, he realized the street, usually annoyingly noisy from heavy automobile and pedestrian traffic, was also silent. After all, it was just after ten at night. He knew it would be over eight hours before Washington commuter traffic again commenced its daily push through the city.

Fully dressed, Persy gathered the remainder of his months of research and placed all of it into a large, unlabeled box which he then taped heavily with shiny brown packing tape, and tucked into the back corner of his walk-in closet. Dark suits, his favorite, hung neatly arranged by shade and season, accompanied by his ties, shoes, and dress shirts, all classified according to color and style.

It was time to go, get it over with, be done with it. This is what it all came down to. The ten years he had worked faithfully and diligently for the Congressman would soon come to an end. He knew it to be as true as his skin was black. He had put his life into his job. It had come to define him. He had worked with Congressman Jackson to build a political stature and reputation for excellence that countered the mediocrity and middle-aged, "fat and happy", "don't-rock-the-boat-if-I'm-still-in-it" attitude of so many of his Black Caucus colleagues. He had helped steer Jackson's career, and the Congressman's undying energy and hunger to successfully widen his political base to include thousands of angry, disillusioned young African Americans, from monied buppies to hand-to-mouth hip-hoppers, looking for real, risk-taking leadership. And Persy had, word-for-word, slaved over an array of legislation over the years only to translate it into the most strategic of laymen's terms for the benefit of the Congressman's most ardent and deep-pocketed contributors. And because everyone with a special interest inside the Beltway knew that it was Hill staffers who held the strongest reins of influence over the nation's legislators, Persy had allowed himself to be coddled and lunched and gifted with everything under the sun, at times outside the confines of lobbying reform protocol—all in the name of pushing the Congressman's agenda.

Persy reached gingerly inside of the top drawer of his expensive cherry wood dresser and pulled out a large brown-tinted bottle of Myer's Rum and walked into the small kitchen of his apartment where he retrieved a liter of refrigerated Coca-Cola. He mixed the two in a tall glass with much more rum than coke, as carefully as a George Washington Hospital surgeon separating Siamese twins, and drank the blend as if he'd been walking the Sahara for weeks without a drop of water. Tears flowed silently from his eyes as he finished the drink that had become his habitual comfort over the past months. Persy's father Isaiah would slap him with such force as to knock the memory out of him if he knew that his only son's life of excellence and undaunted activism had become that of a drunken, suicidal blackmailer.

Persy slowly pulled on his long, puffy, down-stuffed jacket, a black, knitted cap, and thick, black Aramis leather gloves, and reached for his keys, hung ritualistically on a nail by his bedroom door and leaned down to grab the three packages that lay sealed on the bed. He took one more look into the mirror before him. Persy Pritchard, devoted civil servant, proud African American man and community firebrand, once long-time believer in honesty and integrity, the sanctity of law and the word of God. He wavered, his focus thrown off by the trembling in his chest and the alcohol percolating in his bloodstream. He had no choice anymore. Things had gone too far. Too far to go back now. He stood and walked deliberately toward the door. Persy's upper arm muscles tightened around the packages stuffed under his arm as he hesitated for several contemplative seconds, pulled the door closed and shuffled out to an appointment he knew he couldn't miss. Several stops lay ahead of him before the meeting would take place, and time was short.

3

"What are you looking at? You stay in that window long enough, that draft gon' make you sick and you won't be no good for Christmas. I don't kill myself at that dead-end job to come home and have to take care of a grown woman who gets sick from sittin' in a window when the cold is blowin' in. One day you gon' learn. Wait 'til you have babies of your own, you'll know why I worry you all the time 'bout gettin' sick. You my only child, baby, come on away from that window now. Phyllis, did you hear me?"

"Yeah, all right, Mama, I heard you," Phyllis said, not looking away from the window. Her mother was going on and on as she always did. "I'm just watchin' Rodney and them goddam fools outside. Damn, midnight, and they still out there on the corner sellin' that shit. I guess their business don't have no nine-to-five…"

She slowly drifted back into her thoughts, ignoring her mother's pleas to come away from the window and scoldings to stop using profanity in her house. The notorious draft seeped through the lower left corner of the front window, unstifled by the generic-brand plastic wrap that Phyllis's mother had tacked onto all of the windows of the small three-bedroom row house. The house was not fancy, but neat. It sat crunched between dozens of other row houses, some neat, some not. Most occupied, some not.

Twenty-four year old Phyllis Roberson peered out onto the corner of Kennedy and 8th Streets at the four hooded, leather-jacketed men, huddling to keep warm while peeping over their shoulders, on the look out for hopeful customers, the police, or former associates sporting a grudge. They had become a familiar sight recently. She looked across the street at her little '86 Ford Escort, red with a large black gouge on the driver's side from where a distracted driver at the grocery store rammed into her last year.

"Stupid woman didn't have no insurance," she grumbled to herself. "Now I got to drive a hoopty with a black eye, floor board fallin' out, tape cassette busted and bald tires. Damn, I *got* to do better than this." She was tired of driving a car that looked like death was beating down its door, dragging her mother's recycled paper bag lunches to work everyday when it had nothing to do with being eco-friendly but with being cheap, and sitting in the house most weekends because money was tight. Shit, she was a young woman in the prime of her life and wanted to live like she was. She reached into her pocket for a cigarette, then realized she had smoked the last one while watching "America's Most Wanted."

"Shit, can't even smoke a damn cigarette when I need one. I guess I'll be quittin' sooner than I thought…" She let the familiar lingo of her youth roll carelessly off her tongue at home, aware that office life required *Webster's* diction and unsplit verbs. She stuck her finger in her mouth like a baby seeking comfort, and raised her eyes back to the paint-flecked window, back out onto her little window to the world.

She had promised herself that after the abortion, everything in her life was going to change, definitely straighten out for the better. She had finally broken up with Brian after he'd lied to her for the last time. In her vulnerable state, trying to get the hell out of her mother's house and wanting a good man she could build a decent life with, he had promised her anything she wanted to hear. And she'd believed him. *He was gon' quit sellin', get a real job, get his own apartment so they could move in together, and help her pay for school. Well, she was gon' finish school, man or no man.* But after she'd seen him two weeks ago out there with Rodney and his boys, up to the same tired shit, she decided she wasn't having the baby that he didn't yet know about. *She just couldn't.* Phyllis had her own bills and her mother's debts to help pay off. A baby wouldn't have a bank account and couldn't even *bounce* a check.

She'd been working full time as a receptionist for Congressman Jackson for six years, since graduation from D.C.'s tough Ballou High, answering phones, drafting his non-essential correspondence, keeping the front office operating smoothly and keeping her eyes and ears open, serving as office mother and watchdog. Congressman Jackson's constant encouragement for her to finish a college degree had kept her hopes up. Then he could promote her to legislative correspondent, and maybe one day legislative assistant like Rachel Moorshelton. Yeah, that would be the day she could laugh back in Rachel's face, *little Miss So-and-So.* And she had every intention of doing just that. The Congressman was her ticket straight out of the paycheck-to-paycheck misery of life on Kennedy Street. Noise from the right side of the porch interrupted her thoughts.

"Awwww, shit, awwww shit. Come to papa. Come to papa. Ummph, ummph. Awww shit."

"Phyllis, go on outside and get Uncle Jet off that porch," Phyllis's mother yelled from the back in the kitchen. "He gon' freeze out there. I told you about lettin' him sit out there disturbin' the neighbors."

"Mama, that's why you and Aunt Willie need to put him in a home. Don't nobody have time to be watchin' a grown man," Phyllis scowled as she got up from her favorite spot, her nice, warm spot on her late grandmother's old red velvet chair. "Uncle Jet!" she called just barely opening the front door wide enough for the wild-haired man to hear a voice coming from the inside. "Uncle Jet! Come on in now. It's time for you to go on downstairs. You can't sit out there all night."

When the man didn't move from the gray metal porch chair, and continued to rock gently apparently oblivious to the summons, Phyllis leapt outside, tripping over her house shoes, grabbed the man's arm and helped him up and inside, seating him on the dark-green-and-brown mottled sofa, forever sheltered by the hard, sticky plastic Phyllis's mother refused to remove. Pearline Roberson's trademark was plastic— on everything.

Phyllis pulled at the man's coat, while checking his pockets for any leftover cigarettes. "Uncle Jet, we gon' let you sit here for a minute while you get yourself warm, okay. You got to stop sittin' out in the cold. One day we gon' forget you out there."

"Brother, brother, brother, there are far too many of you dying," her uncle sang in a low voice, still oblivious to her presence or the dip in temperature outside. "You know, we got to find a way, to bring some understandin' here today....Aww shit, aww shit, muthafucka, hee...goddam, that's some good shit, that Marvin can sing..."

"Uncle Jet, that language is gon' get you into a helluva of lot of trouble one day. Somebody's not gon' understand you the way we do," warned Phyllis with scolding eyes. "Uncle Jet, do you hear me?" She stared into his eyes, empty of any recognition, his facial muscles twitching.

Before a lot of things had gone wrong, Robert Leroi Strong had had a sharp mind and a lancet tongue, a gift for intellectual gab. Years ago, too many to count now, figured Phyllis, he'd bragged about getting off Kennedy Street and buying his mother a big house on the Gold Coast, up on 16th Street where well-to-do blacks mowed green lawns, took vacations to the Caribbean and sent their children to private schools. Looking at him now, Phyllis saw nothing of the man she was told he once had been. In his teens, he'd picketed white-run stores refusing to hire the black kids in the neighborhood, led organized groups of young people to help rebuild parts of black Washington after the riots in '68, and had testified at city council hearings on flagrant omissions in his school's American history texts of the accomplishments of black pioneers.

Robert's activities had been cut short when he, like thousands of Washington's young, black men in their prime, was drafted into the military—the airforce—and sent to Vietnam in 1969. The family never did figure out how he'd managed to keep childhood Tourette's Syndrome

hidden from military medical personnel, but everyone in the neighborhood knew that Robert, III, or "Jet" as the family called him, was flying
planes, shooting down Viet Cong.

In 1971, Phyllis's grandmother had been informed that Jet was being
sent home, dishonorably discharged, for emotional instability, worsening Tourette's and an incorrigible attitude toward superiors. The
heartbroken woman swore that her boy's mind was sharp, always had
been, and that he must have just seen something over there that his
mind just couldn't take, but the Veteran's Hospital had diagnosed the
young man with a severe chemical imbalance that would prohibit him
from working steady ever again. Back in his mother's house, twenty-
one-year old Jet had refused the diagnosis and treatment and had
packed his bags unexpectedly one night for the West Coast. The family
had figured he was dead after two years with no word. But then Phyllis'
mother had taken him back in, no questions asked when he returned,
visibly more disturbed than when he'd left.

The man now spent his days down in the basement, made into a
small apartment, with the doors allowing access to the rest of the house
kept locked. Despite the VA's assertions that Jet was no threat to anybody, Phyllis's mother had never trusted her brother's mental state, and
detested his uncontrollable cursing and spitting.

"Phyllis," the man said, a rare bit of clarity in his eyes. "Just *look* at
you, all grown up and pretty. You sure took after your Mama." But just
as soon as Phyllis allowed herself to feel optimistic—that maybe *this*
time he would be back for good, Jet's eyes reverted again, claiming that
far-off-distant look, as if he were staring straight through her.

"The truth always got a way of comin' out...hee," he mumbled,
leaving Phyllis once again disappointed, still longing for the Uncle Jet
she knew as a child, the man who'd been the only father figure in her
life. "They're comin'. I know they're comin' for me. I'm just waitin',
you know...the Lord shall reward the doer of evil according to his

wickedness…um hmm. Can't no one hide from God. Shit…" Jet mur-
mured and went silent, his eyelids still twitching wildly.

*   *   *

WITH THE TV DRONING ON IN THE BACKGROUND, and her mother fry-
ing chicken for Tuesday's lunches, Phyllis adroitly led the middle-aged
man down the narrow, wooden stairs to the warmth of his stale,
unkempt basement apartment, gave him a gentle kiss on his cheek and
returned to her favorite spot at the front window, shaking her head at
how pitiful he'd become.

She looked at herself in the window's reflection, seeing the face of a
slightly overweight, honey-colored young woman of average good
looks, glowing from the lights of the Christmas tree. She placed her
hand on her naturally plump lower abdomen, and through the cotton
sweater and waistline of her size fourteen jeans, she tried to feel the life
that was now inside of her, eight weeks old. The thought nagged at her
again. *She just couldn't have a baby now.* She'd never be able to finish
school, and would never get rid of Brian, a brother she knew would
just drag her down. She still had too many dreams to be weighed down
by motherhood.

Half of her friends had had babies in high school. Some of them had
more than one. All but one were living a daily struggle, barely making
rent, burdening mothers, aunts and grandmothers who served as baby-
sitters while they worked, living with any man who would have them
and their children, sometimes even when they were abusive. Phyllis
would have to make her decision by New Year's. The doctor had already
warned her about possible complications from further procrastination.

It was getting late, *10:15.* She decided to head straight to bed so that
she could roll into the office early tomorrow, before all the distractions
from the phone got started and the staff had had time to start picking
at her nerves. She had a lot of paper work to get off her desk before

Congress recessed later in the week, and tomorrow would be a good day to take care of it.

Phyllis plodded into the kitchen, grabbed a drumstick from the foil on the kitchen table and said goodnight to her mother. Once in her small bedroom, she quickly peeled off her clothes, and looked in the mirror for the slightest early protrusion in her belly, again touching and caressing the round of her stomach as if awaiting movement.

Phyllis threw on the same Culture Club T-shirt she'd worn since her days at Ballou High, hopped onto the high-posted bed, quilted in one of her grandmother's creations and set her small alarm clock for six a.m...If she could make it into the office by seven, that would give her a good two hours or more to clear her desk of papers and finish mailing the last of the Congressman's Christmas cards to supporters. During the holidays, most of the staff usually came in later in the mornings, talked on the phone mostly to friends and took long lunches before going home early. The Congressman would appear not to notice, wrapped up himself in the mood of the holidays. But this year was different. The budget ruckus had everybody on edge and they had all been working longer hours than usual.

The long hours, or something, had to be taking a toll on Congressman Jackson. Phyllis could see it in his eyes lately, even if he'd never admit it. She figured that all the unmarried man really needed was a good woman, especially one like Juditha Hurley.

Hurley was the caliber of woman the Congressman should be with, Phyllis thought. As head of the PPF, she sat at the helm of the country's largest and oldest civil rights organization. She was a Spelman College graduate, Harvard law-trained and had cut her teeth at the Justice Department, working her way up from staff attorney to assistant attorney general under the last Administration, that of two-term Republican President Donald Rowland.

The rumor on Hurley—and Phyllis was always quick to ask about any gossip or unsubstantiated news whenever she pulled morsels of

information from her bevy of well-informed if not-so-well paid receptionist colleagues—was that she had at one time been a black nationalist, with connections to the Black Panthers, underground during her
days at Spelman. *One had to wonder, to see her now.* Juditha Hurley,
though well-respected in Washington's elite black social and political
circles, was thought by many to have sold out. She had, said some,
sacrificed her true convictions for a more conservative stance, taken a
holier-than-thou moral tone in her recent public speeches and had
forged a disturbingly conciliatory connection with select members of
the mostly white Republican and overwhelmingly male Heritage
Council, an age-old partisan policy think tank-cum-bully-pulpit from
which many of the current conservative policies on affirmative action,
urban renewal, and welfare reform emanated. Phyllis refused to believe
any of it.

Hurley was a really pretty woman, *a beautiful woman,* Phyllis
thought admiringly. Her dark brown skin was flawless, like the most
perfect soft glove leather, pulled so taut that its pores disappeared. She
had light brown eyes that set off her whole face, commanding the attention of those who stood near enough to her to catch the hazel glint from
any source of light. Hurley was just the type to put a little strut back into
Congressman Jackson's step. And she'd been seen around the office
enough lately to make Phyllis think she was trying to do just that.

The ringing of the phone on the night table abruptly pulled Phyllis'
mind away from her thoughts. She picked it up to hear Brian's
unwanted familiar voice on the other end.

"Brian, it's late and I'm 'bout to go to bed. Not that I have much to
say to your sorry ass anyway," Phyllis said cutting him off before he
could turn on his charm. "I know you were out there tonight with
Rodney and his gang 'a no good street trash. How do I know? Because
I saw you myself....No, I don't even want to hear it. Look, I'm tired of
this. How 'bout the job you were gon' interview for? The apartment
over on Taylor that you told me you was gon' go see? Brian, you're full

a shit! Look, I've gotta go. Yeah, whatever…Um hmm, yeah, I hear you…I'm just not listenin' anymore. Bri, goodnight!"

Phyllis placed the phone down harder than she had originally intended, reached over and switched off her lamp and sat in the darkness, propped against two bed pillows. A crease of street light intruded through the window shade, illuminating the knitted squares of the bed blanket as Phyllis nudged down under the heavy cover. Phyllis worked to shake the anger and disappointment that she felt toward Brian—and herself for having allowed herself to depend on him to shape her dreams, to feel for him, to let him touch her, kiss her, move his hands, the tips of his fingers over her, his hardness inside her.

The fact that she missed him—his strong ebony chest, his lofty cheekbones, the cleft that dented his chin and drew ever more attention to his square jaw line, the soft smoothness of his shiny, tight ringlets of black hair, the mischievous spark in his sable eyes—angered her the most. She had known from the beginning, somewhere in the back of her mind hidden away where she hoped the knowledge would never surface, that Brian was a loser, someone who would lead her on a roller coaster ride of ecstasy, frustration, and noncommittal love. She knew it now, but still loved him despite his flaws, his lies. However, she thought, tugging at her T-shirt, tucked in a twisted fashion underneath her torso, in this new year, she would get over him anyway. He was fine, but he was no good.

With a sense of satisfaction in her decision to overcome the weakness that she had for the silky-voiced Brian, a silent prayer, and a reminder to herself to prepare thank you notes tomorrow to those who had attended the Congressman's holiday office party, Phyllis inhaled the homey scent of cold rub, leftover perfume and old-house musk, and drifted off into a comfortable slumber, oblivious to the invariable sounds of motorists passing down a slush-packed Kennedy Street, and to the light snow beginning to fall. In fact, she was so snug and drowsy wrapped in the cocoon of her homemade blanket, that she also failed to hear the heavy footsteps that made their way forbiddingly across the front porch toward the door of the row house, stopping abruptly as if awaiting a signal to go further.

4

A white camper with Maryland tags pulled up abruptly at the curb, its tires skidding on the frozen snow as it came to a stop. The driver, covered completely in dark clothing, his face hidden from any pre-dawn observer by the shadow of the streetlight post that stood on the corner nearly eclipsing the blue U.S. postal mailbox just behind it, lifted up the camper's rear door, grabbed a corded bundle of papers and threw them against the left leg of the mailbox. He jumped back into the camper's driver's side, and skidded back out into the street just as a pedestrian was approaching the mailbox.

The pedestrian, hooded in a ski jacket on which one could just barely make out the image of the Chicago Bulls logo, moved quickly in the direction of the mailbox, opened the front hatch, peered over his shoulder and ahead of him. Satisfied that the streets were empty, aside from the passing Yellow Cab shifting to make a left turn, he dropped in a small, thin envelope.

The pedestrian slipped unexpectedly on the cold December ice as he stepped over the stack of bound newspapers on the sidewalk. He looked down at the stack as he caught his balance and, seeing the date on the top page, tore away the paper's header and front page headline—*The Washington Post*, Tuesday, December 19, *Speaker of the House Blasingame Denies Dems Claims of Campaign Finance Corruption.* Persy's thoughts were crystal clear for the first time in over a year. At first, disappointment and a saddening sense of betrayal had gripped him. Then over the months that energy had evolved into anger, obsession and a frenzied need to right wrongs so unsavory and unspeakable as to have made him lose his lunch when realization had seized him, rendering it impossible for him to invent any more excuses for what he knew to be true.

"Those motherfuckers will be shaking now. So *god*—dam smug, thinking nobody knows..." mumbled Persy to himself, enunciating every word, as he turned toward the turning cab. "This'll be the new year they never thought would come..." He threw open the taxi door and jumped in as the cab hesitated and then drove off into the early morning. The oranges and yellows of the new day were just emerging over 17th Street, forming a halo over the Old Executive Office Building. He still had one more stop to make—the most critical one yet.

5

Rachel awoke abruptly, saliva sticking to the side of her mouth and a hazy film of sleep covering her eyes, gluing her left eye shut. She didn't immediately know where she was. "Miss Mooreshelton. Miss, uh, Mooreshelton." From a far, Rachel could hear a voice calling her, demanding her immediate attention. She raised her head from her desk only to be blinded for a moment by the early morning sunlight pushing its way over the top of the alabaster buildings across Rayburn's driveway. Wiping her face hastily, Rachel turned around to face Seargent Filipidis, head of Capitol Hill federal security for the Rayburn, Longworth, and Cannon House Buildings who often smiled at her as she departed by the staff exit on late evenings.

"Miss Mooreshelton. We hate to have to bother you," said the sergeant just as Rachel realized the movement of other uniformed personnel in the outer office. "Have you been here all night? Have you been the only staff person here all night?"

Rachel looked around her cubicle. The pad and pencil were on the floor under her chair, her "Practice Random Acts of Kindness" mug was still in its same spot on the desk, its contents miraculously unspilt, and the computer's cursor was still blinking its green iridescence. Her heart jumped so violently that she felt a pounding in her head that took seconds to subside. She looked at her watch—*6:38 a.m.!* It was only then that she remembered. She had never finished the speech!

"Miss Mooreshelton. I need to ask you if you have been here all night," repeated the sergeant, this time with a sign of impatience in his voice.

"There's been an incident involving a member of the staff of this office, early this morning. Would you like some coffee Miss Mooreshelton?"

Finally caught off-guard by the sergeant's last few statements, Rachel mentally surfaced from her sleepy haze, suddenly alert. "Excuse me, Sergeant, is there a problem?" she asked, pulling the long, disheveled braids from her around her face. She crossed her arms, cold from the wind coming through the window left open from the night before.

"Yes. Uhh, I'm sure that you must know Persuvius Pritchard, the legislative director and chief of staff for this office. I see him just about every day when he leaves the building," said the tall, dark-haired man in a faint Mediterranean accent, stepping back to sit against a desk. "Did you see him at all this morning?"

"No, I haven't seen anyone from the staff yet today. I, ah, somehow dozed off last night. I had to stay late to work on a speech for a press conference that Congressman Jackson is holding this afternoon with the Black Caucus." A feeling began to creep through Rachel's body, exacerbated by the draft coming through the open window. Her arms trembled. "What's wrong Sergeant Filipidis? Why are all of these officers here? I don't understand. Wait. Has something happened to Persy?"

The sergeant lifted his body off the desk, pulled a chair from across the room and sat down to face Rachel, a notepad dangling from his fingertips, garbled voices and static emanating from the walkie-talkie in the pocket of his navy, knitted uniform sweater.

"I'm sorry to be the one to tell you this, but Persy Pritchard's body was found fifteen minutes ago over in Folger Park. He was shot several times in the chest and neck. The body had apparently been dragged several feet and dumped in a thicket of bushes. A woman who lives over on Third was walking her dog and ran home hysterical to phone it in. It appears the dog picked up the scent."

The sergeant rose to speak to one of the officers standing in the doorway. The scuffle of his black patent leather shoes halted. Rachel shifted to close the window, the draft now aggravating her, the tips of her fingers beginning to go numb, from the cold and the shock that was starting to set in. She scratched at her scalp, a nervous habit she had developed since first getting braids a year ago. Rachel's stomach churned. Persy was *dead*.

The sergeant returned, ruffling through his closely cropped hair. "Miss Mooreshelton, we've already notified the Congressman. He's on his way from home now. It'd be real helpful if you could call the rest of the staff and ask them to get here right away. Do you have home numbers for everyone? They'll have to use the back staff entrance."

Rachel nodded.

"We've tightened all security. Only essential staff in until we hear further. Miss Mooreshelton, are you all right? Well, again, I'm really sorry to be the bearer of this news. I'll be right in the other room. Would you like some coffee? I can have Officer Perry bring you some…" he offered.

"Yes, please, thanks," she mumbled, fighting denial of what she had heard in the past few minutes. Seconds buzzed by in paralysis. *Move Rachel. She had to find the staff list that Phyllis kept in her files.* She got up from her chair and stumbled over her bag, throwing some of the contents to the floor. She picked up the bits of the photo she had discovered the night before and tossed them back into the bag along with her wallet, Persy's micro-cassette tape and her house keys and placed it in the left bottom drawer of the desk.

She treaded, still shoeless from the night before, into the outer office to sift through Phyllis' files. Like a robot, programmed for action but unconscious of its motions, she opened the top drawer of the file cabinet behind Phyllis' desk and began searching for the desired file, the whir of thoughts running through her mind drowning out the clamor of officer's voices, ringing cellular phones and wet boots carrying the slush of snow into the office.

"Why are you in my files and what the hell are all these people doing in this office?" Phyllis snapped, walking around her desk to face Rachel. "Why the hell are all these officers in this place? You'd think it was the second coming of Christ." Phyllis dumped her hand bag on the desk and glared around the room at the security personnel milling around.

"Good morning to you too Phyllis. Didn't anyone out there tell you what happened?" Rachel snapped back without returning Phyllis' stare. A tear had begun to make its way down her cheek and along the angles of her jaw. "I'm looking for the staff phone list. Where's the file?"

"No, I don't know what's happened. That's why I just asked *you*. What are you sniffling about?" Phyllis inquired snappishly, moving closer to Rachel. "Did someone get hurt? Why are you here so early?"

Rachel looked at Phyllis' chubby, light-complexioned face, noticing the large mole under her right eye that called for attention. Her coarse, reddish hair was pulled back into the silky straight store-bought ponytail she sported two or three times a week, her fingernails long, painted a dizzying mother-of-pearl-and-purple striped pattern complete with tiny diamond studs affixed to every other nail. She knew that the last thing she needed to do was get into a cat fight with Phyllis at a time like this.

"Phyllis...Persy is dead. He was shot to death, found about half an hour ago over in Folger Park. Sergeant Filipidis has already called the Congressman. He's, he's on...his way..." Rachel's voice stumbled and then trailed off as she stared out into the air towards the windows over-looking the building's semi-circular driveway. "I guess they don't know too much yet. He hasn't told me anything else. I just, um, wanted to call the staff. He asked me to call everyone and get them to come down right away....I just saw Persy last night before he left here. We were the last two in the office..."

"Oh, God. Persy was *killed*?" Phyllis' face froze into disbelief as she attempted to absorb the blow.

"Here's some coffee for you," blurted a security guard standing behind Rachel. She turned to see a medium-build, young, black man wearing the same dark blue pants and navy wool knitted sweater as Sergeant Filipidis. "The Sergeant said you wanted some coffee."

"Thanks. Have you heard anything else about what happened to Persy?" she asked, hoping for the even the smallest extra bit of information.

"Officer, we need to know what has happened here!" snarled Phyllis, coming around the desk to face the young man, who stood inches shorter. "One of our colleagues is dead, and you all are bringing people coffee? Why the hell are so many of you in our office instead of outside looking for who did this?! Don't you know the press is going to be all over this if they're not out there already? We need to know…whatttt…has happened!"

The strength in Phyllis' voice faded despite her feisty outer resolve. Her bottom lip quavered as she wiped away at the moisture building below her eyelids. "How could something like this happen to Persy? Lord Jesus, I can't believe it…" She walked over to her chair and sat her body down with a heavy thud, placed her elbows on the desk and clasped her fingers together in an agitated fashion. The tears were now free to fall.

"I'm sorry ladies, but the sergeant's going to have to fill you in as we get more information. I'm afraid that I know about as much as you do." He placed the steaming Styrofoam cup on the edge of the desk and left through the main office door.

"Christ…Christ…Persy…Let me get the staff file so we can start calling everybody. I guess we should call Jerry first since the press is going to be all over this," Phyllis suggested in the authoritative tone Rachel resented, but to which she had become accustomed. Rachel just nodded, her nerves deadened, and walked toward the windows to stare outside. His death would be a stinging blow to the staff. It was as if there weren't enough precarious challenges facing them this session.

Ray Jackson had amassed the kind of power he had long dreamed of—until the Democrats' '94 defeat to the Republicans. Within a matter of months, funding to the Congressional caucuses had been eliminated, the District's delegate vote had been slashed and the affirmative action debate had become political action item number one. And

Virginia's Bill Blasingame, the Speaker of the House, was calling the shots. Blasingame and Jackson served as freshman Members during the same term in 1976 and since, had fought each other fiercely from opposing sides of the political spectrum. The bad blood between them ran deep, typical of the political animosities on the Hill that were as widespread as the unfortunate plague of crack cocaine in the nation's inner cities.

Jackson and his staff had struggled over the past few years to re-invent his position and that of the Caucus. A power base he had worked two decades to build had been nearly wiped out with a few pen strokes of the Republican leadership. The onus was on Jackson to craft a strategy to help his colleagues seize reelection, even in the midst of a political atmosphere ripe with bitterness and racially-tinged inter-party and intra-party one-up-manship and petty side-taking. Always a fierce, and at times vicious fighter for equal rights and a strong voice for the black electorate, Jackson had pledged on the dawn of the Republican take-over to do whatever necessary to preserve the Caucus' fragile power base. Now the Congressman and his staff would have to somehow find a way to stumble through the formidable tasks ahead without Persy. A crystal clear tear dropped from Rachel's cheek to the scuffed, stained-wood floor as she watched Capitol Hill police mix with security guards on the front sidewalk while squad cars blocked the entrance to the building's driveway.

Phyllis located the file and called the Quantico, Virginia, home of Jackson's press secretary, only to be told by his wife that he had just left for the office 10 minutes earlier for his hour and twenty-five minute morning commute to the office. She continued quickly, calling down the staff list, unaware that several of the officers had hurriedly shuffled out of the office.

Rachel raced into her office to pick up her ringing phone. She hesitated to speak, hoping that the caller was not a Channel 9 reporter digging his teeth into Persy's murder before the body could grow cold.

"Hello, Rachel Mooreshelton," she spoke in such a low, hoarse tone, she wondered momentarily if she'd said anything at all.

"Rachel, it's Thad. I tried reaching you at home last night and this morning, but your answering machine kept picking up. I was starting to get worried," the voice said, its anxiety vanishing as Rachel's apprehension also subsided. "The word from my office is that Persy Pritchard was shot last night or this morning. Adele from Blasingame's office just called me when I was getting in the shower. How long have you been there?"

"I see word has already started getting around. Thad, God, Persy is *dead*...I, I was here all night." The furtive words rushed from Rachel's mouth as if she had a terrible secret she could no longer keep. The fingers of her left hand raced through the base of her braids, pulling and twisting nervously. "I fell asleep last night working on the Congressman's speech...The *speech*. Damn, I never finished it...I don't know...there probably won't even be a speech now. I, I woke up and they were here, and the sergeant said that Persy had been killed over in the park. The whole office is full of officers and they're outside the building too. I still can't believe this is happening. It's like a nightmare. He was *murdered*." Rachel cried for the first time since hearing the news from the sergeant.

"Rach, it'll be okay. Look, I'm on my way to the office. Maybe I should come through there first—" he offered uncertainly in his faintly Mid-Western drawl.

"No, you can't. You know that wouldn't be a good idea. What would it look like, a Blasingame aide passing by to visit this office, especially in the middle of *this*? We can't even meet in the tunnel. The police are everywhere and Jackson's going to need me here. I can't leave." Rachel spun around in her chair at the sound of a noisy crowd coming down the corridor toward Jackson's office. As muffled static from security radios came closer, she glanced at her watch—7:05 a.m. The past few minutes had passed in a haze. "Thad, I'll be okay. Look, it sounds like the Congressman must have just gotten here. I've got to go. Look, I'll call you when I get home tonight, okay? Thanks for checking on me…yeah, I love you too."

Rachel stood up, put her suit jacket on, wiped some of the leftover sleep from around her eyes, grabbed her notepad and headed for the outer office as Congressman Jackson entered. She had to pull herself together. Surrounded by Sergeant Filipidis, a flustered-looking Meryl Deal from the *Post*, several officers and Cleavon Grace, the District's controversial three-term mayor and close friend of the Congressman, Jackson appeared tormented, his velvety, dark-chestnut skin ashen, his eyes flush with concern and another, more complex emotion that she couldn't quite place. She thought to herself, "*Now the madness begins.*"

6

"Congressman, who killed Persuvius Pritchard? When was the body found? Do the police have any leads?" Meryl Deal's questions came in rapid fire succession, her microphone pushing its way into Jackson's face. "Did he have any valuables missing? Were there any witnesses?"

"Meryl, I have *no* comment at the moment," grumbled the Congressman, pushing his way through the host of officers. He threw off his black wool dress coat and headed for his office, followed by the sergeant. He spoke out to the reporter without turning his back, suspending her barrage of inquiry. "*Please*! I don't have the details yet. The office will have a statement for the press shortly. *Phyllis*, is Jerry on his way?"

Phyllis had barely blurted out that Jerry Berman was en route when Jackson ordered her and Rachel to join him and the sergeant in his office. The Congressman was all too aware of how an unrehearsed comment to the press could be distorted before the ink dried. Though he and Meryl Deal were good personal friends and he often fed her delicious morsels of information, he was taking no chances with the death of his chief of staff. The Washington press, always perceived as the bastion of objective, no-nonsense journalism, had, in the Congressman's mind, deteriorated rapidly over the past couple of years into a tabloid-like rumor mill. A circus.

Congressman Jackson closed the door, sat behind his large mahogany desk, folded his arms and sighed. "Sergeant, tell us how Persy was killed. What happened out there?"

The sergeant described the scene of the murder to the best of his knowledge, the time the body was found, the number and location of entrance and exit wounds and the current activities of the force in the investigation. His manner was detached, and his words concise, the undertaking one he'd performed more times that he cared to count. A mobile crime unit was out sweeping the scene, dusting for fingerprints, despite the difficulty the snow presented, checking for shoe tracks, signs of a scuffle, hairs, fibers, anything and everything. The body was fully clothed and intact, except that any money Persy may have had in his wallet was gone, along with his keys and any other belongings he may have been carrying before the attack. The brown leather wallet was, of course, being examined for prints. Because of the sensitive, and possibly political nature of the crime and the identity of the victim, the homicide unit had dispatched over a handful of cops, and half a dozen uniformed officers were combing the area for witnesses. Homicide had already departed to notify the victim's next of kin, and the deputy ME was preparing the body, soon to be on its way to the Medical Examiner for autopsy. Filipidis admitted that the falling snow, which had nearly covered entirely any footprints leading from the body and may have covered other critical evidence was a hindrance, but not an insurmountable obstacle to a thorough investigation. He leaned forward with his pad of paper and pulled his pen from behind his ear.

"Now, I'll need to take a statement from each of you about the last time you saw the victim, his mood, his plans for last evening and anything else you can think of. We'll all need to work collectively to piece this together and get to the bottom of what took place," he said, attempting to seem cooperative and encouraging. "My people are on this, Congressman. They know we need to move quickly on this one. Safety on Capitol Hill is essential for the policymakers as well as residents. And the FBI has already called to stress utmost stealth, and may, uh, have to be brought in at some point." With the last statement, the muscle under the sergeant's left eye began to twitch. "But because we have no reason at this juncture to believe this is a politically-motivated homicide, our district headquarters is on top of it. The less publicity, the better for all of us."

"The better for *who* Sergeant? For the *Republicans* who won't back down on the budget, keeping tens of thousands of workers from paying their bills? For the *President* at the onset of an election year?" Jackson quipped, giving the sergeant a disgusted stare. "The better for *you* because you don't want the FBI stepping on your turf and taking control of your investigation? Or better for the grieving parents of another dead *black man*? Sergeant, I want to know who murdered my chief of staff and I don't care how much it screws up the political agenda!" Rachel and Phyllis traded silent stares while Sergeant Filipidis adjusted in his seat. George Filipidis had fourteen years on the force, eight on Capitol Hill. He'd been around longer than many of the elected representatives up here and no one was going to play the damn race card on him in an attempt to influence his investigation. And he'd be damned if he'd let the FBI move in on this one because they didn't think his federal cops were moving swiftly enough on a case that could spook Hill staffers and their bosses. *No* FBI on this one. *Fuck Jackson.*

"Congressman, I didn't mean to imply that—," the sergeant stammered, the strong lilt of his childhood-born Greek accent flavoring his words in his sudden agitation.

"Sergeant," interrupted Jackson, catching his temper and holding it hostage. "I am an easy man to get along with. Cut the political theatrics, and you and I will work together well on this. Let's all concentrate on what's important here—finding who killed the best chief of staff I've ever had, and a good friend to most of the staff in this office. Now, if she doesn't mind, let's allow Ms. Mooreshelton to give you her statement." The sergeant stiffened noticeably, but thought better of a confrontation.

Rachel mentioned that she and Persy were the last in the office the evening before. She also mentioned that he had reminded her that he planned to take the day off, and that she believed he had dropped back by the office later in the evening while she was in the restroom. But she neglected to mention the tape she had discovered or its contents. Revealing that she had *borrowed* it would probably just serve as an embarrassment, she thought, especially since it was unimportant.

The sergeant questioned both Jackson and Phyllis, neither offering any bit of information that particularly sparked his further attention. According to the Congressman, Persy had dined with him at the Hilton gala and had apparently left early, around nine, looking a bit tired. But the entire staff had looked a bit tired lately. Nothing unusual there. Filipidis sat back and reviewed his notes and turned to look at Rachel.

"Ms. Mooreshelton, you've told me that you were the last one from the office to talk to Mr. Pritchard. Do you recall at all what time he left?"

"It must have been just around 7:15. Most of the staff has been leaving a little earlier in the past few days since its so close to Christmas, but he and Chuck were here a little late," Rachel said. She felt as if she were an unemployed, mother of three near to eviction being given one chance at a job interview that would keep her kids off the street. She knew her memory and her words were critical. *God, this whole thing was unbelievable.* The Sergeant strained to hear her comments over ringing telephones and the conversation of officers on the other side of the Congressman's office door. "You know, things are normally slower than usual the week before Christmas. But since there's no settlement on the budget, some have been staying late. Like Chuck and Persy. The only reason I was still here, though, was to finish a speech for the Congressman. At one point I thought maybe I'd heard Persy or Chuck come back for something and leave. But I never actually *saw* anyone. I had intended to be out of here by ten or so, but like I mentioned earlier, I fell asleep."

"Did Pritchard mention to you where he was going after the PPF dinner? Or is that when he came back to the office? Did he say or do anything out of the ordinary when he came back? Did he appear agitated or nervous in any way?" questioned Filipidis. Rachel shook her head *no* to each question. She told Filipidis that she hadn't actually seen Persy when he came back, just thought that she'd heard him.

"Sergeant, I'm afraid that there was nothing that would have led me to believe that we'd never see him again," she strained. "I wish…I wish I could remember something, but there just isn't anything." She slumped down into the wooden chair and put her hands over her eyes, crying quietly.

In her mind, she went over it again. *"Ms. Mooreshelton, is there anything else that could help us find Mr. Pritchard's killer?"*

Rachel stared at the Congressman's shoes, visible from under the desk. The scene was surreal. All she wanted to do was rewind the past few hours and become just another exhausted, overworked legislative aide for a U.S. Congressman, not a woman being questioned about the murder of a colleague.

7

By nine that morning, the entire staff had assembled and had been questioned. Several uniformed officers and two Hill detectives continued to mill about, telephones continued to ring, the press continued to plead for a comment from the Congressman. But for Persuvius Pritchard, life had ended. Two bullets to the chest and one to the neck had stopped him in his tracks.

Thoughts of Persy flashed through Rachel's mind all morning. She wanted to remember the last thing Persy said to her the night before, the very last words. She tried to recall the precise expression on his face the night before, whether it had been a sheepish grin or an exhausted frown. She wanted to know what on earth he was doing in Folger Park at dawn on a weekday morning. And why he hadn't said anything to her last night when he'd dashed in. She also wondered if similar thoughts were haunting the rest of the staff. It was a sobering moment to say the least. Life and all its ups and downs had suddenly become so precious. It made Rachel want to reevaluate her own.

The Congressman attempted to calm the nerves of his staff. After leading them in a vigil, a silent prayer for Persy, he spoke to them with heartfelt emotion, his face drained. He encouraged everyone to do their best to get some work done since the budget battle wouldn't end in light of their colleague's death. Rachel knew that none of them would be able to concentrate on *work*.

Many cried. Some just stared into space, lost in grief. Jerry Berman roamed the office, pacing, his head shaking intermittently as he stared at the floor. He had been charged with drafting a statement for the Congressman to give to the press. But the initial shock had yet to subside.

Congressman Jackson had temporarily retreated to his office. Rachel noticed that his light on the switchboard was on. *He was probably calling Persy's parents,* she thought. *"Those poor people, and so close to Christmas…"*

Congressman Jackson issued a statement to the press at noon. Journalists from the *Post*, the *Times*, the *Washington Afro-American*, Channel 9, Channel 4, *Roll Call*, the Bible of Hill staffers, and even CNN crowded into the Congressman's inner office. Washingtonians had quickly grown weary of the aggravating budget and furlough talk being beat to death on every broadcast and the media was poised to add a little variety to late-breaking news.

Jackson's somber look paled in comparison to the anticipation in the eyes of the press. Jerry Berman handed Jackson a one-page statement memo, spotted with handwritten notes emphasizing questions to which Jackson should offer no comment.

"Ladies and gentleman, early this morning, the body of my long-time chief of staff, legislative director and dear friend, Persuvius Pritchard, was discovered in Folger Park. He was the apparent victim of a random robbery." Jackson paused and adjusted his eyeglasses. He read on.

"Our office would like to extend our sincerest condolences to Persy's family and friends. Persy was well-loved amongst his colleagues and his presence in this office will be sorely missed. Our office is cooperating in every way possible with law enforcement to apprehend the doer of this heinous crime. Should anyone have any information that might help the police track the culprit, we urge you to contact your local district headquarters. It is more important than ever that we all work together to prevent the crime that plagues our society." The Congressman looked up from the paper in his hands, and paused, his Adam's apple rippling slowly in his throat.

"I am quite sad during this holiday season to know that yet *another* African American male is dead due to…gun violence. Today, a black man's mother and father and loved ones are forced to mourn his death because the community at large let him down. *Our* communities *must* rally together to save our children from the devastation that hits thousands of American families every year. Thank you, and God bless you."

"Congressman Jackson, have Pritchard's parents been informed?"

"Congressman Jackson, do the police have any leads?"

"Congressman, will this tragedy bring the Democrats and Republicans together on welfare reform?"

"Congressman Jackson, do you think that Persy Pritchard is another victim of black-on-black crime?"

"Excuse me, Congressman, does anyone know why Pritchard was in Folger Park when he was killed?"

"Has Pritchard's murder been ruled a random homicide?"

The reporters spoke all at once, each jockeying for an answer. Microphones pointed in Jackson's deep earth-brown face as he began to sweat from the glare of camera lights. He fell silent momentarily. The man who always had something to say, something so eloquent to say, was at a loss for words. The pain of Persy's death seemed to reach way down deep inside of his soul. The Congressman hastily offered that there was nothing more. The office would continue to update the press periodically throughout the day.

Rachel stood in the doorway, gazing at her boss. His shoulders were slumped despite his attempt to maintain composure. He looked out into the sea of reporters, and Rachel once again thought that she noticed more than just grief or concern in his eyes. In the years she had known and worked for him, she'd never seen that look. An uncomfortable feeling swept through her. It was more than grief. It was far beyond disappointment. That look. She was *certain* this time it was…*fear.*

The day wore on at a snail's pace. Over two dozen Members of the House, Democrats mostly, dropped by to give their condolences, many of whom had worked closely with Persy on pushing through last session's crime bill. Even Mayor Grace, attired in his trademark kente-cloth bow tie, had taken time away from the District's own emergencies to linger about the office, catering to the Congressman's grief. Reporters and curiosity-seekers milled in the hallways, while the police munched on late fast-food dinners and huddled to talk in corners. Rachel, Phyllis and the staff bit on fingernails, pulled at hair and groped to accept reality.

Darkness fell once again on the Rayburn horseshoe.

Twenty-four hours had passed since Rachel had seen Persy for the last time...

8

He pulled the cover up close to shield his face from the freezing wind that was kicking his ass. He had slept harder than usual, all day. Maybe longer than that. But old white Mary, with her soft snowy flakes, had kept him warm. He was feeling no pain. He slowly shifted his long, 35-year old torso under the worn, brown blanket to cover the full six-foot-five inches of his frame. He had learned to inhale, then move, inhale, then move a little more, careful not to breathe in his own stench, arising from clothes and hair and a body that had forgotten what water felt like, unless it was rain.

The lonely, unheated, wool-blanketed tent behind the main dumpster in the back alley of The Towers apartments on C Street was a far cry from the spacious five-bedroom colonial in L.A.'s posh Brentwood with the theatre-vision TV and the closets of fine clothes that Raheed "the Speed" Stinson had enjoyed just eight years earlier. The agents were gone. The women had long since disappeared. The commercial endorsements had evaporated. The acclaim. The parties. The friends. The money. All were a memory that his conscious grappled to hold onto. Raheed was worse than a has-been. Heroin, cocaine, alcohol and a bastard of an inflated ego had cost him his NBA contract, his Los Angeles Lakers jersey and his swollen bank account. Like a thief in the night, the white lady—that soft, sweet, flaky powder from hell—stole his game, stripped his dignity and raped him of his dreams.

Raheed inhaled, and shifted again to clutch the same syringe he'd used for six months. A clean one could be a bitch to come by. He'd lost everything, but he held close to his syringe. She was his woman and he knew she'd never leave. He coddled her, warmed her, protected her and craved the moments when she would speak to him through the eye of her needle while hot, syrupy liquid shot through his veins.

He had come home to his hometown of D.C. a broken man. His family had put him in rehab six times in eight years, then twice he had gone on his own, but each time she had called him back. Raheed had a ten-year old daughter, Jasmine, he hadn't seen in five years. His mother cried all the time, begging him to do right. His father had barred him from their middle-class red brick home on Kearny Street. He had robbed his own family for money to feed his five-hundred-dollar-a-day habit. And had served twenty-two months in Lorton for assault and battery on an ex-girlfriend when she wouldn't withdraw money from an ATM at Thomas Circle. *Shit, the bitch was a tight ass. The least she could have done was helped him out until he got himself straight. But naw, she had to go get loud. Called him a motherfuckin' junkie. Well, he'd shown her. Her face still ain't back right.* For the past three years, he'd had nowhere but alleys, grates and bridge overpasses to call home. But he still couldn't shake the heroin—she'd been with him through thick and thin—and he'd eventually embraced her.

Raheed wiped at the untamed stubble on his face. His face was shot to hell. He had been a pretty boy. Spoiled by the ladies. His sensuous copper-brown skin, gently waving, dark-brown hair, deeply dimpled cheeks, strong, arching nose and long, muscular limbs ensured that women stayed close. And he had sparkled in the Colliseum before thousands of fans. Pure wickedness. Racing like magic down the court, his keen eyes would zone in on the basket like a tiger poised to kill its prey. *Dunk. Swoosh. Bam. Pow.*

Raheed picked up the dented, silver spoon that he had found in the trash at Phillip's Seafood House over on the waterfront last week. He pulled the small, plastic zip-lock bag of snow-like flakes from under his knitted hat and poured it lovingly into the hollow of the spoon. Crack had never been his thing. Coke just didn't do it for him. The pure essence of Snow White herself was enough to keep him company. His pulse danced. His mouth watered. He flicked a lighter and guarded the flame from the piercing wind with the palm of his left hand like it was life itself. It cooked slowly, little white bubbles rising up and down above the copper-red-blue flashes licking at the air.

Raheed threw the lighter to the side. The hunger in his veins made his whole body quiver with anticipation. With the spoon in his left hand and the syringe now in his right, he thrust the syringe into the glistening, milky clear fluid. His thumb nimbly pushed upward, drawing the heroin into the syringe. It was done. The reaches of ecstasy, of life giving force were now in his hand, moments away from blessing his veins.

Raheed pulled up the thick sleeve of his knee-length Wizards jacket, wrapped a withered rope tightly around his lanky arm and spotted his favorite green line, in his favorite bruised spot, an inch low of the interior of his elbow. The needle penetrated his marked, leathery, weather-worn skin at just the right angle, and the syringe's contents hit its mark as Raheed's thumb plunged downward.

It was good. Real good. *Real good.*

"Hey man! Get your ass up!" shouted one of two hulking, faceless figures standing over his tent. "Do you have a hearing problem? I said up on your feet! Police!"

Before he could move, hands had grabbed him violently out of his make-shift shelter and jolted him to his feet. He was thrown up against the back wall of the apartment building with excruciating force, and patted down roughly with gloved hands.

"All right, don't move, look at the wall. He's clean Mike. Why don't you check his stuff," said one of the plainclothes detectives, his tone abrasive. "What's your name? Why don't you tell me where you were all last night into early morning?"

Stony silence.

"What's your name, man?" the officer asked again, jerking Raheed around to face him. The dark-haired white officer, wearing a ski jacket with Vale tags hanging from his zipper, looked into Raheed's filmy black eyes. At just five-foot-six, Rick Venable stared up at the homeless man and winced. The odor was worse than a week-old corpse. And his eyes were as glassy as smoky marbles. "*Goddam!* You're high as a mother-fuckin' kite. Hey, Mike, check for narcotics. I said what's your name?"

"Stinson. Raheed Stinson," he mumbled, his eyes flitting back and forth between the two cops, landing on the darker one. "I ain't done nothin' man. I swear I ain't done *nothin*. Cut a brother a break."

Twenty-nine year old Detective Mike James had just been awarded his gold shield a mere two months before, but he knew well that the stumbling black man up against the wall seemed to fit the sketchy composite that his supervisor had shoved at them back at headquarters. The tight-assed bastard, Gravino. As if the same composite didn't fit half the black men in D.C., including himself. He and Rick had already searched six other homeless and had come up with nothing. Most homeless wouldn't know what to do with a loaded piece. *He* knew. He had grown up around them, off of 13th, most of 'em harmless, just down and out, or mentally ill, but nine times out of ten, not dangerous. He knew how degrading it felt to be hassled by the cops for doing nothing but being black and male.

But this was his job, one he'd chosen to do, hoping to watchdog his colleagues' behavior with young black men as well as taking perps down. Even though Rick had already done a very cursory rummaging through the odorous pile, Mike rifled loosely through the man's blankets and bags, looking back for a moment at the towering man, who looked vaguely familiar, as if he'd seen him on TV or something. Something shiny and black hit the cold tar with a heavy click and thud. *Damn, not you man, damn*, he thought, suddenly realizing just who he'd be forced to take in.

"Rick, look at this," grumbled Mike, a fair-skinned black man the size of George Foreman. The thumb and forefinger of his gloveless right hand dangled a .38 caliber revolver. The needle of the syringe lay protruding from under the blanket tent, unmoved. The intoxicating voodoo flowing through Raheed's body was so awe-inspiring to him, so gravity-defying that he failed to fully comprehend the jerk of his arms and the click of handcuffs before he was led to a waiting, unmarked Ford Taurus.

9

"The untimely death of Congressman Jackson's chief of staff Persy Pritchard is just another sign of the moral decay in our society, the growing lack of humanity in our ranks. Persy Pritchard's murderer is not the only one responsible for his death. We all are," Rachel sat, still wearing her coat and holding her remote control, listening to Speaker of the House Bill Blasingame on News Channel 8, his words dripping with forced sincerity. *"Without welfare reform and increased federal funding for the nation's prison system, others will fall prey to the violent behavior of the hopeless. The Republican Party has been working diligently for a compromise with the Democrats on welfare reform and the budget. They, however, also must be willing to share the responsibility for the safety and welfare of the American people. I and my colleagues in the Congress, offer our condolences to Congressman Jackson and the family of Persy Pritchard. May he rest in peace."*

"The bastard," she sneered.

She turned her TV back off, pulled off her coat and shoes and dragged her exhausted body into the kitchen of her eighth floor Connecticut Avenue condo. Her father had insisted that she live in this building, in this area of the city. He had purchased the two-bedroom condo to keep Rachel from renting a dismal, but eclectic loft efficiency in Mount Pleasant, a neighborhood where the city's Nicaraguan, Guatemalan and Ethiopian immigrants mixed comfortably with blacks, and hip, yuppie whites eager to gentrify. The warm earth tones of her handpicked furniture and wall hangings and the strong aroma of mixed

African violet potpourri gave her the strong sense that the place was hers, and not in her father's name. She looked up at her wall clock. *Eight o'clock*. Her telephone rang.

"Hey, Rach, let me up," said Thad, calling from the intercom outside the building.

She pressed the entry code and waited for his knock.

In early February, the two of them had sat side by side in a crowded Appropriations Committee hearing in the Cannon Caucus Room with perspiration from the body heat soaking their clothes. Thad's attention had shifted from the drone of Congressman McAllister's syrupy Texan drawl to the scrawled rendition of a more interesting scene, a funnier scene—his hands gripped around McAllister's neck, while McAllister strained to smack him with his Chairman's mallet.

Sitting next to him, her elbow mashed into his upper arm, Rachel had felt every scribble he made. She had peered over to take a look at whatever it was that brought a smile to his face at an otherwise monotonous moment and saw the cartoon. She couldn't help but laugh. The two of them had sat during the rest of the hearing, trading cartoons and silent laughter.

Over the months, the two would find one another during other hearings, equally as monotonous, to scribble caricatures of the committee Members, share written opinions of the lethargy of these *very important* events, and take serious policy-relevant notes when necessary. One day in April, as the crowd of lobbyists, college students and other aides filed out of the immense hearing room, Thad had asked if she'd join him for lunch. He wanted to know more about life in Congressman Jackson's office, *so he'd said*. Noticing the look in his eye, *that look*, the one that had told her he might be interested in a little more than discussing the Congressman, she had surprised herself by saying yes. And she kept saying yes week after week after week. And he'd been there for her since.

When Rachel opened the door to let Thad into the roomy apartment, she collapsed into his arms, embracing him tightly. "It's okay

Rachel. It'll be okay. There's nothing we can do about it now," he said, comforting her, his large alabaster hands caressing her ebony neck, burrowing into the thick mass of her braids.

Rachel stood back and let her tear-stained eyes look at him, *her Thad.* He had the cool good looks of Brad Pitt—wavy golden hair, piercing gray eyes, solid square jaw and a shadow of a beard. She inhaled his essence—shampoo, musky cologne and the scent of winter cold that he carried so well. How could she ever doubt her love for this man. He made her laugh. He held her close. He listened to her worries and made them his own. When they were together, alone, the fact that he was white was an aside, an afterthought, pushed into the dark corners of her mind. But still always there, jerking at her conscience.

"Thad, this has been the most horrible day," Rachel cried. "There are no leads and the whole staff is scared. The police are saying it was probably a random shooting, that somebody was just after his money, but maybe it *wasn't*…Who would want to hurt someone like him? I swear people are crazy."

Thad held her closely and led her to the sofa.

"Shh, Rachel, I know today's been an ass-kicker. I mean, my God, Persy is *dead*," he said, sitting her down with care on his lap. "Let's try to forget about it. I hate to see you this way. You need to get it all off your mind…just for a little while."

Thad reached up to stroke her face, to wipe the tears away. He carefully moved to undo the top button of her blouse. She looked down at him, and suddenly all of the grief and exhaustion began to melt away.

"God, I love you Thad," she whispered as he caressed the soft mahogany skin beneath her blouse. He kissed the inside of her neck, knowing precisely where to slide the tip of his moist tongue. His touch made her tingle with anticipation. The two fell haphazardly onto the plush sofa, the ugly day forgotten, life's realities swept aside. The glisten of her dark skin resonated under the soft glow of lamplight, a stark contrast to the milky-white of his muscular, untanned body, rising and falling in spontaneous motion. Rachel's insides exploded and goose bumps rose up on her skin as Thad entered her with just the right amount of tender force to make her moan uncontrollably. Thad tore all the sexual myths she'd heard about white men to shreds. The brothers she'd been with in the past had it going on, but Thad held his own too with no problem at all. The strength in his legs and in his hips never ceased to amaze her.

The two lay together later in the evening, wrapped in the afterglow of their lovemaking. Stray clothing was strewn about, abandoned on the hard-wood floor, the sofa arm, and the coffee table.

"Rachel, Christmas is next week. We've avoided this topic long enough, and I, uh, think we need to talk," Thad said sitting up to face Rachel, somewhat hesitant to disturb the look of bliss on her exquisite, sculpted face. "We can't keep going like this."

"Look, Thad, I know I need to talk to my parents about us. But now…the holidays…it's just not the right time." Rachel placed two fingers on either temple as if she were hoping to drive away a splitting headache. "Thad, we know that we love each other, but our parents just won't understand. It's a shame that in the nineties, we're having this dilemma, but Thad, my family just won't accept this relationship."

"Rach, I'm willing to fly back to my little town outside of Dana, Ohio, to announce to my entire family that I have fallen madly in love with the most beautiful woman in the world." Thad smiled at Rachel and poked at her small, round nose. "They and the whole goddam town will recover from the news at some point. I'm willing to take the risk of being disappointed by their reaction."

"Thad, let's not ruin a perfect evening by getting into this, alright. Pleeez, my day has been bad enough," sighed Rachel, beginning to stiffen to his touch. "I just can't deal with this today. It's too complicated. I can't just tell my father, a staunch supporter and fundraiser for the Democratic Party and owner of The African American Journal in Baltimore that his only daughter is romantically linked to a 32-year-old, white Republican from a racist little town in Ohio. *And* an aide to Speaker of the House Blasingame no less!"

The Washington-Baltimore corridor was home to the most economically affluent and politically powerful African Americans in the country, and third-generation Jamaican-American Henry Mooreshelton and his family were among them. His feelings about white people were simple: play their games in the business world to get ahead, to garner the resources needed to become self-sufficient and fight like hell to build your own economic empire. Spend your money in the black community, live in the black community, when able, support whatever political party that supports your people's agenda, despite historical allegiances, and multiply within your race, to ensure that future generations will have all the advantages for even more dynamic achievements. And that was the way things were supposed to be according to Henry Mooreshelton. *Period.* Thad just didn't understand how strongly her father felt about these things, especially when it came to his own children.

"Oh, okay, so I suppose we'll continue to sneak around forever...Is that what you expect to do?" Thad ran his fingers furiously through his hair as he stared down at Rachel, waiting impatiently for her reply. "Rachel, I feel like I'm hiding our relationship because there's something wrong with us being together. But there isn't and you know it. Are you that afraid that your shining star will dim in your father's eyes? Does he have so little unconditional love for you that knowing about us would make him treat you like he does your brother? I know that's what we're really talking about here. It's your *father*. He's the one you're always trying so damn hard to please!"

Thad jumped up from the sofa, his bare feet treading across the wooden floor as he quickly retrieved his scattered clothing. He was really sick of this shit from her. The days when the Lovings were persecuted in the sixties for their interracial marriage were long over. This was Washington. Sure, there were assholes everywhere, but people were mostly progressive and open-minded. Rachel was always so uptight about their racial differences. *If he was willing to catch shit from his parents about this, why wasn't she? What was the big fucking difference?*

Rachel watched angrily as Thad reached for his navy-blue, Tommy Hilfiger winter jacket. Her silent rage and frustration showed in her sullen, coal-black eyes.

"Thad, come on sweetie, let's not do this. *Please*, not now. If we can just wait until after the holidays, I can think of a way to talk to my parents…." She reached up to grab the collar of his jacket to pull him back down to sit on the couch.

"Rachel, I have to go. Let me know when you have enough courage, and enough *faith* in us to go public. I can't keep hiding my feelings like this. This is bullshit. This is hard for *both* of us," Thad said, shaking his head in frustration. "I may be a Republican, but I'm not the stereotype conservative, racist piece of shit that your boss would love to pigeonhole me as. I can separate my political convictions from my personal life. Can *you*?"

"But, Thad, think about it, isn't our politics a big part of who we really are?" she questioned as she watched him reach for the door. Her heart raced. She didn't want him to leave. She needed him tonight, but she just could not tell him what he wanted to hear. Not tonight. "Isn't it almost *too much* of who we really are?"

Thad looked at her longingly, hesitated momentarily, then opened the door. He knew that being with a black woman would be a little more of a challenge than dating a Nordic blonde. He'd always had a few black friends, even in high school in Dana and especially during the two years he'd spent in Botswana in the Peace Corps after finishing up at Brown. Thad had inherited his father's no-nonsense, conservative Republican stance on economic issues, but not the intolerance of Jews and people of color who Elias Derrickson swore were stripping him of his country and his birthright. But this conversation between him and Rachel had gotten tired, stale. He walked out.

Rachel pounded her fist into the arm of the sofa and sat wrapped in her blue bed sheet, angry that the evening had gone wrong. Not even feelings for Thad could wipe away the impending sense that her life was at a crossroads. Whose happiness was more important? Her father had never forgiven her for taking the job with Jackson against his strongly expressed wishes, and she'd been trying to make up for it ever since. He was a stubborn, self-centered controlling man—and half the time a hypocrite to boot—and Rachel knew it, but she still played the role of the little girl seeking to please daddy.

Rachel wandered over to the large window that spanned the length of her dining room and looked out into the blustery night sky. She stared out at the glowing image of the landmark Washington Cathedral, its gilted spires springing up from the surrounding trees, a breathtaking view that always helped to clear her head.

There were too many things happening at once. Too many confusing things that was clogging up her thinking and preventing her from getting a decent night's sleep. Persy's death sure as hell wasn't going to help matters. Yarrick's AIDS had him in the hospital for the third time. Thad was working her last nerve with this talk of talking to her parents about him. And budget stress at the office was kicking everyone's ass. At this point, crafting the speech for Jackson would come as a welcome relief from reality rather than a burden of her job. Due to Persy's unexpected death, the Congressman had postponed the press conference until January second. He had mentioned to her as she was leaving the office that the theme of the speech must be renewal. People must believe, he had said, that the new year should bring with it hope for the future and a discarding of those things past about which we can do nothing. Hope. Faith. Trust. A new beginning. *It would be a new beginning*, she thought to herself with sudden, renewed assurance. *She would make it a new beginning.*

Somehow, she would get over this hump with Thad. She hadn't anticipated that things would get this way. Well, she *had*, but the reality of it was hard to swallow. Living in the middle of it and telling her family and friends about Thad was more difficult than she'd originally figured.

Things with Thad had been so easy in the beginning. He was smart and funny and affectionate and thoughtful, all those things *Cosmopolitan* and *Essence* and *Glamour* told a woman she should have in a man. She'd wake up on some mornings and find him gazing at her, taking in every pore of her face, every crinkle in her hair. The two of them would tramp to the kitchen and make breakfast together, the cool sounds of Wynton Marsalis, Incognito or George Howard flowing through the apartment like a spring breeze, while they talked incessantly about favorite old TV shows. Every Sunday morning, they made love on Rachel's living room couch and then, still naked and wrapped together, they read the thick Sunday edition of the *Washington Post*, in complete silence, each absorbed in the juicy news impacting the city. Complete, comfortable and loving silence.

As the relationship grew, as their feelings for each other grew, Rachel knew that she would have to confront the issue of race, and all its unwanted implications. But even more conflicting in this town where politics ruled, the issue of party weighed heavily on her mind. Rachel had procrastinated month after month over all of this. Thad had yet to meet one of her friends, though she had met a few of his. She had procrastinated not only because she feared she'd have to go into battle with Dawn and Saundra and Yvonne to defend her relationship. It was more than just the unavoidable confrontation she knew she'd have with her parents. Her father would flip out and accuse her of turning her back on her whole race and her mother would stand right behind her father like she always had.

It was the battle she waged with *herself* that kept her from introducing the man that she loved to the other loved ones in her life. The feeling— that she was somehow betraying the black man, betraying herself, betraying her parents' dreams—though buried down deep, would surface and nag at her. The disappointed, disapproving stares that she and

Thad got from the brothers, just standing in line for a movie, or waiting for a table at Georgia Brown's or walking down the aisles at the Safeway, would get under her skin and make guilt rear its ugly head. *Who are they to look at me funny,* she would think, *the brothers have been toting white women around like proud peacocks for years. So what, I'm with a white man. I didn't seek him out. He found me.*

Talking to herself always had a way of making her feel a little better, for a while. Now things had come to a critical point with Thad, and she knew denial of the inevitable wasn't going to make it go away. She *would have to* make a new beginning.

And somehow, she would make her father understand her feelings for Thad. Or try living life without his approval for every damn step she took.

Rachel reached nonchalantly for her shoulder bag and retrieved the micro-cassette. In handwritten letters on its front, someone had scribbled *Tape 2.* "Maybe a little 1970's news and music to lighten the emotionally downtrodden this evening," she quipped to herself. Then as quickly as she had picked it up, Rachel thought otherwise, aware of just how sleepy she was after not sleeping well at her desk the night before. She should get to bed early. Had to make up for lost sleep. The actuality of Persy's death was beginning to settle in. Death. It made her shiver.

Rachel tossed the cassette back into her bag, turned off the lamp by the ruffled sofa and headed toward her bedroom, safe, and away from the commotion in the office, away from her father's heavy, disapproving tone, away from the friends from whom she had to conceal her love for Thad, away from Persy's death. *Away from death.*

10

Phyllis peered out of the fogged window of the L2 Metro bus as it slowly pulled away from the intersection of Kennedy Street and Georgia Avenue toward downtown. She sleepily watched the street signs go by. Jefferson Street. Ingraham Avenue. Geranium Street. Decatur Street. The dark night had given way to a cold, drizzily gray morning. As the large bus heaved its way down Georgia Avenue, dodging potholes that the District of Columbia government had long since ignored on this side of town, she commenced her daily commute to the office.

As the bus pulled in to each stop, groups of weary passengers boarded in heavy silence. An old man, his face swathed in five-day stubble, blew his nose loudly into a yellowed handkerchief. A stooped woman, smelling of rubbing alcohol and mildew, passed Phyllis as if every move brought a new twinge of pain. Phyllis' eyes met those of a small, dark-complexioned boy sitting on his mother's lap, mucus running down his face, his ashen, ungloved hands wiping incessantly at the relentless stream.

Phyllis turned her attention back to the window, watching the all too familiar scenery disappear behind the bus in a blur of faded browns, whites and grays. The boarded-up Mount Zion Church of God. Al, Jr.'s Liquor and Carry-Out, its windows taped with signs advertising discounts on Budweiser and Coors. The Roundtree Funeral Home and Memorial Chapel with its brick edifice rising up and away from the surrounding rowhouses already had a line of mourners out front dressed in dark colors. Yum's Chinese Take-Out with iron bars running vertically down its two storefront windows. ShayShay's World of Hair, the windows behind which Phyllis could already make out women sitting in curlers and under helmeted hairdryers. Phyllis was a DC girl, a "Chocolate City" baby. She knew Washington like she knew her ABCs.

Georgia Avenue had at one time run through the heart of the black middle class and its business community. It had been a place of exceptional pride, a gem in the community. Grand churches, doctors' and lawyers' offices, black-owned banks and well-patronized clothing stores and markets had lined its sidewalks. Though still the locale of many of the city's black-run businesses, many of the doctors, lawyers, accountants, large tithe-generating places of worship and their patrons had abandoned Washington for the safety, lower taxes, better public schools, bigger homes and improved public services available in the surrounding Maryland and Virginia suburbs.

The District of Columbia government, mired in its own unending budget struggle and handicapped by a lack of political leadership on its city council and an impotent, though charismatic mayor, had long sought to attract the best and the brightest of black business back to Georgia Avenue. The thoroughfare was now home to hundreds of struggling Korean and Chinese-owned take-out spots, liquor stores, pawn shops, funeral homes, fast food drive-throughs, hair salons and oft-boarded-up storefront churches.

A small renaissance of sorts had begun in recent years. A smattering of newly-opened African and vegetarian restaurants, a few used car dealerships, auto insurance agencies and a block-long, full-service car wash were enjoying hard-won success. And of course, Howard University sat on a hill as it had for over a century as a beacon of black academia.

The Metro bus passed a billboard reading in giant green letters *D.C. Cares for You!* sponsored by the Council to Promote Washington, D.C. The city's mayor and council had proposed plan upon plan to draw big business back to its urban community. A new sports arena, a community-wide recreation center and hospital were the key to revitalization of the nation's capitol in the hearts and minds of the city's officials and community activists.

The embattled mayor, Cleavon Grace, reelected after a long fight with alcoholism and gambling addiction, sought to bring back the glory days of his first administration. The mayor's solicitation of a prostitute, caught live on a resident's video camera eight years earlier, had spelled a quick and controversial end to his brief reign. In a move that stunned the black power elite and the media, Congressman Jackson had publicly sworn his support and pledged that he'd never turn his back on his Vietnam war buddy, no matter how far he'd fallen. And the mostly black electorate of Washington had also shown the nation that they had short, forgiving memories, and had voted Grace back into office two years ago after a nasty, racially-divisive election. Despite his warmed-over charisma and flashy promises, congressional control over the city's finances, however, left the actual fate of the city in the hands of Speaker of the House Blasingame, a Congressional oversight committee on the District of Columbia, and a recently established, objective control board of economists and financial wizards.

Despite the problems of the city's politics, the media stories of drug-related murders, the racial rifts, and the hopelessness she saw creeping ever deeper into her neighborhood, Phyllis loved Washington. She may have complained day in and day out about the drug dealers outside her window, the piles of trash that often lay uncollected for weeks on the streets that she called home and the thirteen-year old, junior high school-age mothers who thought their babies made them grown. Phyllis may have prayed every night to her grandmother in heaven to put in a good word with God to help her off of Kennedy Street, away from her past and her present. But she knew deep inside, looking out the fogged bus window, that she loved this place. D.C. was her home.

But she also feared it. When her sixteen-year-old cousin Deandre had been shot to death on the steps of Thornton High School four years ago, his death had hit hard—and close to home. News cameras had waited outside her mother's home, where Deandre and his mother, her Aunt Willie, had lived with them for eight months.

"Yet another District teen shot in a hail of violence," the TV had blared. Deandre's death had scared her, more than she had ever been scared. Her tough exterior had cracked, and a consuming depression had settled over her family. Her mother and aunt had fought over how the community's generous contribution would be spent, Phyllis retreated into herself, not knowing how else to cope with the shock, and Deandre's father, never around when his son needed him, had drowned his guilt in cheap, corner-store liquor.

But the pain and the shock had eased with time. Phyllis had taken an offer from her girlfriend Lashawn to go to an eleven 'o clock service with her at the 13th Street Fellowship of Faith Church of God, and it was there that she had sought peace. When Reverend Sampson placed his solid hands on her trembling shoulders and asked her to take Jesus into her life as her Lord and Savior, her legs had buckled and the heat of the energy inside her and the pounding voices of the mass choir had brought her to her knees. She had promised to God that she would live a life worthy of His holiness, and she had prayed until her head had ached for the soul of her cousin, another casualty of the ruthlessness of the streets. She knew that she had to do right, to be something, *for him*, the little brother she had never had.

The news of Persy's death played over and over in her mind. To her it was like watching the hourglass that sat on the living room TV. Each grain of salt was just another dead body, another life wasted. And more and more were being sucked under by the force of the gravity, with nothing to stop the next grain from dropping.

The day after, she thought. *The office would be a goddam mess like it was yesterday, worse maybe, now that the press was digging into Persy's life and death.* She'd seen the front page *Washington Post* headline as she was grabbing her lunch from the kitchen counter a few minutes ago.

Congressional Chief of Staff Found Slain on Capitol Hill.

She had liked Persy. He was an intelligent man who had run Jackson's office with distinction, and was responsible for much of the success Jackson had enjoyed these past ten years. With his wire thin limbs, mocha-colored skin, and inquisitive, perfectionist nature, Persy was highly organized, and knew the ins and outs of key policy matters like the back of his hand. He read like it was a matter of life or death—liberal policy papers, conservative publications—anything and everything to keep Jackson on top of any matters vital to Jackson's constituency and the nation's African American leadership.

Another dead black man. Phyllis sighed at the sad and disquieting, but recurring picture in the media of prone bodies, covered in yellow coroner's quilts. The kaleidoscope of images raced through her mind. Persy. Deandre. Black men. Shot. Stabbed. Dead.

Crime and its steady and particular attack on the black communities of Southeast and Northeast Washington had further split the city into black and white, rich and poor. Phyllis knew that Persy's death could intensify the racial divide in many of the city's neighborhoods. Affluent, white District residents would push themselves farther into the Northwest pockets of Friendship Heights, Chevy Chase and Glover Park. Additional police patrol cars would surface in these areas just after a death like Persy's, to ease the fears of those with money and a well-used vote. Meanwhile, residents of Anacostia, Lincoln Heights, Trinidad and Petworth would continue to wait too long for a needed ambulance or fire truck. The city's budget crisis had resulted in severe pay cuts for metropolitan officers, causing many to seek tempting higher salaries elsewhere and some others to respond slowly to emergencies or fall short on investigations, especially when the victims were poor and black.

"Shit, I am *not* gon' do this," Phyllis mumbled to herself, using her pinky to wipe the moisture from her eyes. Despite her strong faith, Phyllis' tongue was still no stranger to colorful speech. It was just her way. "*Damn*, Persy, why did this have to happen? Why'd you have to end up bein' another one?"

*   *   *

TO LIGHTEN HER MOOD, Phyllis began to write thank you notes to those who had attended the Congressman's annual holiday party—constituents, other Members, non-profit executive directors, corporate benefactors, lobbyists, city officials, select job seekers, and occasional political opposition from whom he or Persy might need a favor.

Phyllis glanced down at the long, guest book list of attendees. Congressman Manuel Gonzalez-Jimenez and wife Marta. Dr. Marsha Diallo, Chair, Political Science Department, Howard University. Howard Manning, AT&T External Affairs. Marshall N. James, President, NAACP. Congresswoman Delta Thomas and husband Renaldo. Juditha Hurley, Executive Director, Putting People First (PPF). Larry Leibowitz, Law Offices of Cohen, Leibowitz and Greene. His Honor Cleavon Grace, Mayor, District of Columbia. Speaker of the House William J. Blasingame and wife Allison.

Bill Blasingame and wife Allison, thought Phyllis again to herself, remembering the pair at the party. It could be described as odd at best that Blasingame and his wife had shown up at the Congressman's year-end affair. It was no secret to anyone that Congressman Jackson and Bill Blasingame had long fought politically over affirmative action, welfare reform, campaign finance reform and a host of other issues—always on opposing sides. There was no love lost between them on a personal level either.

Blasingame's appearance at the Congressman's party had sent a moment of silent agitation through the well-dressed crowd in the expensively decorated private room at the Watergate. Throats were cleared, looks were exchanged, backs went rigid.

Blasingame, attired in his customary conservative, dark gray suit and speckled tie, entered with his wife Allison on his arm, dressed in a chic, red silk designer suit, its skirt just above her stockinged knee. Allison Blasingame had an exotic beauty rarely seen in Congressional wives. Most were older, more reserved, more cultured and less stunning. Allison's tawny skin tone and long and shiny, russet, wavy hair belied her poor Tennessee upbringing. The slight slant in her eyes, the fullness of her lips and her leggy, hourglass figure made her look far more like a runway model for Donna Karan than a Congressman's spouse.

Blasingame, a wealthy, well-known Richmond surgeon in the days before the headiness of politics summoned him, and one-time chairman of the powerful Ways and Means Committee, in great contrast to his breathtaking wife, was a pale, slightly overweight man with a paunch where a trim tummy had once been, blotched skin, jowls hanging under his pudgy face and spiky, graying hair. His face was craggy like an old basketball deflated after years of grueling dribbles. His thin lips parted to show perfectly aligned small, white teeth as he smiled on-cue to those in attendance, well aware that his presence was undesired.

Why had Blasingame showed up at Congressman Jackson's holiday party—uninvited? The question stumped everyone on Jackson's staff. *Except Persy.* He was the only one who had greeted the Speaker and his wife with any real expression of cordiality. *Almost as if he expected them,* puzzled Phyllis. The others allowed themselves only perfunctory greetings and strained, small talk with the Speaker. But Persy's demeanor that evening after Blasingame's arrival had seemed deliberate, almost as if he were putting on a performance. But for *who?*

The city bus stopped begrudgingly before the Metro Center subway station. Phyllis returned the box of cards and party list to her oversized burgundy satchel and pushed her way into the crowded station, encircled by hundreds of other Washington commuters scurrying to jobs across the snow-laden city.

11

As she trudged up the left side of the Rayburn Building's driveway, Phyllis looked up upon hearing the boisterous flapping of the American flag overlooking the massive building, whipped about by the freezing December wind.

Nausea slowed her pace as she gripped her abdomen. She gazed upwards, summoning the will to keep walking, her satchel weighing her down and the cold, moist wind hindering her steps.

"Ah, damn, morning sickness. I ain't got—don't have time for this right now," she mumbled under her breath, correcting her own grammar. If she had known pregnancy would be like this, she never would have had sex. She'd thought they were being careful. *Obviously* not careful enough. "Oh, please make this go away."

By the time Phyllis had made her way down the long passageways of the building to the Congressman's office, a small crowd of officers, press and curious passersby had already gathered outside the main entranceway.

"Excuse me, please move," she said gruffly, pushing her way through the throng. Once inside, she threw down her heavy satchel and sought out Rachel, who, as the office early bird, she knew would have already arrived and who would probably be manning the ringing phones.

"Hey, Rachel, what's goin' on? Any new news?" she asked once she found Rachel just putting down her phone.

"Well, actually, yes," Rachel said. "Sergeant Filipidis says that they have a suspect in custody. Someone they picked up last night for questioning. He's black, *of course*."

The two exchanged weary, knowing glances. Both were all too accustomed to suspects in homicide cases across the city being black men, a tired reality that made African Americans throughout the metropolitan area shake their heads in constant disgust and disappointment.

"*Goddamit*, Rachel. This black on black violence has gotten on my last damn nerve," blurted Phyllis, her eyes rolling. "Sometimes, I just want to move away from here, you know, like out to the suburbs, Prince George's or Montgomery County, as far as I can get from all this craziness. Washington is my home and everything, and I love this city. But I'll be *damned* if I'll let it take my life."

After a brief, mutual silence, Jerry Berman charged into Rachel's office, his tall, wiry frame in motion and the few remaining hairs on his balding, freckled head standing at attention in the staticky air.

"Good morning, ladies. The Congressman would like to see everyone in his office for a few minutes for an updated briefing about Persy. Jill will catch the phones while we're in there, Phyllis." Phyllis could already see the petite figure of the staff's college intern, Jill Rosencrantz taking a phone message in the outer office. Every season of the year saw an invasion of college and graduate students eager to experience life on the Hill, hoping to rub shoulders with power and add something impressive to their resumes.

The entire staff, including the Congressman's Appropriations Committee aides, gathered quickly and quietly in Congressman Jackson's large office, which featured a massive mahogany desk, leather chairs and matching cabinet set, overflowing with periodicals, books and policy papers. Wearing his gold, wire-rimmed glasses, silver-and-navy tie and blue-black suit with a well-starched pin-striped dress shirt underneath, the Congressman's crisp outer appearance contrasted with the worn look on his face and the concern in his eyes as he sat down to address them. Sergeant Filipidis opened the door just as Jackson opened his mouth to speak.

"Sergeant, good of you to join us," Jackson uttered, with a tense smile. "I was just going to update the staff on the status of the case. I'm sure we would all benefit from *your* handling of this briefing. Please," he said, gesturing to a leather-backed armchair.

Anticipation mounted in the room. The phones suddenly and eerily went silent, as if on cue. A pin cascading to the speckled carpet would have been heard upon contact in the still, strained quiet of the moment. Dark blue cap in hand, the sergeant took a seat and looked around the room at the dozen or so members of Congressman Jackson's staff.

"Last night, we apprehended a suspect who we believe may be Mr. Pritchard's killer. The suspect is a black male, a 35-year old vagrant who occasionally sleeps in Folger Park. We believe that the bullets found in Mr. Pritchard's body match those of the .38 caliber revolver found on the suspect. Our SID lab is analyzing the slugs now and, ah, Ballistics is taking a look at probable entrance and exit wound angles to determine the proximity of the shooter to the victim. We, uh, hope to have some answers by later this afternoon."

"It appears that Mr. Pritchard may have been the victim of a random mugging gone wrong. Our suspicion is that the suspect became agitated. Perhaps Mr. Pritchard argued or hesitated to give up his wallet or other valuables. In his agitation, the suspect probably shot him, dragged the body into the bushes to hide it from sight and fled the scene."

"However, ladies and gentlemen, I must emphasize to you that this is still an ongoing investigation. And we'd also still like to determine where Mr. Pritchard may have been going in the wee hours of Tuesday morning. We appreciate your cooperation with the police department in suppressing any unauthorized information to the press until we have unquestionably linked the suspect to the homicide. We know that you're all anxious to know what happened to your colleague. And we're doing everything possible to pin down the culprit. It does, however, appear at this time that Mr. Pritchard was probably just in the wrong place at the wrong time."

The staff exchanged teary glances as the sergeant rose to leave.

"Sergeant," spoke Congressman Jackson. "Is it okay to have someone on the staff clear Persy's belongings from his office? His mother called this morning to request his personal effects."

The sergeant cleared his throat, his fingers toying unconsciously with the rim of his hat.

"Yes. Yes, I believe that would be all right. Our people have already been in his office to investigate. There's nothing in there that we can see that's connected to this case. We've just about completely ruled out any premeditated foul play. Now, if you'll excuse me, I'm headed back over to the district station to be present for the next round of suspect questioning."

"Sergeant," the Congressman spoke once again, standing to challenge the uniformed man face to face. "Please call our office if there's any news. If you've got the guy, we want to see him charged and put away. It's unfortunate enough that this had to happen. Our office is devastated. We're at a loss without Persy. We at least need to have the assurance that his killer will be brought to justice, despite the fact that the victim isn't a WASP from Chevy Chase."

With a quick look of contempt and a crimson face, the sergeant stared the Congressman in the eye.

"Congressman, I assure you we *are* doing everything possible to close this case. This is not about black and white, sir. It's about finding whoever killed Persuvius Pritchard." The door could be heard slamming behind him.

The Congressman's intercom interrupted the still tense atmosphere.

"Yes, Jill. We're in a meeting, no calls," he said impatiently, still thinking about the sergeant's last words.

"Uh, Congressman, it's, it's President Gray. He's on line three for you," Jill stammered.

"President Gray...," Jackson's demeanor was abrupt, rushed. "Folks, we'll have to finish this up later. If you'll excuse me. Jerry, I still need that next statement to the press. They need fresh meat to chew on.

Phyllis, call the White House and double-check my seating placement at the dinner tomorrow night, please. Last time some idiot sat me next to Glenn Boxer from the NRA."

The staff began filing out quickly.

"Phyllis, will you and Rachel please begin packing up Persy's things," he asked as an afterthought.

Both women nodded and turned to leave, heading down the short corridor to Persy's closed door. Rachel felt an odd shiver of apprehension, an irrational sense of foreboding.

Phyllis' nausea came back just as she reached for the knob to open the door. She and Rachel looked at each other, apprehension gripping them both.

"God, help me. I guess someone's got to do this," Phyllis said, turning the brass knob to enter the office of the dead man.

*   *   *

AFTER SEVERAL MINUTES OF SEARCHING AND PACKING IN the natural twilight pushing its way through the wide windows of Persy's office, Phyllis flipped on the ceiling light switch, causing her to squint momentarily from the sudden brilliance. She moved back over to the closet and continued removing Persy's jackets and knitted sweaters from the dangling hangers. In the bottom of the closet, a stack of old issues of *Time* and *Newsweek* had been placed meticulously next to similarly stacked back issues of *Roll Call*, the NAACP's *Crisis*, and *Black Enterprise* and *Emerge* magazines. The shelves of the long closet were lined with the *Journal of Foreign Affairs*, *The Chronicle of Higher Education* and various other periodicals, some dog-eared or rumpled, others apparently unread or just barely skimmed through. Page markers and written notes poked out of the magazines and books at random, evidence of Persy's inexhaustible appetite for knowledge.

Rachel's murmurings from the other side of the room caught her attention.

"What are these? *Anthony*...." Rachel looked up at Phyllis, her expression dazed. "*Anthony*..." She nearly dropped the contents of the file folder she held in her trembling hands.

12

Thursday, December 21

"Soon I will be done, trouble of the world, trouble of the world, trou—ble of the world…" bellowed the heavy-set, light-brown woman, robed in gold and black. The choir hummed in low tones behind her as the sadness of the front pews enveloped her, tears falling from her keen eyes, rolling down the creases of her bosom. "Soon I will be done, trouble of the world, I'm going home, h-O—M-e…to my GO—d." The lead singer went silent, lowered her head and stepped back to join the rest of the choir.

The reverend stood at the podium and looked down below to the open casket. He grabbed at the kente cloth draped over his robe and shouted out to the grief-stricken congregation. "The colors of this African cloth are bold and bright, the colors of the human heart. Warm, forgiving, in praise of the wonders of life. Brave and beautiful colors, the green of the earth, the yellow of the sun, the red blood of our race," He reached his hand up to his balding head and wiped at the beads of salty sweat that had begun to surface, intensifying the shine of his skin beneath the sanctuary lights.

"These colors," he exclaimed, "dare to survive against the evil and heartache that ravage our society, our people. But today, this December 21st, just days before the commemoration of the birth of our Lord and Savior Jesus Christ, the colors of the kente cloth mock me as I see only gray, the colorless spirit of the evil that has claimed our communities, that has claimed the life of our brother, Persuvius

Pritchard." The reverend held his arms outstretched, gesturing down toward the lifeless body in the white, gilded casket. His voice grew, his enunciation pointed.

"Persy gave his young life to this community, only for *it* to take his. At a tender 33, he had overcome the perils of poverty to give of himself as a motivated public servant, serving for 10 years in the office of Congressman Raymond Jackson, Jr. How proud we were of him and his continuing devotion to the community from which he came. And so today, the color has drained from my soul as I look down at brother Persy, shot down on a cold morning this week on his way to work—the victim of yet *another* random murder in this nation's capitol. Darkness has pierced our world today, and we may feel right now that we may never again see the light, that we will continue to mourn for our children lost to the gun violence in our streets. *But*, my brothers and sisters, I am here today to tell you that the Lord moves in the darkness! During our darkest moments, He is there to guide us. And so it is during times like these that we must keep strong in our faith that God will see us through—to the day when the bright colors of the kente cloth can be seen clear of the dark shadow that hangs over us this morning. May God take brother Isaiah and sister Hanna into His mighty hands and soothe them in their time of grief. And May the Lord have mercy on the soul of the killer who has taken one of our best, our brightest…"

First Pilgrim Baptist Church was awash in grief. Row upon row of dark-clothed mourners cried, wailed and blessed aloud the soul of Persy Pritchard. The anguish that hung in the air nearly suffocated the faint stench of the polluted Anacostia River that had seeped surreptitiously under the doors and through the poorly-ventilated windows of the house of worship. Phyllis reached forward instinctively, placing her hand on Mrs. Pritchard's shoulder to comfort the weeping mother. Mr. Pritchard's 60-year old, caramel-brown face seemed to have aged in the past few days from the pain of his only child's death.

His worn carpenter's hands held those of his wife as they began to receive condolences from friends and relatives.

From opposite ends of the pew, Rachel and Phyllis swapped knowing, uneasy glances, both aware of what the other was thinking. The contents of the file folder they'd come across in Persy's office was like dead weight on their minds. The old photos with the familiar face but the unfamiliar name and a cryptic note in Persy's handwriting had them both spooked. Rachel's stomach knotted up from hunger and concern. Persy's written accusations about Congressman Jackson had killed her appetite. She blinked hard in an effort to erase it from her mind.

In the back of the sanctuary, a woman stood silently, and walked out toward Martin Luther King, Jr. Avenue, virtually unnoticed, tightening the scarf on her head as she treaded out into the freezing rain, still falling from the day before. She wasn't staff. She wasn't family. She wasn't friend. Rachel could just barely pick up the oddly matched shade of the woman's eyes and her light-brown scarf.

*　　　*　　　*

DETECTIVE MIKE JAMES TOSSED THE CASE FILE ON A WOOD VENEER desk that had seen better days and roughly rubbed his honey-brown fingers through his closely-cropped, rust-colored goatee. His ex-wife Renata had called and managed to ruin his day from the get-go. They'd argued over who would have 3-year old Marcus for his birthday weekend in January, despite the fact that Mike had been awarded custody last summer in the divorce settlement. *If she hadn't slept around with that lame-ass attorney on her job down at the District general counsel's office, they wouldn't be playing tug of war with Marcus.* Since Mike's days playing second string quarterback at North Carolina, he'd had a weakness for the ladies. *He* was the one who'd always had the wandering eye for the opposite sex.

But Renata Taylor was a sweet cognac-colored beauty who had rocked his world and had kept him faithful for five years of marriage until she messed up trying to sleep her way into a higher income bracket. After partying a little too hard down south and only using his textbooks for doorstops, the registrar's office at Carolina had sent Mike a big expulsion slip after he'd paid no attention to multiple warnings. With his father, retired district lieutenant Elroy James backing him up, he had bucked the trend of his do-nothing street crew by hustling his way into the police academy where the sober realities of dead bodies, crack addicts and abused children had straightened him out fast.

Mike got something out of what he did for a living and he knew he was good at being a cop. It was his calling in life to chase the bad guys. But Renata hadn't been happy. He didn't make enough, even with over-time five days a week, to maintain the lifestyle his wife wanted to live. So she had fucked around behind his back and gotten caught. Thinking about seeing his wife buck-naked in bed with Kenneth Galbraith III, a pussy muthafucka with a prep school dick to match, made him want to bomb every law school in the country. And now she had the *nerve* to fight with him over Marcus. Ooh! In an effort to shake his frustration and anger at Renata, Mike focused his attention back onto another, more immediate concern.

He stood over his desk and stared at the file, trying to figure out why something about this whole case wasn't sitting right with him. It was typical at times to close a case within a few days, without incident, and lock the perp away for a few years to do some heavy time for rape, vehicular manslaughter, murder one, armed robbery or whatever other heinous infraction committed. But this case was sloppy and too many little pieces of the puzzle were being overlooked or ignored for the sake of a quick indictment. Or at least it appeared that way and was actually pretty obvious to Mike's practiced eye. But no one had questioned any aspect of the investigation so far, including Mike's partner Rick, who had been called out to the scene over in the park minutes after

Pritchard's body was found. An hour had transpired before Lieutenant Gravino had summoned Mike to Folger to assist.

His massive physique, outfitted in pleated, mud-brown slacks, a crisp off-white dress shirt and a colorful designer tie, with his gold badge clipped onto his brown leather belt, the rookie detective made his way across the 4th Street Southeast district headquarters. A stream of weak mid-afternoon sun forced its way through the small windows of the concrete slab building, the icy rain having let up for the moment. The district office consisted of about three thousand square feet of space housed within two stories located comfortably on a semi-quiet residential street of federal-style row houses in the heart of Capitol Hill. A dozen or so second-hand desks filled the main room of the headquarters building, arranged conveniently behind a wide counter by the entrance, manned by a rookie uniformed officer. Two dozen unis and plain-clothes detectives criss-crossed each others paths as Mike lowered a white paper cup under the water cooler spigot in the makeshift kitchen for a refill. He spotted Rick Venable taking a seat back at the desk adjoining his own. They needed to talk.

"Hey, James, man, the lab'll have the print analysis to you guys in a few," said fellow detective, Horace Freeman, slapping Mike on the back, his ready smile plastered on his face as usual. "That's too bad about that brother, Pritchard. It's ironic, man. A black man trying to do something to advance his people, doing something good, you know, and he gets shot down in cold blood. Murder with a capital M. I tell you it's a cryin' shame."

"Yeah, man, I know," offered Mike, shaking his head in mutual disappointment as he gulped the cool spring water. "What's worse, it mighta been another brother took him out. Look, thanks for the heads up on the lab info, bruh. I'll catch you at the gym later."

Mike sauntered back across the room, sat down in his metal chair, tucked a pencil behind his ear and cleared his throat. It could be a little sticky asking a bunch of questions about an investigation that Gravino had clearly given his partner Rick the lead on.

"Hey, Ven, Freeman says the prints should be called in from the lab at any minute," he uttered, tapping lightly on the case file before him. "You think we got our man?"

"Stinson? You've seen him squirm. He's guilty as hell," said Rick Venable with a confident grin on his narrow face, his green eyes settled squarely on Mike. "I'm about ninety percent sure on this one, man. He's the shooter, no doubt. *You* were here when I got the call. The guys over at the SID already confirmed the slug and residue match. Mike, we've got him on more than just circumstantial—*we* have the weapon. As big as Stinson is, his junkie ass'll be somebody's girlfriend in Lorton by next week. He'd probably fuck a goddam waterhose to feed that bad ass habit he's runnin' with. What a loser."

"Admittedly, the guy threw away a career that boys in inner cities across the country would kill for, but Rick, man, that doesn't make him a murderer. I've read the case reports three times. Don't you think it's a bit out of the ordinary to skip a more thorough sweep of Pritchard's office at Rayburn or the apartment over on 12th? If the shooter was out to rob Pritchard, why didn't he just take the whole damn wallet, not just the money that was in it? And where did Gravino get the eyewitness description fingering somebody looking like Stinson? I talked to Mrs. McCarty this morning to get a tighter ID. She said *she didn't* give a description to anyone on the force. Everybody's been so quick to assume that Stinson is the perp, that Pritchard was nothing more than a stray victim of a petty robbery, man. I'm not so sure Stinson is the one we should be holding." Mike leaned forward and loudly shuffled papers on his desk. He looked Venable dead in the eye, his deep voice dropping to a whisper. "Is somebody from up top pulling strings on this one or *what*?"

Thirty-eight year old Venable, a seven year veteran detective awaiting the outcome of the sargeant's exam he'd taken just two weeks earlier, shifted abruptly in his chair, causing it to squeak annoyingly against the scuffed, teal-colored floor tiles.

"Mike, I can't believe you would ask me some bullshit like that!" Venable shouted in his southern Virginia drawl. "This is me you're talking to. Mike, I've been on top of this case since McCarty placed her call in here Tuesday morning. We've been as thorough as we need to be. You *know* that."

"Rick, man, I'm not trying to criticize your handling of the case. It's just that—" In the midst of Mike's response, Venable's phone rang, throwing them both off. As his partner picked up the receiver, Mike sat back in his chair and threw his size 13 feet up onto the desk, pulled the pencil from behind his right ear and tucked it between his teeth. Rick was was definitely holding out on him. He could sense it as strongly as an identical twin sensing harm to his sibling. That smug grin, the minute twitching of his lips. The two had only been working together for two months, not enough time to know each others every quirk or habit, but Rick's lip twitching had already become a clear sign of uneasinesss. His thin lips had twitched in the same way last month down at Judiciary Square when Venable had testified in an Eastern Market murder and sexual assault case. Venable had come clean to Mike later that he'd lied about some make-or-break details revolving around his interrogation of the suspect involved. Just about every cop Mike knew had lied or bent the truth at one time or another to save his own ass or to ensure that a perp was sent out to Lorton. He wasn't exactly innocent himself. But he'd never fuck with a case like Pritchard's in this way. *Never.* Something was up.

Rick Venable hung up the phone. A disturbed look surfaced on his otherwise self-assured, mustachioed face.

"Harris says there were no prints on the .38. It was clean. Nothing," he said, raking his small, wide-knuckled fingers through his longish brown hair. "Hell, Stinson probably just cleaned it up before he fell asleep. Everything else fits like a glove. I told him to go back over that piece with a fine tooth comb until he finds something."

"Rick, when we pulled Stinson out of that tent, he was so fucked up he didn't even know he was being arrested, man," Mike said, biting down on the pencil eraser. "How the hell was he lucid enough to wipe a gun completely clean? I'm telling you Rick, there are some things about this case that I'm a little uncomfortable with. Maybe we should talk to Gravino."

"Mike, that *won't* be necessary. Let me deal with this. I guarantee you, this whole thing is being done by the book, *strictly,*" whistled Venable through his teeth in an exasperated tone, his dark bushy eyebrows arched.

"Yeah, man, well you deal with it the *right* way." Mike had given Venable the benefit of the doubt, but he'd blown it. Some cases were always given short shrift in the system. Dead black males, prostitutes, junkies and poor white trash seemed to make up a disproportionate number of such cases. They were society's throwaways. It made him sick. They may have had the weapon, but it had no prints, and the circumstantial evidence was nonexistent. And the motive? As intangible at the time as a ghost. Robbery. But no money found on the perp. And too many other unanswered questions for Mike to just look the other way. Persy Pritchard's case wasn't going to be closed this easily. Not if it was up to him.

13

Phyllis slammed down the phone at her desk and listened to the soft vibrating twang of the receiver settling into its cradle from the force of its fall. It rang again, the very sound of it irritating her as she tried to shake her nervous mood.

"Good afternoon, Congressman Jackson's office," she spoke in as unperturbed a voice as she could summon. "Yes, Ms. Hurley, he's still in the office. Would you like to speak with him again? If you'll hold just one moment, I'll get him for you."

After putting through the call, a brief smile flashed across her face. She delighted in thinking that the Congressman must be getting pretty serious about Hurley. She had already put through no less than three calls from Hurley that day.

She imagined herself in Hurley's place, running a nationally-recognized, well-funded organization. Classy. Sophisticated. A real mover and shaker. Her elite social circle included the likes of Vernon Jordan, Washington insider and close confidante of President Gray; Eleanor Holmes Norton, Washington's delegate to Congress; Ofield Dukes, long-time, high-profile public relations guru; Bob Johnson, founder and president of Black Entertainment Television, the popular late Secretary of Commerce, Ron Brown, and Mary Lynn Rutledge-Gray, the self-assured, highly visible wife of the President.

If Phyllis could just play her cards right, and finish school, maybe she could work toward a life like that. Money. Influence. Famous friends. Interviews on the evening news. *Happiness.*

"A baby'll ruin all of that," she grumbled, feeling the ceaseless hunger that now forced her to eat two lunches. "But Lord, *what am I supposed to do?*" She stared upwards, clasping the silver cross that dangled around her ample neck, and summoning a being she felt greater and more powerful than herself.

At that moment, Seargeant Filipidis stepped through the office door from the busy hallway.

"Hello, Ms. Roberson. I need to speak with Congressman Jackson if I may, please," he said. He remained standing, holding a two-way radio in his right hand, as Phyllis got up to summon her boss.

Congressman Jackson, dressed in his black wool coat, emerged from his office with a slightly ruffled facial expression nearly masked by his interest in the sergeant's visit. He held a stack of papers under his arm, poised to dash to the Capitol for the vote.

"Congressman, I wanted to come right over with the news from our lab," said the sergeant, fiddling with the radio, neglecting to shake Jackson's large, extended hand. "The lab results are conclusive. The slugs extracted from Mr. Pritchard's body are an identical match to the gun found on the suspect we're detaining. The lab supervisor also feels certain that the residue from the barrel of the .38 matches that discovered on Mr. Pritchard's clothing."

"It looks like we've probably got our shooter. Of course, the son-of-a-bitch swears he didn't do it. Even broke down and cried. Swore he'd never kill anybody. Said he was asleep all night on top of a heated grate in the alley of a building on C Street. The guy has a list of priors, served time for assault and battery, and has three charges on drug possession that were dropped. Fell through the cracks on technicalities. He cried like a mama's boy in the interrogation room. Typical, I'm-not-guilty performance, I'm afraid. Not only is the suspect a junkie, he's a former pro ball player. Played with the Lakers for four years. It's a damn shame. *Damn* shame. Anyway, we're still on the look out for evidence that might point in other directions, though. But it looks like this one may be pretty open and shut. Every once in a while, we get lucky right away. We—"

"BZZZZZZZZZZ"

The buzzer on the round, wall clock above the main office entrance resonated throughout the office, signaling the impending vote at the Capitol.

"Sergeant, we're relieved to hear that you've cleared this one up quickly," said Jackson, his face breaking into a charming smile, his demeanor easing. "I'll inform the rest of the staff when I get back. I've got an important matter to vote on in the House Chamber. I'm afraid I've got to leave now. Why don't you fill me in on the details on the way out. Phyllis, if Ms. Hurley calls again, tell her you don't expect me back in the office later this afternoon, hear?"

I thought he just said he was coming back later, she thought.

The sergeant and Congressman Jackson departed hurriedly out into the hallway, their footsteps echoing down the corridor.

The bullets match the gun found on the suspect? puzzled Phyllis under her breath. *Maybe Persy was wrong all along. Maybe he was just in the wrong place at the wrong time. Maybe there's nothing to be worried about after all. But…those pictures…Maybe somebody's smarter than Sergeant Filipidis* and *his Capitol Hill police…*

Phyllis opened the staff file, still sitting open on her desk from the day before.

Rachel Mooreshelton—202-371-9223.

Knowing that Rachel would probably not return to the office later in the evening after the Committee vote and the Supreme Court ruling, Phyllis picked up the phone. She slowly and meticulously dialed Rachel's number as if the slightest misdial could be lethal. She whispered a careful message.

"Rachel, this is Phyllis. The sergeant says the bullets in Persy's body came from the gun they found on that suspect they're holding. They're probably going to close the case. They think they've got the person who killed Persy. But…well, maybe they don't. Those pictures might…I don't know, but maybe they're wrong. Call me when you get home. You've got the number, I think. We ain't gon' just sit on this, Rach. We *can't*. Bye."

Phyllis put the phone down gently. Her breathing was hard and her eyes darted around the room. The rest of the staff were absorbed in their work, on the telephone or otherwise preoccupied. *None of them know do they? Something is not right. It's just not right.* She wished that she had never helped Rachel clear Persy's things. She wished she had never agreed to stay silent. *How could I be such an idiot?* She wished Persy had never been killed. She wished those people had never been killed, that those gunmen had never even walked into that bank.... *She wished she didn't know....*

14

Rachel stepped hastily into the cab. The day's gray skies had disappeared into darkness. Ominous clouds had passed southward, opening the heavenly expanse of night to share its diamond-studded stars with the universe.

"Old Ebbitt Grill, 15th Street, please," she said settling into the worn, rear seat of the rattletrap taxi. The cab turned left and sped up Constitution Avenue toward downtown.

On one hand, she felt exhilarated, triumphant. The Committee had voted to appoint a special prosecutor to launch a thorough investigation into Speaker Blasingame's fund-raising practices during his previous campaign. In November, the *Post* had published a two-part expose of serious alleged campaign improprieties, leaked by an anonymous source close to the Speaker. Reportedly, the allegations were just the tip of the iceberg. Names had been bandied about. Speculation still pervaded the Hill as to who might have exposed the Speaker. Well, now that person would have to come forward if the investigation were to proceed. Now, it was almost as certain as the moon was full that both the Justice Department and the Federal Election Commission would commence their own scrutinous probes into the Speaker's campaign activities, placing him yet further under the federal microscope, and in the media's hot seat. The *Post's* allegations were detailed, far-reaching and brutal. The Speaker's long, prosperous career now hung in the balance, and he knew it.

Of course, thought Rachel, *Congressman Jackson was thrilled. He'd had a grin on his face as wide as the Anacostia River.* Reporters from the *Times*, *The African American Journal*, her father's paper, and *Newsweek*, had all been on hand on the steps of the Capitol Building to interview Jackson and other Democrats, hoping to acquire juicy, biting quotes to provide fodder for a Republican response. Many of the reporters had also questioned the Congressman about the investigation into Persy's death, to which he answered with a curt, "No comment at this time." Again, Rachel sensed from what she knew to be a distressed tone that Jackson was uncomfortable with Persy's murder and the investigation. Strangely enough, she had a nagging feeling that it wasn't due to grief alone.

On the other hand, Rachel could not mask her disappointment in the Supreme Court's ruling that yet another majority-minority district, drawn along racial lines to better ensure election of a minority representative to Congress, was unconstitutional under the 14th Amendment. The ruling served another blow to the Congressional Black Caucus.

Members from the Washington, Maryland and Virginia chapters of the NAACP, students from Howard University Law School and others had gathered outside the imposing white, granite Supreme Court on Maryland Avenue to protest the Court's decision. Peculiarly, Rachel had not seen Juditha Hurley or representatives of the PPF in the crowd. She couldn't believe that Hurley had not used the ruling as yet another opportunity to grandstand or another avenue to self-promotion. *Then again, Hurley had been allegedly linked lately to the Heritage Council.* Rachel had heard lots of rumors recently.

Rachel emotionally examined the sea of angry faces—black and white alike—shouting, calling, chanting. Signs were thrust up and down, back and forth, jockeying for camera coverage or the eye of a probing reporter from *Time* or CNN.

Rachel let her mind drift. The cab turned up the wide stretch of Pennsylvania Avenue in the direction of the White House. Rush hour traffic crawled at its customary pace. Night-blue Lincoln town cars, Metro buses and a parade of other cars, vans and four-wheel-drive vehicles inched down the icy street. As her cab pushed forward, Rachel admired the historic beauty of Washington that she so often took for granted during her hectic daily routine.

The National Museum of Art, the whiteness of its huge mass glowing eerily from dozens of bright lights shining up from its base. The National Archives, standing at attention, its wide columns majestic. The Justice Department, its squared, hard corners signifying the serious work to be done up and down its maze of red-carpeted corridors. The Ford Theatre, where President Lincoln's cruel fate still drew wide-eyed tourists.

The cab again turned, this time onto 15th Street. Looking over her shoulder, Rachel could just see the Washington Monument ascending slowly above the trees across from the Department of Commerce. *There's the big pencil*, she thought, smiling, remembering her childhood nickname for the imposing sight. The point of the Monument pierced the darkness like a magic wand, sprinkling stars throughout the night sky.

This was why she loved Washington. Its history. Its politics. Its good. Its bad. Its *power*. It could drain her idealism, zap her emotions in the midst of ugly legislative confrontations, and chip away at her hope that the 435 Americans representing the millions would do right for the sake of what's right. Washington had brought the reality of politics to her doorstep and dropped it with a thud. But somewhere, underneath the egomania, the influence peddling, the compromising of ideals and the finger pointing, underneath all of that she knew there was something good worth hanging around for, worth working for.

"That'll be, ah, $5.35," said the cab driver in a vaguely familiar foreign accent. Rachel reached in her wallet, handed the man six wrinkled, single bills and stepped out to see the huge, well-known, gold letters that spelled out the name of the historic Washington bar and cozy restaurant. For over fifty years, Washington old-money insiders had gathered at the Old Ebbitt Grill to gossip, deal make on a handshake and commune within the walls of the exclusive establishment. In recent years, its antique oak walls had begun to attract a younger set, young yuppies and buppies from law firms, Capitol Hill and the press, in search of a good beer.

Rachel had never really taken to the restaurant. Not enough brown faces in the place to please her. In the past few years, after the relief of graduation from Princeton, she had made a point to spend time at the city's black clubs and bars, with her girlfriends. She loved the hot throb of house music and Old School tunes with extra bass. The throngs of people, of all shades of brown and beige, mixing, talking, and dancing under sultry, dim lights.

As she adjusted her rumpled coat, a stinging breeze slapped its icy hand against her face, paralyzing the tiny hairs on her neck, and forcing her eyes to surrender droplets of frigid tears.

She stepped through the heavy revolving door. Old Ebbitt Grill, in stark contrast to her usual spots was well-lit. Rich oak paneling and brass fixtures adorned the interior, and elaborate stained glass and burning candles illuminated the crowded bar. Gladys Knight's *I Heard It Through the Grapevine* could just barely be heard, piped in as filler behind the cheerful chatter of the clientele, attired in loafers, casual blazers, button-down shirts, and worn jeans.

She and Thad had visited the bar just two weeks ago and had had a great time, wrapped up in each others glances over a bottle of White Zinfandel and a shared plate of spiced shrimp. But tonight, the happy faces and idle small talk just fueled the uneasiness and growing sense of alarm that she had tried her best to suppress all day.

Rachel hung her coat on top of others on the tipsy, standing coat rack and unexpectedly found a stool at the bar near the entrance.

"Hi, there, what can I get you tonight?" asked the smiling bartender, his tall, slender body sporting a white dress shirt accented with a burgundy bow-tie and suspenders. The bartender stared momentarily at

Rachel, noticing the disturbed, frozen look on her otherwise lovely, cherubic face. "You look like you could use something warm."

"Yeah, uh, thanks. I'll have a Bailey's coffee please." Rachel pulled absentmindedly at her wool turtle neck, the dread rising from her stomach feeling as if it would choke her. *6:45.* She glanced back toward the bar's revolving glass door out into the dark, busy street outside, still jammed with traffic fleeing to Northern Virginia and Maryland suburbs. Thad had not yet arrived. The cheerful conversation and holiday spirit around her, after only minutes, buzzed in her head like a raging alarm clock that she couldn't turn off. She peered up to the small TV above the bar framed by bottles of Absolut, Jack Daniels, and Tanqueray.

"Tonight on Eyewitness News at Seven, the House Ethics Committee votes today to appoint a special prosecutor to investigate charges of campaign finance corruption in the office of Speaker of the House Bill Blasingame.

Partisan impasse, will the Republicans and the President resolve their budget squabbles before the winter recess?

Turning back the clock? The Supreme Court hands down a controversial ruling today on the constitutionality of race-based congressional districts.

A city in trouble, Diana Sinise reports on the mayor and city council, embroiled in yet another battle over painful budget cuts.

And a former Los Angeles Laker will face a grand jury tomorrow in the Tuesday shooting death of the chief of staff of one of the nation's most prominent Members of Congress.

Later on Eyewitness News, is your youngster eating too much? Roger Donovan has tips for keeping your kids away from fat. Don't go away, Channel—"

Two large hands encircled Rachel's throat without warning and squeezed playfully.

"OH! my God!" gasped Rachel, clasping her hand to her heart, throwing her head around to look at Thad who was grinning slyly. "You scared the shit out of me! Dammit Thad, you know you can get hurt doing that to people. And, anyway, I'm not in the mood for fun and games right now. As if my nerves aren't already on the tip of a ledge ready to jump. Don't do that again, okay? I just can't take it right now."

"Yeah, hello to you too, Rach. I'm just trying to lighten things up. This hasn't been the best week for either one of us. I know you've heard the news about the Speaker." Thad leaned over to give Rachel a quick kiss, his cold cheek brushing against hers. "Let's try to get a table. I'm starving. I, uh, missed lunch today. Allison Blasingame was in the office most of the day with those kids, about ten of them. You would have thought I was there to baby-sit."

"Thad, you know I can't stand Allison Blasingame or your sleazy boss," Rachel said, picking up her coffee mug to move toward the wooden booths. "but I have to admit I think her work with foster kids is commendable—more commendable than marrying the Speaker. She's really into those kids from Social Services."

"Alright already, we're not going to discuss my boss or the Ethics vote. The last thing I'm trying to do is end up in an argument tonight, okay?" The two sat across from each other in a small windowless booth in a corner near the restrooms. They quickly ordered from a stocky waitress who took their requests with indifference. Thad reached inside his black business pouch and pulled out a brown, light-weight clasp envelope and hesitantly handed it to Rachel.

"Look, I think you should take a look at this. One of the interns handed it to me this afternoon, unopened," he said, lowering his voice to a whisper. Rachel tugged at the tiny, silver clasps, reached in and pulled out a copy of a newspaper clipping—a photo, dated August 12, 1972. In familiar handwriting *San Francisco Chronicle* was scribbled above the picture. A blazing fire leapt at her from the file photo, firemen battling its flames at dusk. Rachel peered down at the caption.

Rescue teams fight an evening blaze on Denver Street after being summoned by a neighbor who smelled gas. Arson is suspected in the Saturday blaze which apparently took the life of 26-year old Anthony Ford, a prime suspect sought in the June 12 robbery in Oakland where 3 perished, including the suspect's wife, Queenie Wasserman. San Francisco police are trying to determine whether suicide may have been a motive in the setting of the blaze. The coroner's office has attempted to use military medical records of the former Army medic to ensure a positive id, but the body of the dead man was burned beyond recognition.

"Thad, what is this? So? This is a picture of a fire in San Francisco," muttered Rachel, staring at Thad and shrugging her petite shoulders. Then a sudden flash of recognition spread across her face, illuminated by the soft glow of the candle on the table before her. "Wait a minute. A fire that killed *Anthony Ford*…in August of 1972…prime suspect in a June bank robbery? But then…"

"There's more, stick your hand back in there and see what else you might pull out." Thad nervously sat back in the booth and waited for Rachel's reaction to the remainder of the envelope's contents. She removed a cassette tape, numbered "one" and a handwritten note, in *Persy's handwriting*. She knew his handwriting anywhere. She'd had to read more of his scrawled memos and notes than she cared to remember and his loopy scribble was distinct.

"What is this?" she asked of no one in particular, as she began to read the note with apprehension.

It's amazing how someone at the highest reaches of government can fool the people for so long, especially in this information age in which the press digs into every nook and cranny of a politician's existence. But some remarkably escape scrutiny, when they may deserve it the most. My disappointment consumes me. My faith—a faith in law and justice and of the goodness inherent in most people—has been shaken at its core, betrayed by one of my own…and others. And no one, including you, especially you, are innocent of the madness that power and influence spreads through our elected officials—our pillars of society.

The corruption and hopelessness of the times is rampant…and I am an unwilling **witness** *to its devastation. Two years of searching and probing, only to find that my darkest suspicions of some of our best, some of our most courageous, are true. And that kills me. And it will destroy you, who have attempted to reduce our influence to dust. You want to keep it all for yourselves. You see, I understand the angry white male. But you are not his salvation. You are his thorn. Persuvius Pritchard.*

She flipped the note over. A series of numbers were scrawled haphazardly. NB 006120028, 216401882, 220441056, 221602345, 216389921, H.R. 1218, H.R. 1517, 2301 Bladensberg, prop. file #68-01, #72-05, #100-00, Rosewood & Hall.

"Jesus," Rachel whispered, goose bumps rising quickly amongst the wispy, dark hairs on her arms. "*Persy*. So, it *is* true. According to him, it sounds like it *is* all true." She clutched the note as her right hand stretched up to cover her lips. "Oh, my God. What are we going to *do*? This is crazy."

"Rach, what are you talking about? I don't get it…what is he talking about?" Thad leaned toward Rachel, his voice in a hushed tone. "All this rambling about dishonesty and politicians…what was wrong with him? Do you really know something *about this*? Why the hell would he send this stuff to *Blasingame's* office of all places?"

"I found some torn photo scraps and a weird tape in Persy's office the night before he was killed. I didn't really think anything about any of it. I just thought the stuff was interesting, you know. So, I thought I'd keep the tape for a day since Persy told me he was taking the day off on Tuesday." Rachel stopped, slightly exasperated from the emotional mixture of denial and bizarre truth ringing in her head.

"But the tape had some news audio on it about three people murdered in a bank robbery in Oakland, California by a group of intruders. The audio claims the armed intruders were members of the Black

Panther Party. The robbery took place, I guess, during the Nixon Administration because the news woman went on to mention something about Nixon, but then the tape cut off. That seemed to be all that was on the tape."

"And the photos—they were actually just torn pieces of pictures of three men standing, I think standing on a street somewhere. The place didn't look familiar. But the faces had been torn off. I just didn't really think anything about it, but—" Rachel tugged at her braids and moved her fingers frantically through her scalp, her pulse racing wildly.

"Thad, something's wrong. Something is really *wrong* here and—" she sat back in silence, staring at the black-and-white photos that lined the wall of the booth. Snapshots of Members of Congress shaking hands, giving speeches, standing in Old Ebbitt Grill, slapping each others shoulders—all white men.

"What is it? I mean, what is this all about Rachel? I'm still in the dark," Thad pleaded, grabbing for her left hand, laying limply on the table. "What's with the clipping, and the tape and note and those numbers?"

"I don't know. But things that I've seen in the past few days give me a bad feeling. What I'm thinking just can't be right. *Can't* be." She leaned forward and looked Thad in the eyes—those mesmerizing gray eyes that had swept her away soon after they met.

"Yesterday, Congressman Jackson asked Phyllis and me to clear Persy's things from his office. That was a strange experience, you know, packing up a dead man's belongings, but, I guess somebody had to," she paused to catch her breath, looking around her, suddenly feeling an awkward paranoia as if everyone in the restaurant were listening.

"We were packing his books and magazines and stuff into boxes and, well, the sun was starting to go down so the office was getting darker. Phyllis went over and turned the overhead light on and then I saw this file folder under Persy's laptop case. Before I put it into the box I noticed it seemed to be unbendable, you know, like there were some pictures or something inside, Persy posed with the Congressman, or family maybe.

Well, um, there *were* pictures—polaroids—but they were old. One was of a black man in his twenties, with a cocky smirk on his face, standing out near a street corner, wearing a black leather jacket and posing with what looked like an assault rifle. Another was the same man, maybe in his twenties with his arm over the shoulder of a blond, white woman. The face of the third person wasn't there. The date on the pictures said *summer, 1971* and *Anthony, Queenie* was written at the bottom. A third name had been blotted out so hard with a black pen there was nearly a hole in the photo. I didn't even have to think twice to know that the second picture, which was torn, was the missing piece to the scraps I had found on Monday night. Except the second pair of legs turned out to be that of a *woman*, not a man."

"Yeah, okay, some old pictures. What about them? How is this all related, or is it?" asked Thad. "Look, sweetheart, we're getting ourselves all wound up for nothing, right? This package that came to the office was probably sent by some nut. The same package was probably mailed to twenty other Members. There's always some disaffected voter out there trying to scare someone. Maybe somebody just wanted Persy to look bad, look crazy or something."

"No, Thad, I don't think so," argued Rachel, tightening her grip on Thad's hand. "You don't get it. The pictures of *Anthony*…they're—"

"Here we go folks," interrupted the waitress abruptly. "Cheeseburger well-done and Ebbitt club sandwich. Can I get you anything else?" She blurted, looking back toward the kitchen as she placed the platters in front of Thad and Rachel. The two shook their heads and the woman walked listlessly back to the kitchen.

"Thad, *Congressman Jackson* is in the pictures. It's *him*," whispered Rachel, pushing her cheeseburger aside. "I think *Anthony* in the pictures is *Congressman Jackson*. I know that cocky smirk anywhere. I can't explain it. I don't really understand it. But the only explanation scares the *shit* out of me, and Phyllis wants to go to him tomorrow to ask about it. But she *can't*. We *can't* until we figure out what it's all about. I think Persy already had. He had scribbled another note that was in the file, rambling on about dishonesty, the black man's code of silence and God's wrath and how he couldn't live with the knowledge of something so bad. It was almost like a suicide note, but, um, I guess somebody got to him before he could do it himself."

"On the back of the paper, there are handwritten notes in the margins with the letters *AGFB* and scribbled words like, *FBI, Tennessee* and *Washington Post*. Thad, what's on this tape? Did you listen to it?"

"Well, hello Rachel. And how are you this evening?" Startled, Rachel looked up into the ebony brown face of Juditha Hurley, her hazel eyes glowing under the lights, giving her an almost menacing expression.

"Oh, uh, Ms. Hurley…I'm, uh, fine, and you?" Rachel offered, working to regain her composure. "I know you must be as upset as the rest of us about the Supreme Court ruling today."

"Yes, well, the clock is ticking further backwards everyday," Hurley said, her penetrating eyes fixed on Thad. "Some people have to be run over to fork over equal opportunity. But at least we did have a coup of sorts in the hanging of the Speaker. He'll be finished by the time the special prosecutor is done. The rumor is that George V. Moskowitz from Cohen, Leibowitz and Greene is slated to get the job."

"Ms. Hurley, Thad Derrickson." Thad reached out his hand toward Hurley. "I work for Speaker Blasingame, and I don't think anything will come of the whole matter. It's just a publicity stunt being pulled by the Gray Administration. *Anything* to put an end to the Republican revolution."

"I *know* who you are, my dear," Hurley stared back at Rachel, her eyebrow arched. "Keeping strange company these days, Miss Mooreshelton? I'm a little surprised at you. I hope we're not talking policy this evening…" Rachel and Thad exchanged quick glances.

"Ms. Hurley, it's been a pleasure to meet you. Have a nice evening," said Thad, strong suggestion in his deep voice. Hurley smiled wickedly and strolled off to join a group of well-starched white men and women at a large table in the back of the restaurant.

"Great. Now she knows that we know each other. I'm sure she can't wait to tell the Congressman who she saw me with," sulked Rachel, looking down at the table.

"She should be the least of your concerns right now," Thad returned. "Look let's get out of here. If we hurry, we can get over to the Library of Congress before it closes, look through some of the old clippings for more info on this stuff. It *does* all sound pretty crazy. Maybe we can get some answers over there. Come on. Let's just leave the food."

"Thad, I don't know how much more of this I *want* to know..." said Rachel, her voice unsure and her fingers gripped tightly around the envelope as if some strong force might try to steal it away. "Congressman Jackson could never hurt anyone. This, this Anthony couldn't be him, but I know that it could be. What about that fire? Who's face is missing? Is the *missing* face Anthony? If all of this didn't have anything to do with the Congressman, why else would Persy have been so upset?"

"There's only one way to find out Rachel. Look, let's go. We've gotta hurry," Thad and Rachel paid for and left behind their uneaten food, hot steam still curling over Rachel's cheeseburger. Rachel grabbed her coat, nearly knocking over the coat stand. She looked back over her shoulder as they departed hastily, to see Juditha Hurley staring at her through the crowd of strangers, her steely hazel eyes and the draft from the revolving door both sending a shiver through Rachel as she and Thad raced toward the Metro Center subway.

15

Phyllis held the remote control firmly and pushed play. She sat back in her favorite red velvet chair, parked next to the radiant Christmas tree as the smell of fresh pine floated through the small row house. Oprah Winfrey spoke to her from the 20"-inch set, taped from earlier that day. She figured a good shot of TV would take her mind off reality and thrust it into a dark shadow for a while to clear.

"Today on Oprah, we'll explore an experience that none of us ever wants to live through—a mother's loss of a child to gun violence. The proliferation of illegal guns in this country coupled with an escalating drug trade in cities and towns across the nation and violence in the media, has raised gun related deaths of young people under the age of twenty-five to over 20,000 annually. A sad statistic but true.

Verda Washington's son Jawon was shot to death eight months ago on a corner in her southeast D.C. neighborhood, and she's here today to share her story of grief, anger and helplessness. And Joanne Sfarga of Seattle, Wa—"

"Pearl! Pearl! It's cold Pearl. Shit, shhhhhhhhittttttttttttt, dammmit. Hmph. Hey! Hee, hee. Pearl!" Phyllis jumped at the sudden sound of Uncle Jet rapping loudly at the front door. She unlocked the large bolt lock which kept the miserable cold and anything else out that might be lurking. Uncle Jet stood in the doorway, his eyes ablaze and his tightly curled, graying hair unruly and spittle running down his face from his quivering lips.

"Uncle Jet, damn, you scared the shit out of me," Phyllis complained, still catching her breath. "You can't be out here howling on the front porch. Why didn't you use your key to get in downstairs?"

"Umhmm. Shittt. And...I shall punish them for their ways and reward them for their doings....Therefore shall the land mourn, and every one that dwelleth therein shall languish," cried Phyllis' uncle, gripping her arm tightly, his eyes pleading for understanding. "...the people that doth not understand shall fall."

"Uncle Jet, what are you *talking* about? Look, let me get you downstairs before Mama gets home and screams at you. You know she doesn't like you being up here." Phyllis slowly maneuvered her uncle through the narrow hallway, opened the locked basement door and led him carefully down the stone steps to his unkempt living space. Her uncle continued to spit, jerk and raise his arms while mumbling verses from the Great Book.

"He hath blinded their eyes, and hardened their heart..." he mumbled, looking gently up at her as she sat him on his unmade bed.

He was getting weirder every day. It just wasn't natural for anyone to act that way. He was like a child who awakens from a nightmare, but can't be calmed. *This preachin' and shit is startin' to sound downright scary...*

Phyllis's eyes widened as she looked around her uncle's small, cluttered living space. She rarely ventured down here. It was dank and dungeon-like with solitary light bulb dangling from the ceiling. Uncle Jet's bed and personal possessions were crammed haphazardly into a corner of the large room, which also housed the washer and dryer Phyllis' mother used twice a month to wash all of their clothes. Not that Uncle Jet was ever tidy, but tonight books, old check stubs and endless junk were thrown around the room as if the man had, in a fit of frustration or rage, spewn his belongings in every direction.

There were dozens of first-edition books, *The Fire Next Time, Native Son, Fire and Ice, Manchild in the Promised Land, The Collected Teachings of Mao Tse Tung,* and what looked as if they were original, signed, hand-written notes of Huey P. Newton—all yellowed with their pages curling inward like a child's lock of hair. With her uncle seated, still mumbling, though now in whispered tones, Phyllis sifted through the papers that littered the floor, so old that their edges had turned brown. She wondered where in the world he had squirreled all of this away and why he had pulled it all out just to throw it around the room. Many of the papers appeared to be internal FBI memos, press releases, untitled pages of reports with the FBI's prominent logo imprinted on the masthead as well as internal memos on Rosewood & Hall letterhead, somehow involving the prominent Georgetown lobbying firm. There were old, opened and unopened envelopes without return addresses that had been sent to Jet, all to the same P.O. Box number. She checked some of the faded postmarks. *Atlanta, GA April 1976. Washington, D.C. November 1978. Washington, D.C. February 1979. Washington, D.C. November 1995.*

"Uncle Jet, what the hell *is* all of this?" she asked, holding up a handful of brittle, stained memoranda.

The man's eyes focused on hers as they rarely did. He lightly patted the books that lay on the bed next to him.

"Now you see? They are comin' for me. Just a matter 'a time…" Jet laid his frail body onto the bed, wrapped himself into the fetal position and closed his eyes. He had said what needed to be said, and had shown what needed to be shown. In his confused mind, God's work had been done.

*　　　　　*　　　　　*

PHYLLIS RETURNED UPATAIRS TO THE COMFORT OF THE LIVINGROOM, still a little disoriented over what she had seen in the basement. *Oprah* was still on, tears streaming down her face while she sat hand in hand with an older black woman, shaking and crying as she told how her son was killed in cold blood.

"Oh, God, please. This is not what I need to be looking at. Death, death, death. You'd think there ain't no good news in this *damn* world," she grumbled to herself, pressing the stop button on the remote. Memories of Deandre invaded her thoughts, his crooked grin, his cocky swagger, the way he used to drink up all the milk and leave the empty plastic jug in the fridge just to annoy the ladies of the house. His swollen body at the morgue, his closed eyes bulging, his beautiful coffee-colored skin turned sallow. Still and dead. Oprah's face disappeared and a cable channel eight news report popped onto the screen of the TV.

"*Tonight, internal affairs investigators paid a surprise visit to a warehouse on Bladensburg Road, northeast where the Property Division of the D.C. Metropolitan Police is responsible for housing and classifying hundreds of stolen weapons and thousands of dollars in cash bundles seized annually from crime suspects. D.C. Chief of Police Hamilton "Ham" Draper has offered no comment this evening to Eight News in connection with how and why thousands in drug money and weapons have turned up missing. Foul play within the ranks? Gerald Tanuda is live in northeast with—Click! Wheel of Fortune! With your host Pat—Click! Coming to you in an exclusive on BET, here's Mary J. Blige and her latest release on Video Soul—Click! This movie is rated-R—Click!*" Phyllis channel surfed until something of interest caught her eye.

"*I want the American people to know that as President, I am doing everything possible to resolve the budget impasse with the Republican leadership,*" spoke a smiling, bright-eyed President Gray, after Phyllis pressed the button on the remote for channel four. "*We want our people back to work, our government back in full operation and our political parties working together in Congress to do what's best for our country. During this holiday season, the people of this great nation need to feel secure— secure in their jobs, secure in their neighborhoods and secure in the fact that the government does and will continue to work for you.*" Phyllis sat back to listen, spurred by the President's earnest expression and caring demeanor. She liked President Gray. She had cast her first ballot ever for the man who had shook her hand during his campaign when he'd visited black-owned businesses along Georgia Avenue two summers ago.

"The untimely death this week of a young man in his prime, a man working to make our government a better one underscores the importance of community and crime prevention. Persy Pritchard was shot to death on his way to work in the wee hours of a dark morning here in our nation's capitol. His death came as a blow to his boss, and my long-time friend, Congressman Raymond Jackson, Jr., and his family in Southeast Washington, D.C. His death also came as yet another blow to law enforcement in our nation's cities, and to all the citizens who expect to be protected from those who hold so little regard for human life. Persy died alone and unprotected and it is our job, at the local, state and national levels to better ensure the safety of the American people. I intend to propose stronger gun control enforcement in the new year and increase the budget for law enforcement, in the hope that more young men like Persy will grow into old age.

I bid the American people a good night and a safe and joyous holiday season. God bless you all. Goodnight." Phyllis caught the last twinkle in President Gray's emerald-tinted eyes before the camera cut away to political pundit, Storm Haley, for post-address commentary.

9:03. Phyllis turned the channel to *Friends,* just as she noticed a dense, wet, foggy haze beginning to settle over Kennedy Street. She walked into the kitchen to get a glass of milk to quiet her rumbling stomach. The tiny life inside of her demanded to be fed. She nuzzled her abdomen with the palm of her hand.

"Alright, alright, I'm gonna feed you. Don't worry, it's comin'," she whispered, staring downward. The conflicting feelings about the baby entered her mind again, pushing forth from the back lot of her conscience. Replaying the scene of Oprah's crying guests in her mind, she wondered if it were even worth bringing another delicate life into such a crazy world. But then, on the other hand, life was so short, why not experience all the happiness there is to have? She and the baby could be happy on their own. Why wait for motherhood if God had already given her an opportunity? Maybe it was meant to be…Brian had left no less than ten messages for her since yesterday. She had refused to return his calls, despite her mother's complaints about Phyllis *lettin' that man wallow while you play selfish*. She had kept her mother in the dark about Brian's lies. Pearl Roberson had been just as charmed by Brian's luscious good looks and polite manners as Phyllis had been. For some reason, Phyllis couldn't bear to tarnish his image in her mother's eyes as he had done in hers. Her mother had hoped so much that Brian was the good man her daughter deserved. *For now, why ruin the illusion?* Phyllis had figured.

On her way back into the living room, glass of milk, and a plate of steaming, leftover baked chicken and green beans in hand, Phyllis was instantly aware that she had not heard back from Rachel. Quickly placing the plate down, she reached for the phone and dialed Rachel's number, still lingering in her head from earlier. Rachel's answering machine again picked up. *Damn*, grumbled Phyllis as the greeting played. *Beeeeeeeeep.*

"Rachel, did you get my message earlier today? This is Phyllis," sighed Phyllis, pacing back and forth in the narrow hallway between the living room and the kitchen with the cordless phone. "I need you to call me as soon as you get home. We gotta talk about this thing with the pictures, and I'm not sure if you heard about the upcoming arraignment of that man bein' held for Persy's murder. Damn, Rachel, where are you? Call me." *Click.*

A knot in her stomach tightened, both from growing hunger and the tension that she feared would bring back the nausea that had ruined her morning. She grabbed her plate of food and plopped back into the chair, seeing the colorful Howard University brochure and application that had arrived last week. It was her dream to complete a degree in communications at Howard, like her friend Shelley had. *That degree would get her off on the right foot.*

"This ain't no goddam game we playin'. Rachel needs to get her ass home so we can talk about this," Phyllis hissed aloud to herself, staring at the application. "She got some nerve tellin' me what I will or won't do, what I should or shouldn't do. Her ass is gon' get me fired she keep playin' around. I'm gon' talk to the Congressman *tomorrow*. He'll explain all this shit. I don't care *what* she says. Just because she already got her college degree and she sittin' pretty over there in her Connecticut Avenue condo don't mean *shit*. She ain't gon' fuck up the little bit I got."

Her food getting cold, she picked up the phone again and dialed Rachel's number. The *same* greeting saying the *same* thing played once again in her ear. *Dammit Rachel.* She couldn't shake the bad feeling that had toyed with her nerves all day. A twinge of nausea that her strong will couldn't keep down, gnawed at her insides. *God dammit Rachel, where are you?*

16

A smoky film of mist from the north moved stealthily across the sky, covering the whiteness of the moon and the sprinkle of stars as Thad and Rachel ran into the 13th Street entrance of the Metro Center subway station. They raced down the escalator, their feet barely hitting each steep step.

Almost surreal in its appearance, the station opened up before them, looking like a space station from a Star Trek movie. The high ceilings and taupe-colored, squared shapes carved into the surrounding stone walls served as temporary shelter to the hundreds of holiday shoppers and nighttime partygoers waiting for the sleek silver trains to scoop them up and whisk them off. The two jumped onto a Blue Line train toward Capitol South station and sped off into the darkness of the narrow tunnel.

Thad and Rachel sat next to each other in silence, neither daring to speak further about their suspicions until well away from a listening crowd. Rachel looked around the train car. Aside from a few young college students, the passengers were quiet, their subway faces—no eye contact, intense stares at the carpeted floor—intact. Rachel worked to catch her breath after their race to the station, but realized that her breathlessness was spurred more by fearful anticipation than physical exhaustion. Thad reached for her hand with a quick, wavering glance. She held it tight, the damp cold of his familiar palm easing her alarm only for a moment.

After several minutes that seemed to stretch into an hour, the train stopped at Capitol South and Thad and Rachel strode hastily through the station and out into the shiny wetness of First Street. *8:30*, Rachel's watch read. The two slowed their pace to a brisk walk, confident that they would have at least an hour to burrow through stacks of microfische. As they reached the steps leading up to the main entrance to the Jefferson Building which housed the main hall of the Library, two dozen or so people were heading in the opposite direction.

"Wait a minute," said Rachel, grabbing Thad's arm to slow his stride. "Thad, these people are leaving. There are too many people leaving at the same time. But it's only 8:30."

"Excuse me," Thad called out to a thick-set, older woman hurrying down the steps. "The Library is still open isn't it?"

"Oh, actually, they made an announcement half an hour ago that the Library would be closing early tonight and tomorrow due to the holidays. They're closing now. 8:30."

"Shit," Rachel whispered into the air, throwing her arms up in frustration. "Now what? I can't wait on this. I've got to find out tonight what all this stuff means. I can't let Phyllis go to the Congressman tomorrow. We can't just go in there making accusations or asking a bunch of questions if we're not even sure whether Persy was right." With droplets of moisture on her troubled face, Rachel squatted on the stone steps and covered her eyes.

"And what if Persy *was* right? Then what? What if the Congressman killed Persy to keep his connection with this robbery from getting out? Then what do you think he would do to *us*? He may have been the *shooter* who *killed* those people. *Dammit.* This is insane! Congressman Jackson would never hurt *anyone.* How could a man who has devoted the last twenty years of his life to improving life for others be the same person who killed three people? I *know* that man. I've worked for him for *four years.* It's impossible. There's just no way anyone could hide something this bad for over *twenty five years*, especially a Member of Congress!" Tears began to make their way down Rachel's face, her gloved hands now balled into tightly clenched fists.

"Rach, let's go. Come on, let's walk back to my place, okay? We can figure out what to do when we get there," suggested Thad, reaching down to pull Rachel to her feet. "I don't know, maybe we can get back here first thing in the morning before work. That might give us some time. There's nothing else we can do tonight. Think about it, Anthony *could* have been the guy with the missing face."

Rachel pulled away from Thad and jumped up and ran ahead of him in silence. An impulse gripped her.

"You're probably enjoying this aren't you? You would *love* to see Congressman Jackson go down, wouldn't you?" Rachel shot at him, spinning around to confront him, her eyes watery. "You love this whole damn thing. I bet you can't wait to run to Speaker Blasingame with all this, right? *Admit it* Thad, deep down inside, aren't you just jumping up and down with a little joy right now? Another Democrat brought to his knees. Another *liberal* Democrat bites the dust. *Damn you.*" Rachel walked fast, the tail of her red coat trailing behind her.

"Congressman Jackson is one of the only Members of our *righteous* Congress still willing to admit that he's a liberal. And you just can't stand it, *can you*?" Rachel shouted, abruptly spinning around again, her angry face gleaming under the streetlight. "You and your Republican revolution have people thinkin' that's it a bad thing to be a card-carry-ing liberal. Well, *all* of you can go to hell! I'm proud to be a liberal. If it means caring about the plight of others, and reaching out a helping hand to those in need who just can't do better for themselves right now, then, *hell yeah*, I'm a card-carrying liberal, and proud of it, god-dam it. But you, you selfish Republicans. Anything for a *buck*. Anything to hold it all to yourselves, just like Persy said, so willing to step on the backs of those who're responsible for you being where you are! You would *love* to see Jackson go down. A *black liberal*, at that. And one of the few *well-respected* black powerbrokers with tireless conviction who has stood up time after time for the issues that impact his community."

"I can't believe you would think that!" Thad yelled out after her. "Do you think I would use a time like this when your job could possibly be in jeopardy to score *political points*?! Don't you realize that most Republicans like me are decent, God-fearing Americans who raise their children to respect others, work hard and love their country just like anyone else? Do you think so little of me that you think I would do anything to *hurt* you? Rachel, you *know* that I don't think that way. Where are you *going*? I live the other way!" Thad stood in the middle of the sidewalk, his hands stuffed into the pockets of his long, brown coat, his face flushed with confusion, his wet blonde hair matted to his forehead.

Rachel ran for several blocks, letting the cold droplets of dense mist hit her face and the frosty air race through her braided hair. She stopped running and looked down at the grassy area of Folger Park where the yellow "Police Line Do Not Enter" tape lay tangled in the branches of leafless bushes. She stood, momentarily paralyzed with confusion, fear, disbelief and denial.

"Persy, *please* tell me that this is all wrong. Tell me that you were wrong," she cried softly, her squinted eyes trained on the yellow tape, phosphorescent in the murky darkness. "Didn't you know what this would *do* to us? To the staff? To the Black Caucus? To *faith* in black politicians? Why would you dig up *lies* like that? *Why* would you do this to us!?" Thad caught up with her, placing his large hands lightly and hesitantly on her trembling shoulders.

"Let's go, Rach. This isn't going to help, sweetheart," he said, looking around cautiously, suddenly uneasy about standing in the spot where a man had been murdered just days before. "I promise, we'll come back in the morning, okay? I want to help you with this, okay? Look, we don't really know for sure who was who in the photo. Regardless of what you think, I am *not* happy about this. If it's true that Congressman Jackson is actually the Anthony Ford that killed those people, it would hurt everybody, not just your office. Not just you. This is not about politics. This crazy thing is about innocent people being killed."

"I *know*. But you can't tell me it's not about politics *too*, or that it *will* be when the shit all hits the fan," Rachel mumbled, turning to face Thad, wiping the moisture from her eyes. "Do you know what this will *do* to black elected officials in this country? It'll knock them back twenty five years. And the Black Panthers—I'm sure the FBI would love to reopen files on productive, tax-paying African Americans all over the country who've long since taken off their black leather jackets, cut their afros and laid down their guns, because twenty-five or thirty years ago they were young and angry and desperate and went to extremes to improve conditions for their people. The Panthers don't need a stain like this on their backs. What if the organization had nothing to do with the robbery? And God knows what a scandal like this could do to President Gray's chance at re-election. *Jesus*, this is bigger than embezzling public funds or bribery! This is *murder*! *Triple* murder! And maybe Persy's death *too*! So I *do know* it's not just about *me* or *my office*. *That's* what scares the shit out of me!" Thad felt Rachel's shoulders shudder again, sensing that she really feared far more than just political fallout.

Through the rainy drizzle, Thad hailed a cab which slowly came to a stop, its headlights reflecting off the wet tar of the street.

17

At Fifth and G Streets, Northeast, the cab pulled to a stop in front of a small brick apartment building. The street had fallen quiet, the only sounds those of cars passing on distant streets. The tension from Rachel's earlier outburst still smoldered. The two had shared a heavy, uneasy silence during the cab ride to Thad's first floor one-bedroom apartment.

"Thad, I'm not going in. I, uh, need to go home," Rachel muttered as Thad moved to get out of the cab.

"What? Rachel, just come in for a few minutes. Come on," his eyes pleaded with her, his hand reaching for hers. Rachel got out and stood against the back door of the cab.

"I really just want to go home," she whispered. "I'll call you as soon as I get in, all right?"

"Rach, don't do this. Dammit, *don't do this*. Don't push me away." Thad slammed the palm of his hand against the cab, causing Rachel to flinch and her shoulders to stiffen. "Rachel, you know I'm not black, and I never *will* be, and I'm not a Democrat, and I probably *never* will be. But *I* am *not* the bad guy here. I *love* you. I'm a *blond, blue-eyed, white boy* from Dana, Ohio, who happens to *love* you, and nothing that hurts you would *ever* make me happy. Hell, you ought to *know* that! But I shouldn't have to keep—Dammit, I'm just tired of apologizing to you for who I am, or what I'm not, or constantly trying to convince you that this thing between us is possible, that it'll work if we both want it. Our relationship has nothing to do with this mess with Congressman Jackson. Don't keep me out of this."

"I'm sorry, Thad. I'm just frustrated over this whole thing, and I just lost it. I know that something like this is going to put smiles on a lot of bastards' faces, your boss being one of them, and I, I just don't know what to do with all this," Rachel admitted, her shoulders softening only slightly as Thad's hands gently embraced her upper arms. "But, I *know* you wouldn't go to him with this. I should have never said those things, all right. This has just gotten more complicated than I would have ever thought," She quickly sensed a growing discomfort from an apology to Thad that she didn't entirely mean. The cab driver honked his horn impatiently.

"I've got to go," Rachel whispered under her breath, her body taut, while the motor of the cab idled. She looked up at Thad apologetically, wanting to ease the strain.

"Thad, if Congressman Jackson really is somehow involved in this mess, how in hell do you think he managed to bury it all this time?" Rachel questioned, not so much looking for a reply from Thad as she was digging for an answer somehow from within herself. "How could he have fooled everybody so long?"

"Not that this is a great comparison, but how do some serial killers stay on the lam for years without suspicion? I have no idea how Jackson could have pulled it off, but that fire in San Francisco could have sealed his new identity as Ray Jackson," Thad offered in a muffled voice, watching a couple walk quickly down the sidewalk, a huge umbrella protecting them from the mist. "Doesn't someone do background investigations on new Members of Congress like they do on people working for the CIA or the FBI? How could he have gotten around that if he's not really Ray Jackson, you know, if there was a real Ray Jackson who actually died in that fire?"

"I don't know. The FBI surveilled the Black Panthers for years, watched them like hawks, paid off informants and infiltrated their ranks, so I have trouble believing that someone could get around all that, other than somebody sleeping on the job during a background check. I guess if he took on the identity of Ray Jackson, whoever he was, then he was obviously smart enough to use his social security number and everything else. Maybe the real Ray Jackson's parents were dead and he had no other family to counter Ford's claims to his identity. Or *who knows*? But, it looks like he *did do it*." Rachel said shifting her body to duck back into the cab. "But this is still not all making sense…What is the *AGFB* and *Tennessee* and the *corruption* that Persy scribbled about? And the numbers he documented in the note."

"Rachel, look, why don't you stay here? Just come in—"

"No. I'll call you from home," she said, closing the door to the cab, and rolling the window down partially. "You know I love you, and I'm, uh, sorry."

"I know. Be careful." Thad paused, peering at Rachel through the haze as he moved away from the cab. "We're okay, right?"

"Yeah," Rachel mouthed, staring back at Thad as the car pulled off into the drizzle, its tires rolling noisily over water puddles.

Rachel tried to understand why she had to get away from him. Her brain was numb. She just didn't want to be around him. Her nerves were too frayed to have to explain her feelings, to even know *how* to explain them. Thad just didn't grasp the impact that Jackson's downfall could have on the perception of the black public servant, the black man, the entire African American community. He didn't understand that no matter how much money her daddy made, Rachel would fight an uphill battle for the rest of her life for respect in the American context—from white America. She knew too well that white America defined who and what deserved that respect, and more often than not her own people bought into it whether they were willing to admit it or not. If a powerful man like Congressman Jackson went down, respect for many of the rest, by association of race, would go down with him. She wished she could just bury her ugly suspicions and make them go away.

Her colleague was dead, her job was at stake, the admiration, bordering on awe that she had held for the Congressman for years was faltering fast, and a growing fear was festering in her that she could no longer deny. Rachel just couldn't focus on *Thad's* feelings right now. She knew she'd probably just hurt them more by staying with him another moment.

She sat in the back if the cab working to push aside the guilt she felt over the things she'd said to him. He hadn't deserved being screamed at like that, and she knew it. Her nostrils inhaled the musty scent of sweat, smoke and incense in the cab and her ears the staticky sounds of an old Aretha Franklin tune on an am station. She wiped at the fogged window. Her mind started processing rationally again. Tomorrow, she'd call in sick, even though it would be a bad move on her part. After the Supreme Court ruling, the office would be buzzing, the press would be calling and her presence would be needed. Jackson would be furious with her for not showing up during a time like this unless she was on her death bed. Not to mention the work on the budget that would be pushed into the late hours of the next evening. Chuck Marinelli would be looking for her to take up the slack on the budget figures. But all that had become suddenly unimportant. She remembered what it was like as an eighth grader to overhear Yarrick, a senior in high school, talking to his lover over the phone, the confusion and panic she had felt when she realized the meaning of his words and tone of his voice. She knew that if her father ever found out that his only son was gay, it would change the dynamics of her family forever. And it had, in worse ways than she had imagined.

Rachel pulled the gray, numbered cassette out of the envelope, wondering what on earth more Persy could have known that could answer some of her questions. That same feeling of confusion and panic that filled the conscience of an eighth grader pushed its way into her life once again. Tomorrow, she had no choice but to call in sick. Phyllis would have to give her just a little bit more time. There was no other choice…

"So, you ready for Christmas? Bought all them presents for every-body?" asked the driver in a husky voice full of phlegm and cold. Christmas hadn't crossed her mind all week.

*   *   *

RACHEL FIDDLED WITH THE LOCK TO HER APARTMENT IN THE quiet, eighth floor hallway of The Essex condominium. A TV played in the neighbors' unit next door and the aroma of Italian food seeped down the hall from elsewhere. She opened the door, stepped inside, dropped her bag on the rose-colored area rug near the door and turned the lamp on. Rachel knew immediately that something was wrong. She was meticulous with her belongings, always keeping everything in its place, and everything was not in its place.

"Oh God," she whispered, almost too conscious of the sound of her own voice. Like a deer caught in headlights, she stood rigid near the open doorway. The greeting on her answering machine played over and over again. Files on her dining room table lay where none had been when she had left for work and she could see the bathroom light on from beneath the crack in the door. Her hands grew stiff, her mouth opened just enough to whisper, "Oh God."

She listened carefully for the slightest sound coming from her bed-room. She ran to the answering machine, slamming her hand down to stop the repetitive sound of her own voice. The recording cassette had been removed. Her head buzzed. The panicky feeling that had been a numbing achiness since yesterday was now a full-fledged attack. She picked up the phone and dialed Thad's number. After eight rings, she hung up and dialed again, her eyes squinted, alert for the slightest movement from anywhere in the apartment. No answer. *No answer.*

Shaking, the phone still in her hand, she pressed the code to reach Dorothy Huddle, the desk attendant on duty in the lobby.

"Dorothy, this is, ah, Rachel in 810. Has anyone been here to see me tonight?" she asked in as steady a voice as she could. "Maybe someone who you don't know?"

"Oh, Rachel, hello dear," said the 69-year old woman. "No, I don't think you've had any guests tonight. Were ya expectin' somebody honey?"

"Um, no, not really, but no one has asked for me at all? Anyone you didn't recognize?" quizzed Rachel, alarm growing.

"No, dear, I don't believe so. Oh, but I did see a familiar face come through the lobby. I think I've seen him on TV, maybe on a game show or somethin'. Oh, well, enough about that...Is something wrong young lady?" Dorothy waited patiently for a reply.

"No, no, Dorothy, nothing's wrong. I, I just thought that maybe someone might have been looking for me, that's all. Thanks, um, anyway. Never mind." Rachel dialed Thad once more. Still no answer. Unseen by her, one of the files slid off the dining room table and hit the floor loudly. Somewhere in her bowel, something erupted. Her mind shut down and instinct took over. Rachel dropped the phone, raced to the door, grabbed her bag and ran down the hallway to the elevator. *Hurry!* Five. Six. Seven. Eight. The door opened and she vaulted into the elevator and frantically pounded the first floor button. Rachel pressed her body into the farthest corner of the small elevator and trembled in paranoid silence. When it came to a stop, she lunged forward, around a corner to the left and out the side door of the building to Fessenden Street where she could just make out the shape of her car, a red, '86 BMW, a college graduation gift from her father, at the end of the block.

Rachel spun around to the sound of the door opening behind her. Riveted, she stood inert as a small, silver-haired woman with arthritic fingers held something out to her.

"Hon, I think you might have dropped this out by the elevator just now. You dashed through so fast, I didn't have time to get to you." The woman handed her the cassette. "You be careful racing around out here. The streets are slick, you know. Are you *sure* you're all right?"

"Thanks, Dorothy. Um, yeah, I'll be okay, thanks." Rachel darted up the block, and jumped into the car, feeling the cold leather seat against her pant legs. She sat in silence and inspected the car, relieved when she could find nothing amiss. She stuck the keys in the ignition and turned on the headlights.

She braced to consider her options. She could take the Beltway to 95 straight out to her parent's house in Baltimore County and stay there for the night. No. Her father would ask questions, lecture her, argue with her. A definite no, not there. Cheryl's efficiency apartment in Adams Morgan—too many questions, too much idle talk, too many friends in and out. She could call her Uncle Davis out in Silver Spring from a pay phone up the street at the gas station, but she hadn't visited him in almost a year. The *police*? Right. And say *what*? Her idea of what was going on was was too incredible! No one would believe her. She would go to Thad's, but he hadn't answered the phone. She threw the car into first gear, turned right at the bottom of the street onto Connecticut Avenue and sped down the wide thoroughfare toward downtown.

The little BMW, its faulty windshield wipers gliding hesitantly across the front windows and the stripped gearshift making painful squeaks at every shift, headed southeast toward Capitol Hill. Thad's was the only place she could go and not have to explain her presence at eleven o'clock on a Thursday night, her hysterical mood, the reason why she couldn't go home to her apartment and the reason why she couldn't call the cops.

"Ha!" Rachel screamed at the top of her lungs, a crazy grin breaking out across a face hidden by tangled braids. Laughter engulfed her and she smacked her right hand against the steering wheel violently. Hysterical crying laughter bellowed through the car as it raced passed spotty traffic down North Capitol Street.

"The Congressman is the boogeyman ten times over, Persy's dead and little aliens are crawling through my apartment moving my things around! Merry damn Christmas Rachel! Happy Kwanzaa! Well, you knew politics was a bitch!" Still breathing heavily, Rachel looked down at the passenger seat at the cassette Thad had given to her earlier, snatched it and shoved it into the tape player.

She pushed the car into fourth gear and drove around the perimeter of the hulking figure of Union Station. Persy's exhausted, inebriated voice mumbled from the car speaker.

"*The caption from the San Francisco Chronicle picture reads, the Mitchellson's of San Francisco became little Gail's foster parents after her mother, Queenie Wasserman, was fatally wounded during a robbery at an Oakland branch of California Federal in June. Well, I saw that picture. Three people smilin', a big, blond white man, Grady Mitchellson, his brown-haired wife, Sandy, and a three-year old girl, Gail, with long curly hair and light brown eyes and an emotionless expression that tells me she'd rather not have been there. The perfect all-American white family.*" Persy's edgy voice paused for several seconds. Rachel turned up the volume and maneuvered the car around Stanton Park circle, accelerating down 6th Street northeast.

"*It's something how a little white girl could stir up so much trouble for so many people. The Republican revolution won't last long. People in this country are gonna get tired of their bullshit and we'll knock those damned Republicans out on their asses. I know it means that one of mine is going down with you, but it's all over,*" Persy rambled, the voice growing agitated, angry. "*I know it all. Jackson, Tennesee. Nice place to visit. And the PPF, so damn righteous, absolution is out of her reach….It doesn't stop with him. It might have started with his crime, but we know it doesn't stop there. Damn you all to hell.*"

White girl stirring up trouble? Rachel slammed her foot on the brakes and clutch in the no parking zone in front of Thad's apartment building, ejected the tape, stuffed it into her bag and pulled out two keys Thad had given her last month for emergencies. This was an emergency. The lights in the apartment were out, so she let herself in, pushing at the boxes that had blocked his doorway for two weeks. The door was heavy.

She walked through the darkness to the floor lamp in the far corner of Thad's small living room. She was not prepared for the sight revealed by the sudden burst of light.

Thad's lifeless body lay haphazardly across the boxes that blocked the doorway. Rachel's head burned as if a stone were being rubbed feverishly against it to spark a fire. Without thought or instinct to guide her, she fell to her knees in shock and just stared, too paralyzed to scream or cry. Just enough energy to stare, a dream-like state having enveloped her. Somehow she mustered enough momentum to drag herself across the room to the body. Thad's head hung over the far end of the boxes, his torso and legs splayed slantways across the box tops, his left arm tossed backwards, his right tucked underneath his body.

A low moan emerged involuntarily from somewhere deep within her. Rachel reached out and touched Thad, as if her touch would bring him back. It didn't. She knew he was dead. All at once, her heart was shattered into a million tiny pieces and her throat was choked with a strangled cry. Fear like she'd never known before throttled her whole body. It was the nightmare where the bad guy was chasing her, right on her heels, except it was real. Thad was dead.

After a moment, Rachel's instincts began to take over and her mind once again regained its grip on reality. Before jumping up in panic to flee the apartment where a killer could still be lingering, Rachel stroked Thad's blonde hair, silent tears streaming down her face. That's when she noticed—Thad's throat had been slit.

18

In the misty cold, Mike James dropped his sleeping son off at his parents' home on Jonquil Street in a serene, middle-class residential neighborhood just inside D.C. near the border of Maryland. Despite his strong belief in sleeping at home every night with his son Marcus, tonight he had to head back over to the station now that his partner and other shift colleagues were off-duty.

Since the divorce, Mike had tried to make life as stable as possible for little Marcus under the circumstances, and hated like hell that his three-year-old still had to be shifted back and forth every other weekend to his mother's apartment in Wheaton. He took his breaks to pick his son up every afternoon from the Owl School on 16th and then to his parents home until his shift was over. The two awoke every morning to the cartoon sounds of "Power Rangers" and threw Cheerios at each other across the kitchen table while Mike packed Marcus' lunches. His son was his life. His little man. For the moment, he'd given up everything else—dating, hanging with the fellas, a more regular work out schedule at the gym—to devote full-time to his spitting image. Nobody would ever be able to say that Mike James was a black man who didn't take care of his child.

Stinson's arraignment was scheduled for eleven in the morning in courtroom nine in the pale, white marble courthouse at 6th and D Streets, northwest near the heart of downtown. Mike had hoped to have this opportunity to read Venable's case reports on Persy Pritchard's death more thoroughly without suspicion while his colleagues were away. His movements were motivated more by strong hunches than solid proof of something awry on the force's part. He'd have to be real discreet. The force was already under fire in the press for tens of thousands of dollars and dozens of stolen weapons missing from the Property Division. *The last thing he needed was his name added to the list of problems the force had to dig itself out from under.*

Mired in thought, Mike could still feel the pull of the cumbersome bullet-proof vest that he wore often lately, even when he was off-duty. Washington area police were suffering from low morale and just plain fear in recent months due to a rash of random police ambushes by ruthless criminals in search of vengeance or some form of twisted respect from their peers. Jumping back into his truck, left idling in his parents' driveway, Mike tried to ignore the stiffness of the vest to focus on what he needed to do later.

At midnight, he would show up at the headquarters, claiming to have mistakenly left his house keys. It would give him just enough time to get back into the lock-up to chat with Raheed Stinson, without the violent intimidation that Venable had laid on so thick after Stinson had surprisingly waived his right to an attorney. Stinson's face was a mess of bruises as if he'd lost badly to a Mike Tyson fresh out of an Indiana penetentiary. Mike would take a different approach, in search of the truth.

*   *   *

RACHEL TOUCHED THE SMALL, BUT DEEP INCISION JUST ABOVE THAD'S larynx with shockingly little blood to indicate its existence. Such a tiny cut had robbed him of his young life. In a rush of sadness and fear, she grabbed her bag, threw her ravishing, rope-like braids back from her face and ran out of the apartment, crying uncontrollably. Only a couple of hours ago, she had feared that everything was about to go haywire. Now it had. In her bewildered haste, she bumped into a neighbor returning home from coffee at Starbucks, jumped back into the aging BMW and sped away into the pellets of sleet that crackled against the street, her car weaving as if an alcoholic were at the wheel.

*   *   *

MIKE DISCREETLY LED RAHEED STINSON, HANDCUFFED AND SORELY bruised, out of the lock-up into a small interrogation room. In the dimly lit and sparsely furnished, windowless room, Mike stared across the table at the fallen basketball star, and shook his head in disgust. As if it weren't enough that he could lose his shield for conducting an unauthorized interrogation, here he sat before one of the country's former premier ball players, now homeless, suffering from narcotics withdrawal and looking *bad. Real* bad. *How could the brother let himself drop this low? Some young brothers out there would sell their souls for what he'd had.*

"Yo, man, why you got me in here in the middle of the night?" asked Stinson, leaning back as far as he could in the hard metal chair, wary of Mike's intentions. "I've already told y'all everything I can tell. I didn't kill *nobody.* Your partner is buggin', man. I could press charges for what he's done to me. Some kinda brother *you* are. You ain't done shit to help me up in this camp."

"Are you finished?" Mike leaned forward over the back of the chair in which he sat and wrapped his hulking arms around the sides of the table. The air in the room was still and Stinson's odor invaded Mike's nose like the smell of open garbage wafting through an apartment window. He stuck a toothpick in his mouth. "Look at you. Bein' a hoop man can't help you in here, can it? Let me tell you something, *my brother.* If you killed Persy Pritchard, then know that I'll do everything I can to make sure you're locked away so long your mama won't even recognize you. But if you didn't have nothing to do with this, I'll fight to get you cleared. You hear what I'm saying?" Stinson stared at the floor through swollen eyes. He nodded his head.

"I need you to tell me again where you were from Monday night through Tuesday afternoon, in detail. And you tell me where the gun came from, and where'd you get the money to score the heroin if you didn't shoot Pritchard?"

"Man, no matter what I say, you ain't gon' believe me. Everybody's already made up they minds that I killed that brother. What else can I say?" Salty tears surfaced in Stinson's eyes, making him wince.

"Raheed, you have any kids?"

"Yeah, a daughter. She's ten. What's she got to do with anything?" The thought of his daughter seemed to send another twinge of pain through Stinson's body.

"Have you seen your daughter lately? Are you a part of her life?"

"Naw, man, I haven't seen her in a long time, five years. Her mother don't want me around her. I guess I'd just be a bad influence."

"When she thinks of you, do you want her to always think of you as just a junkie ex-ballplayer of a motherfucker livin' in the streets like a dog? 'Cause you know I don't have to tell you that that's what you are, right?" Mike stood up and began to pace back and forth in front of Stinson, his eyes never leaving the suspect's face. "You got a chance to come clean right here and now. Take responsibility for what you've done, *like a man.* You haven't done shit for your child have you? Well, god-damit, take responsibility for *this*! For killing one of your *own brothers.*"

"Man, I told you, I haven't hurt nobody. I served my time for stuff I done. Get off me," Stinson wailed, shiny tears running down his once-handsome face, now the size of a lumpy, beaten-up pumpkin. "All my shit's been taken from me. You know the white man don't want a brother to have nothing and I don't have *nothing* left. I'd probably be better off in jail anyway, but I didn't kill *nobody.*"

"All your shit has been *taken* from you? Man, please," Mike shouted, standing over Stinson, his large fingers in the man's face. His sudden disgust for him made his stomach turn. "How about you *gave* it away for a goddamned high? Fuck the bullshit. Nobody put a gun to your face and made you throw it all away, did they? No white man stuck that needle up your arm. You did that shit by your damn self, man. Pathetic piece of shit. Now, you need to come correct and tell me why you shot a brother who was doing something with his life."

"I didn't do it. I'm not a killer. I didn't kill nobody, man. I swear," Something in Stinson's eyes, and trembling, pitiful body language told Mike the man was telling the truth. It was a strong pull in his gut that made him believe this man who had sacrificed the good life for a smelly, cold tent in a back alley. Raheed "the Speed" Stinson broke down and admitted to stealing the CD-changer from his brother's car to purchase his last high and followed it up with his spiel on his whereabouts the morning Pritchard was shot. As far as the gun was concerned, Mike had already figured it was a plant. Whether Rick had done it or not, he wasn't sure, but someone had planted that piece on a Stinson so stoned or sleeping so hard that he'd had no idea of another's presence. He was a sorry-ass excuse for a black man, but he hadn't killed anyone.

"Alright Stinson, I actually believe you, man," Mike offered, sitting back down to face the accused. "But, obviously, no one else does. Did you talk to anyone or see anyone hanging around your tent either Monday night or early Tuesday morning? Known or unknown to you?"

Raheed rubbed his dirty hands through the matted waves of hair on his head and scratched at his face.

"Naw, I didn't see no one. I don't know where that gun came from. I haven't ever even had no gun. I was sleeping all night Monday after I got my stash. I saved it for the morning, you know, like for *breakfast.*" Raheed's caramel-colored face, pock-marked like a dried Cheerio, broke out into a devilish grin as he responded to the look of dissatisfaction in Mike's eyes. "That's when you and your boy crept up on me. I hadn't been nowhere since like nine o'clock Monday night. It ain't right for me to be in here for this. Y'all just picked any brother off the street to pin this on. I know how it works. I guess you figure my life ain't worth nothin', right? Well, you don't care nothin about that brother Pritchard either if you let me take the fall for somebody else who's still gone be out there. 'Cause *I* didn't do it."

Mike got Stinson to swear he wouldn't mention their little "discussion" to anyone and put the man back in the lock-up. Told him he'd send Venable back in to finish the job if he so much as hinted about their late-night conversation. Headed back to his desk, Mike knew that Internal Affairs would eat up a case like this like it was juicy tenderloin. But he wanted to take care of this one himself.

✳   ✳   ✳

SLEET BOUNCED OFF OF THE SMOOTH FINISH OF DARK-BLUE PAINT ON the Lincoln Towncar as it pulled up quietly and paused in front of the rowhouse at the corner of 8th and Kennedy Streets, its engine idling. The stars and stripes of the District of Columbia tags stood out only because of the curious insignia imprinted in the left bottom corner.

Within the small house, darkness reigned with only stillness as its companion. Only a stray car or two made their way past, the occupants too preoccupied with turning a radio station or lighting a cigarette to notice or care about the expensive automobile that was double-parked and taking up half of the street. The sound of a single set of footsteps disappeared behind the house and several minutes later could be heard again, accompanied by a second set of feet, scuffling hesitantly across the sidewalk and into the waiting vehicle. "They" had come for Jet Strong.

✳   ✳   ✳

MIKE JAMES PULLED THE PRITCHARD CASE FILE FROM THE PILE ON Venable's desk and headed toward the men's bathroom down the hall. He placed the file on top of one of three white porcelain sinks and walked over to an open urinal to relieve himself. His nerves had been stomping his bladder all day since the tense conversation with his partner. He had to laugh, thinking of what he was doing, sneaking around like he was. It was like a scene straight out of a B-grade mystery flick. A *bad* B-grade mystery flick. He grabbed the yellow file folder just as a uniformed officer with his thick, navy coat and cap on entered.

"Hey man," said the thin, dark brown man as he headed directly toward a urinal. He spotted Mike's shield but didn't recognize the face. "You on shift?"

"No, actually I had to make a run back up here to get my house keys. Got all the way home and couldn't get into my house. I'm on seven to three." Mike stood awkwardly, the file held tightly in his left hand.

"Jarvis. Todd Jarvis," said the officer, extending his hand before turning back toward the L-shaped urinal. Mike hesitated for a split second.

"Uh, Smith. Ron Smith. Homicide." The lie stuck in his throat. He swallowed it back down uneasily, stepped into a closed stall and sat on the toilet. *Damn, why didn't he just tell the man the truth?* He waited. Jarvis' footsteps finally moved toward the door and then stopped.

"Alright, man, have a good evening. Nice to meet you," said Officer Jarvis.

"Yeah, man, same to you." Mike sat back on the toilet seat, struggled to ignore the stench of the dingy men's room and flipped the file open.

Todd Jarvis paused outside the bathroom. He'd worked the 4th Street station for three years and had never seen the man in the stall. Never seen the name either. *Ron Smith. Maybe someone else knew the brother. He seemed nice enough, though.* He jiggled his keys and strolled outside to the blue-and-white D.C. Metro patrol car across the street. His partner sat waiting.

Where's the damn print analysis? Mike wondered, bewildered. There were notes and official report papers missing that had been in the file earlier that afternoon. It was Department policy that files were to remain intact, papers were never to be removed. *Where the hell was the rest of the file? Why was somebody fucking with this case? Why Persy Pritchard's case?* The leftover fried chicken, collard greens and candied yams that Mike had eaten two hours earlier hit the bottom of his stomach like a boulder slamming into the earth after careening down a mountain. The stall was exactly where he needed to be.

19

Mike closed the driver's side door of his sleek, new black Navigator with D.C. vanity plates reading 1GoodCop and stretched his hulking frame as much as the space inside the truck would allow. The late December D.C. weather was doing its usual seasonal acrobatics. Mike looked out beyond his dashboard at a dry, gray Friday morning, unseasonably warm for the weekend before Christmas at fifty two degrees. While the Navigator warmed up, Mike sat out front of the concrete stump of a headquarters building in the early morning chill. He checked his reflection in the rearview mirror. Not bad for a brother pushin' thirty, he thought. Aside from a slowly receding hairline, his boyish good looks remained intact. His baby-faced handsomeness was set off by a cuddly teddy-bear exterior, despite his sinewy 220 pounds. And he had an ever-present twinkle in eyes the color of ripe walnuts. The kind of sexy innocentness a mother-in-law loved, and that other brothers knew could charm the skirts off their wives if he had the inclination to do so. He had always reminded his mother of a wrestler-sized version of a young Smokey Robinson, without the crooner's velvety voice.

His ability to be at once sympathetic but tough, and at times menacing had helped him extract information from suspects and witnesses in the past who his colleagues had given up for hopeless. His capacity to connect with the men and women, young and old, brought in for questioning, was a strong point, a career asset. And he felt that his skills had worked for him last night with Raheed Stinson.

With a city resident population made up of seventy-five percent African Americans, it was no surprise to anyone that well over eighty percent of those arrested in the District were black—a fact no one could get around even if one preferred not to admit it. Of the 400 detectives on the Washington D.C. Metropolitan Police Force, shockingly less than half were African American. *So what the fuck else was new? Everything was always off-balance,* Mike felt. *But, hell, I'm not going to cry over it. Shit, I'm trying to be part of the solution, not the problem.* Disparity or no, Mike James knew himself to be one of those young, black detectives who could relate to many of the perps as others could not. He'd come from the streets himself ,and it was only by the grace of God that he'd escaped them.

He held a crumpled piece of paper in his right hand. *Dr. Davendra Salvi, D.D.S., 1225 31st Street, N.W, Suite 300.* In his search through the Pritchard case file, he had come across the name of the registered owner of the .38 found on Stinson. Stinson would be transported over to the municipal courthouse in a couple of hours and Mike thought he'd pay the good doctor an unscheduled visit before the arraignment.

He drove first to his parents' home to wish his son a good day at nursery school and to remind his mother to wrap Marcus' Christmas gifts, and then took a fast, winding shortcut through Rock Creek Park to Whitehurst Freeway. The smooth sounds of Frankie Beverly & Maze flowed through the truck's interior from the CD changer in the trunk. Mike managed to hum along though his thoughts were a million miles away. He exited right along the canal and turned left into the pricey paid parking garage of the Potomac Executive Suites Building, one of city's most exclusive corporate addresses, even in the midst of Georgetown's tony high-rent district. The rich wide, speckled marble building sat just six stories high overlooking the murky waters of the Georgetown Canal, separated from the Potomac River by the highly-trafficked Key Bridge into Northern Virginia. Its top two floors consisted of million-dollar penthouse condominiums with balconied, conversation-piece views of the water, while the lower floors housed three law offices, the Rosewood & Hall lobbying firm, two small, but well-endowed trade associations and a wing of medical offices, mostly plastic surgeons, high-priced dentists and a wealthy podiatrist.

Mike walked through the heavy glass doors into a lavish marble lobby that put Buckingham Palace to shame. On his way to the 14 karat gold-plated set of elevators, his eyes settled on the glass-encased reception desk of Rosewood & Hall to his left. The lobbying firm was a retiring Congress Member's dream, damn near Nirvana, and many of them ended up there after several terms in Congress, exploiting their contacts and legislative savvy for big bucks. *Huge* bucks. Three years earlier, Rosewood & Hall's spin doctors had successfully re-packaged a recovering Cleavon Grace, helping to boost the former community activist back into the political arena. And Peter Rosewood, son of a well-to-do tobacco farmer outside Richmond, had contributed handsomely to Bill Blasingame's coffers for over a decade. As the elevator doors rolled open to receive him, the rookie detective recalled a *Post* story from two years ago about the strangulation death of one of the firm's executive vice presidents, in his home out in Bethesda. *They never had arrested a suspect in that case*, he remembered.

The ornate elevator delivered Mike to the third floor. Dr. Salvi's office sat behind an oak door with a gold nameplate affixed as if to say, *look who's got moulah*. A tiny woman's head could just barely be seen above the top of the reception desk in the waiting room.

"Yes, do you have an appointment with Dr. Salvi?" she inquired nervously in a thick East Indian accent, as she noticed Mike taking in the opulent interior. The same initial response occurred a little too often in his line of work. *Goddam, like a big black man dressed in plain clothes couldn't walk into a doctor's office without suspicion that he was there to hurt somebody. The same old shit.*

"No, I don't," he replied and at the same time withdrew his gold shield, to her surprise. "Mike James, D.C. Metro Police, Homicide. I'd like to ask Dr. Salvi just a few questions involving a homicide case. Is he in?" Her face noticeably relaxed. Any tension in the air evaporated.

"Oh. Well, I'll see if he's still in with a patient." The woman's long, jet black hair trailed behind her as she hastily disappeared behind yet another heavy oak door. Mike dropped his heavyweight's frame into one of several plush black leather chairs and settled his feet into carpet so fine that it was a shame to walk on it in anything more than bare feet.

A slender, middle-aged man of medium height and a gentle bearing walked through the door and held out a well-manicured hand. His shiny black hair was peppered with gray at the temples and his deep reddish-tan skin revealed only tiny wrinkles at the corners of his bespectacled eyes. *Money, money, money. The man exuded wealth, old East Indian affluence. He probably had more greenbacks in the bank than Mike would probably see in a lifetime.*

"Detective James, I'm Dr. Salvi," he uttered in a soft, cultured voice complemented by a light, sing-song New Delhian cadence. The man's expression hinted at confusion over the detective's unexpected visit. "My assistant tells me you're here about a *homicide case?* I don't know how I could possibly be of assistance…"

"Dr. Salvi, I'll get right to the point. I know that you're a busy man. A young man by the name of Persy Pritchard, chief of staff to Congressman Ray Jackson, Jr., was shot to death on Tuesday morning in a park on Capitol Hill. Perhaps you've heard the story on the news or read about it in the paper?" Mike examined the man's expression care-fully for any sign of recognition. There *was* none. "I believe that my partner may have dropped by to question you earlier this week." But the tone of his statement came out more like a question as the foggy expres-sion on the distinguished dentist's face remained unchanged.

"No, detective, I'm afraid that I have no idea about this unfortunate incident. Why would the police wish to question *me* regarding this young man's death?" Now, either Salvi was a damned good liar, or he honestly knew nothing about the case, and had not been questioned by Venable about Pritchard. The *case report* said otherwise.

"Dr. Salvi, the .38 caliber revolver used to shoot Mr. Pritchard is registered in *your* name. The gun was found on a suspect who'll be arraigned this morning," Mike offered, now just about as baffled as the good doctor. He could feel his temperature rising and the room closing in on him. Great big letters flashed in his head. COVER UP! This whole case was fucked! But *why? Why would Rick want to do a half-assed job on this investigation and lie about it? He had to know that someone would check behind him. Maybe he wasn't the only one involved. And no one had expected Mike to stick his black ass into the middle of it. Something had happened out there to Persy Pritchard. Something someone wanted to hide.*

"Dr. Salvi, did you know the gun was missing?"

"Oh, yes, it was stolen out of my Mercedes two months ago while I was on Capitol Hill attending a Congressional hearing. I immediately filed a report and an officer came to my office to ask me some questions," said the man, rubbing his forehead and looking at his watch. "You know, with all these drive-by shootings, especially with the car that I drive, I can't be too careful. That gun was like a necessary evil. But I never took it out of the car though. They never did recover it."

"Do you recall the officer's name who came to talk with you?" Mike braced himself, squinted his dark-brown eyes and prayed to God that the answer that came out of the dentist's mouth would not crush his devotion to law enforcement and his pride in his badge.

"Well, let me think…I believe it was Vittle, Vendall. No! It was *Venable*, a Detective Richard Venable," Salvi said, gingerly patting back his gelled hair and looking again at the expensive Rolex watch that adorned his arm. Mike's senses were suddenly so sharp he could hear the second hand on the doctor's watch. Ticking. Ticking. Ticking. "Detective James, I hate to be abrupt, but I really do have to get back to my patients. If you have any other questions, feel free to come by again. Will I be getting my gun back?"

"Well, Dr. Salvi, we'll need it to conclude the investigation—"

"Detective, I hate to be smug in the face of a murder and I'm sorry about what has happened to the young man, but I would like to have my property back," he said with a note of rising impatience. It was time for him to get back to clients who drove Lexuses, resided in multimillion dollar Foxhall mansions and paid in *cash*.

"Dr. Salvi—" Mike's pager went off mid-sentence, disturbing his mental flow. "Excuse me, can I use your phone?" Salvi pointed in the direction of a custom-built private phone booth just out in the corridor and excused himself.

"This is James," he spoke harshly in baritone, still reeling from the revelation of Venable's questioning of Salvi about the stolen gun. Mike had had no prior knowledge of that case. And his partner Venable had made *sure* to keep it under wraps. But *why*? "Yeah. Yeah. What? I'll be there in fifteen minutes." Life had just spun wildly out of control. Rick Venable and God knows who else were playing hide and go seek with Pritchard's murder case, and he was about to race from the extravagant offices of Georgetown to an oppressive crime scene where a young, white Republican Congressional aide lay dead, his throat slashed. Mike closed his eyes in silent prayer. Only the man upstairs could back this brother up now.

20

A piercing morning sun and the loud howl of the wind against the wide picture window awakened Rachel with a start. Giant capital letters spelling out *Kinko's* ran backwards across the window. A computer sat in front of her just as it had on Tuesday morning when Sergeant Filipidis had told her the news about Persy. Except this computer belonged to a Kinko's at 4th and Pennsylvania Avenue, southeast, where Rachel had fallen asleep at a workstation at the 24-hour copy center in her search for a place to lay her head. And life had changed dramatically since Tuesday morning.

The fear hit her right away. She looked around the well-lit place. At eight o'clock in the morning, the busy Kinko's branch was already buzzing with activity. Well-dressed corporate types and interns from associations located in the neighborhood darted in and out, making copies, printing flyers or buying reams of paper. No one seemed to be paying her any attention. The misery of last evening sent her face into her hands as she tried to get her thoughts together enough to figure out what to do next. The sight of Thad's body and a ghostly image of Persy danced in her head. Where could she go? Who could she talk to?

A telephone rang and shot a pang of alarm through her petite body. It reminded her of the ring of the crank calls that had wrecked her concentration on Monday night. The calls. The *crank* calls. Until now, she had somehow forgotten about the caller's forewarning message. *It's all over for him you know.* She had thought it was just a childish prank. Some fool with nothing better to do. But maybe Persy's killer had told

her exactly what he or she planned to do. How could she have forgotten
to mention it to Sergeant Filipidis?

"Hey, I see you finally woke up," said a twenty-something brown-
skinned man with a Kinko's name tag and spiky short dreadlocks. The
name read "Hassan" in bright yellow letters. "I was startin' to get worried
about you. I thought you might miss a deadline on a paper sleeping all
night like that. You go to school around here?"

"No. Um, I work for a Member of Congress," she replied, trying to
wipe her eyes and pull her braids back into a bun. "I'm sorry I fell
asleep. I'll be leaving in a minute."

"I mean, you know there's no hurry or anything. I just wanted to
make sure you were okay."

"Yeah, thanks. I'm fine. I appreciate the concern."

"Hey sista, we gotta take care of each other. I watch your back, you
watch mine, right? Especially as pretty as you are. I'd watch your back
anytime." Hassan sauntered off with a macho strut, grinning, and
pleased with himself. The ladies couldn't help but to want him. He was
the man.

Rachel turned back around to face the window, the sun's reflection so
bright that it made her sweat under the coat she'd never taken off. She'd
have to call in sick, like she had planned before, before…everything that
had happened last night. She picked up her shoulder bag and checked
its contents. Good. It was all still there. The cassettes, the notes from
Persy, the photos.

She grabbed a cab that stopped in front of the Kinko's and directed
the driver to the Library of Congress. Rap music played loudly from the
front speakers while the young cabbie bopped his head along to the
pounding beat. It was a little on the early side for the earsplitting
rhymes of the late Tupac Shakur, and the noise clogged her thoughts.
She needed to think now more than ever.

"Excuse me, could you please turn that down a little?" she asked
hesitantly.

"Oh, no problem. Whatever you want," he said in a thick Latino accent. "You running late to work miss? You look like you're in a hurry." The driver peered at her through his rearview mirror. Rachel could make out olive-colored skin, deep black eyes and a thick moustache.

"No, not exactly, but I need to get to the Madison Building as a soon as I can." She watched the images of bundled-up bike couriers and pedestrians along the sidewalk, bracing themselves against the frigid gale force winds whipping down Pennsylvania Avenue.

"Did you hear about that guy that was killed last night right over on 5th Street? Worked for the Speaker of the House?" asked the jovial cabbie. "It's been all over WAMU this morning. It's a crazy world out there we live in, huh?"

Rachel clenched her jaw and held her lips together tightly to fight back the tears. Her eyes were red.

"Yes, I know all about it," she said, unable to choke the tremor in her voice. Her utterance was barely audible. In her head, she could hear shots fired, people screaming and the image of a young, militant, black man brandishing a rifle. The same young man in the old photo in her bag. His face was so familiar it made her cringe. But still, *who the hell's face was missing?* "I know all about it. It's a crazier world out there than you think."

*　　　　*　　　　*

RACHEL CLOSED THE DOOR OF THE TELEPHONE BOOTH IN THE basement of the Madison Building lounge and dialed the familiar number of her boss' office. Library of Congress employees and anxious tourists brave enough to weather the nation's capitol in the miserable cold shuffled by, and two hurried-looking men waited outside the booth for Rachel to complete her call. One tapped his fingers impatiently against his briefcase. She watched her hands, shaking like a sunbather's in a snowstorm, as her fingers carefully touched each button.

She had rehearsed the conversation in her head a dozen times in the past five minutes while she sat in the glass-encased booth, holding the phone in her hand. She had to convince Phyllis to meet her at noon so that, together, they could search through computerized lists of microfische logs of newspaper articles and books in search of something that would bring to light so many of the questions tossing around in her head. Like why someone had killed Thad. Phyllis *had* to come. She was the only person Rachel had left to help her. The only person who would understand. Their working relationship had never really been an easy one and a tense, one-way envy had prevented them from becoming the friends they might have otherwise become years ago. Why Phyllis couldn't stand to see another black woman get ahead—except maybe Juditha Hurley—had gnawed at Rachel for longer than she cared to admit. But maybe she *had* been guilty of being a little condescending at times. Maybe more than a little. Now, she wished she could take it all back. Rachel sniffed back her tears and waited for an answer.

"Good morning, Congressman Jackson's office," said a tired-sounding Phyllis. Rachel hesitated for several seconds, sensing a growing weariness on the other end. "Congressman Jackson's office."

"Phyllis. Phyllis, this is Rachel."

"Where the hell have you been?" Phyllis asked in an irritated whisper. "I tried to call you all last night. I left about five messages and then when I tried to call this morning, the answering machine didn't come on at all. Where are you?"

"Phyllis, please, just listen to me, okay? A lot has happened since yesterday. I know it sounds crazy but I can't explain it right now. You can't mention the things that we found to anybody. Not *anybody*. Can you meet me at the Madison Building at noon, in the periodicals section?" Rachel's brown eyes went up toward the ceiling as she prayed for Phyllis' answer.

"What? *Meet you?* Rachel, I don't think you understand why I tried to reach you again this morning, do you? You really *don't* know, do you?"

"Know *what* Phyllis? I know everything about Congressman Jackson and I think I might know what happened to Persy, but I need you to help me. Please."

"Rach, you may know all of that, but you obviously have no idea that the police have an APB out on you right now for killing a Blasingame aide. Some white boy named Ted or Thad or something. This office is a fucking zoo! The phones are ringing off the hook, and the Congressman is locked in his office again. Rachel, what have you done? What the hell is going on?"

"Oh, my God." It was as if an earthquake had hit, sending all of her emotions and thoughts tumbling violently. Rachel could feel her head grow light and could suddenly see metallic spots jumping around before her eyes. In her mind, she wondered if the two men outside the booth recognized her, if they knew she was wanted for murder, if they knew she had become a statistic. A young black murder suspect in America.

"Phyllis, I didn't hurt Thad. When I left his apartment last night he, he was alive. But then I had to go back later and he was dead. But Phyllis, I didn't do anything. You've known me for four years. You know I wouldn't do anything like that. The police are wrong. You have to believe me Phyllis. Please, meet me here at noon and I can explain it all. Phyllis, I'm *begging* you." Rachel could faintly hear Phyllis breathing heavily, and the ceaseless digital ringing in the background of the office's other phone lines.

"Rachel, I've got enough problems in my life right now without getting mixed up in yours. I can't afford to lose my damn job and maybe even go to jail because of you. Like *you'd* do the same for me." The old hostility in her voice was back. "And if you say the Congressman did these horrible things and we've known him for all these years, then maybe I don't know *you* as well as I thought either."

"Our jobs are dead in the water anyway, Phyllis, whether you meet me or not. By next week, all of our jobs are gonna go up in smoke as soon the media gets a hold of all of this. There's more at stake than just our jobs. Persy and Thad are dead because of what they knew. That means you and I might be in danger too. You're the only person who can help me. We're in this one together Phyllis, whether we like it or not."

Rachel gripped the handset so tightly that she thought it would crumble under the force. Again she waited for an answer, hoping that Phyllis could toss aside the history of jealousy and catty bickering that had plagued their relationship to help save them both. There was no more room for the procrastination and indecision that had wracked Rachel's life in the past several days. They had to work together. *Now.*

*   *   *

"Yeah, some lady from Putting People First called in right after we got to the scene saying she knew who Derrickson was with last night," Rick Venable said, standing over Thad Derrickson's motionless body. The room felt awfully cold even though the heat was on. Something about a dead body seemed to bring a chill to any room. Venable looked up at his partner Mike who was busy taking notes and avoiding eye contact.

"What's the woman's name?" Mike asked.

"Uh, Juditha B. Hurley, executive director of the PPF," read Rick from a small notepad. "I was about to head over there after we wrap things up here."

"Rick, man, why don't I question her? You can take care of the neighbor who witnessed the woman running out of here last night. Two heads are better than one, right?" Mike attempted to make light of his anger and the feelings of betrayal that had his stomach tied up in knots. With Rick around, he wouldn't be able to ask Hurley the kind of questions he wanted to. He didn't trust Rick anymore to be thorough on any case.

"Yeah, cool, Mike. Be my guest."

"How long have you guys been here?" Mike looked at his partner for the first time in the five minutes he'd been on the scene.

"We got the call at six-thirty. I was here by seven."

"Rick, why wasn't I called until eight-thirty? You know I'm always supposed to get a page as soon as a body gets called in, man. What's the deal? I know I've only been around for two months, but this is the second time in less than a week that this shit has happened. You're my partner. But I don't know, man, you're just not acting like it."

"Mike, we've gotta job to do here. Have you forgotten about the dead body lying here?" Rick Venable walked around the corpse to stand closer to his partner. His voice dropped low. "If you have a problem with me, we can discuss this later. You got called in as soon as possible. Check with Garner at the desk if you wanna know why it took so long for the lazy asses to page you. Don't get in my face about it."

"I'll tell you what, Rick," Mike shouted. He placed his index finger on the tip of Rick's shoulder blade and pressed down. "If I didn't get a page when I should have, it's not because Garner didn't call it in. It's because you didn't want me to get it, and I want to know why." Rick stood so close that Mike could almost feel Venable's heartbeat. Rick's whisper came out more like a hiss. His eyes looked up at Mike like an assault weapon zoning in on a target.

"Listen to me, you big ass, Evander Holyfield-looking motherfucker. Do not fuck with me. You're a rookie so act like one. If I tell you something, then that's how it is. Period. Do not stick your black ass into shit that's none of your fucking business. I've got the lead on these cases, and I'll handle them however I goddam please. Got it?"

Yeah, he'd gotten it. Mike resisted the temptation to hit Venable hard enough to send him straight to the morgue along with the dead Hill aide. He would remain cool for now, but he had to get the hell away from his "partner." Mike stomped out, leaving half a dozen uniformed officers staring and disappointed that they wouldn't get to enjoy a good brawl. His Navigator roared through several Capitol Hill neighborhoods and past buildings on the Senate side of the Capitol on its way back to headquarters. Venable should have kept his bigot ass down in southern Virginia instead of joining a predominantly black police force in a predominantly black city. He was gonna eat every fucking word he'd said.

*   *   *

"WHERE DO YOU THINK SHE IS?" SUZANNE ASKED PHYLLIS, standing over her desk. "An APB on Rachel Mooreshelton is preposterous! She has got to be one of the most harmless people I know. I mean, I could see the Congressman killing someone before someone like Rachel." *Yeah, hold that thought.* Phyllis couldn't believe she was having this conversation with ditzy Dixon. Her head was about as empty as Phyllis' bank account. If her father, Reverend John Ezekial Dixon, pastor of Atlanta's most prominent black church hadn't contributed so heavily every two years to the Congressman's reelection effort, Suzanne Dixon would be sitting in her father's fiefdom teaching Sunday school—for a living. And even that would be because she was the high and mighty Reverend Doctor's daughter. The stylish designer tortoise-shell glasses Suzanne wore were non-prescription, her appearance as a bright, efficient acting chief of staff was apparently more important than any real substance.

"Phyllis, have you heard from Rachel yet?!" shouted an enraged Congressman Jackson, storming out from behind his locked door. "Have you heard anything new?" Phyllis paused.

"No. No, we haven't heard anything. I called her apartment, but I know the police have probably already been over there anyway. Congressman, are you gonna to be alright? You want me to get you some coffee?" Ray Jackson's brow wrinkled and his whole body shook. Although the office was always overheated in the winter, she'd never actually seen him sweat.

"No! I want to know what's going on with Rachel! First the trouble with Persy and now her. What is happening in this office? Have we lost all semblance of normalcy around here?! I took this job to help my people not bury them. One staff person dead and another one wanted for murder. This is ludicrous!" The Congressman's oversized sable hands clenched into fists. The strong lines of his Masai warrior's face seemed to deepen and double in a matter of seconds. He was pacing now, back and forth before his own imposing portrait, while Phyllis, Suzanne and the others stood shocked by such a rare loss of composure. "This is fucking ludicrous. What are they doing?!"

"Congressman, who are you talking about?" Phyllis asked.

"What?! No one. I just don't know why all of this is happening *now*." Amid the incessant phone ringing, fax tones, and keyboard clacking, Raymond Jackson, Jr. silenced himself, looked up at the bewildered faces of his staff, walked back to his office and closed the door.

Phyllis picked up the phone after several rings. She hoped it wasn't Brian calling for the fifth time, trying to break her resolve to stay away from him. But damn if she didn't miss him. Just the thought of his chocolate-brown skin made her moist in places that hadn't been touched for weeks, except by a rugged old washcloth.

"Phyllis?" She recognized the perpetually worried tone of her mother's voice. Her mother never called her at work.

"Mama, why you calling here? What's wrong?"

"Phyllis, Jet is gone. I been all over this neighborhood and he's gone, Baby. I even asked Mr. Charles down at the Buy Right. You know he always watching everything around here, and he ain't seen him. I'm 'bout ready to call the cops. You know Jet don't just wander off like that. He hasn't been outta this yard in twenty years except fo' when I take him to the VA. This cold'll kill him. I don't even know if he's got a coat on out there. Oh baby, I hope he's alright."

"Mama, wait a minute, whadduyu mean you can't find Uncle Jet? Maybe he's just out in that back alley…Did you look back there?" Her uncle never went anywhere beyond the alley behind the house. And even if he did, everyone in the neighborhood knew that the wild-haired man, who looked like a drunk without a drop of alcohol, and sat on the front porch day in and day out in the cold and the heat was Jet Strong. She knew the neighbors would walk him back home if they saw him beyond the safe haven of his yard. Alarm immediately settled in. "Mama, call the police. Hang up with me and call the police. I'll get home as soon as I can. Hurry up!"

Damn, she still had to meet Rachel. But she also had to find Uncle Jet. What was up with all this insanity? What the hell happened to passing legislation on the Hill? In the past four days, everything had happened but the passing of the budget. The events of the past week had agitated the morning sickness that had become her unwanted friend. She had already thrown up twice that morning and with the news of Uncle Jet's disappearance, she could feel her stomach churning again. *What a damn mess. Everybody was buggin'.* It was Christmastime, but no one would have known it from glancing at the facial expressions in the office of the honorable Congressman Raymond Jackson, Jr.

Phyllis grabbed her purse and told Jill to take over the phones. She was taking her lunch break. With Jet missing, she'd be gone longer than a lunch break. For the rest of the day was more like it. She'd just have to call in from home and tell the Congressman. In the mood he was in, the Congressman would probably go off on her. She'd just have to suffer through his wrath this time.

Her phone rang. Phyllis stared at it, wavering. *Daaaaamn.* She flung the phone to her ear. "Congressman Jackson's office."

"Phyllis, girl, this is Verna," spoke an exasperated familiar voice. "I just wanted to let you know His Honor is on his way over there—just so you know. He been actin' crazier than usual this week so don't be surprised when he shows up unannounced. That man got me writin' out these damn checks again, not telling me what they for. I ain't *tryin'* to get in no trouble one day when somebody come around here snoopin' around into the office budget. What's wrong with you? You don't sound right."

Phyllis clasped the phone, recalling the post-dated, nameless checks her friend Verna, the mayor's special assistant, was asked to write out every month and send off to an unidentified P.O. box in the District. *That damn man was gonna get Verna locked up one day for something illegal, and she couldn't afford to quit with three children at home to feed,* she thought to herself. God, *she had to meet Rachel and she had to see about Uncle Jet.*

"Verna, I'll have to catch you up later," Phyllis said loudly, reaching for her bag. "I gotta run."

She dropped the phone and turned to open the main door to the office, but the knob was already coming in at her like a bullet. Mayor Cleavon Grace was on the other side of the door, his wide nostrils spread across his round face. They collided.

"Mayor Grace. I don't know if this is a good time to see the Congressman. Had you arranged to meet him?"

"No, I didn't," the mayor grumbled, pushing past Phyllis and heading toward the Congressman's closed door.

"Mayor Grace, I don't think this is a good time to show up unexpected."

"Miss Phyllis, did I ask you what you thought?" The mayor stood, wearing his trademark kente cloth bow-tie, with scary indignation stretched across every pore of a weathered face that looked as if it had fought through every vice known to man, and had lost. "Now is he back there or not?" Mayor or not, he had picked the wrong fucking time to talk down to her. Enough people had talked down to her for enough years, just because she didn't have a degree, drive a Mercedes, come from the right family or live in the right neighborhood.

"Yeah, he is Mr. Mayor. I guess I forgot that being mayor of D.C. gives you the privilege to walk in here actin' like you own Capitol Hill too."

The mayor was upon her before she could move. He grabbed her arm and led her aside, outside of earshot and eyesight. He stuck his short, beefy finger in her face. His eyes bulged with fury.

"You watch yourself, Miss Phyllis. You just watch yourself. You'd better act like you know, young lady, or you might find yourself hard-pressed in the welfare line. Or other less comfortable places. Now I'm going in there to speak to the Congressman. Don't you ever talk to me like that again, you hear?" Grace let go of her arm, straightened out his suit and made his way back to Jackson's suite. He disappeared inside.

Fuck this bullshit. He might have thought he could lay his hands on prostitutes but not on her. He'd never been anything but gracious and conversational in the past. Whatever was up his ass better get pulled out before she saw him again. *These folk get awfully high-and-mighty when they get the people's vote. Think they untouchable. If he touches me again, he'll find out just how untouchable he really is.*

21

Before Stinson's arraignment, Mike double-parked outside of 1400 New York Avenue, an expensive address near the White House, and put his siren light on the dashboard to keep the city's ruthless parking enforcement officers away from his car. Of course, a fifty dollar ticket on his truck would never stick anyway, but in his annoyed state, just seeing one of those pink tickets would send him over the edge.

Mike stopped to chat with the desk guard for a minute. The Wizards had crushed the Houston Rockets the evening before and fans across the metro area were still celebrating the rare victory over the two-time national champs. He took the elevator up to the penthouse floor and stepped out into a decadent lobby that looked like it was the national headquarters of a Fortune 500 corporation. The central offices for the PPF occupied the top four floors of the building. And Juditha Hurley's corner office had a killer panoramic view of downtown Washington, including the Washington Monument, the Lincoln Memorial in the distance and a peek at the President's back lawn.

Well, *goddam*, thought Mike. So this was life in non-profit America. The world in which Juditha Hurley lived and worked was about as far away from the bullet-prone, poverty-ridden neighborhoods of the city as black Democrats were from capturing a majority in the Congress. The PPF's modern-day mission was in the midst of turbulent reevaluation by the community that had supported it for over twenty years, and its membership was in decline. Mike knew through the papers that Hurley was fighting an uphill battle to keep the organization afloat financially. But looking around him at the flock of employees passing back and forth, the high-tech monitors, computer systems and the guessable price tags on the furniture within sight, the last problem he would think the PPF had was a financial one. They did have some fine women fighting for his civil rights though, Mike observed, his mind drifting temporarily from the task at hand. Several shapely young advocates in short business skirts walked by, eyeing him admiringly.

"You must be Detective James," bellowed a woman's deep voice from behind him. He turned to see a stunningly beautiful cinnamon-colored woman standing with her delicate hand out, a toothpaste-commercial smile and hazel eyes that bore a hole right through him. "I'm Juditha Hurley. I'm glad you found our office with no problem."

*   *   *

THE COFFEE HE SIPPED WAS A LITTLE TOO BITTER, but Mike didn't mind as he took in every curve of Juditha Hurley's hour-glass figure as she turned away from him to face the large window in her office, deep in thought. Mike also admired the wall of honor to her right. Plaques, awards and name-dropping photos lined the wall, a tribute to the woman's accomplishments and heady contacts. The closest Mike would ever get to any these big names was through a magazine photo or in an American history textbook. Juditha Hurley with President Gray. A very young Juditha Hurley with the late Dr. Martin Luther King. Juditha Hurley in jeans and a long leather jacket with Huey P. Newton. Juditha Hurley with Minister Louis Farrakhan. Juditha Hurley with Indira Gandhi, and countless others. By the look of the photos, Hurley had to have been in her late forties, but time had been very good to her. She didn't look a day over thirty, and as others had over the years, Mike found himself falling fast under the force of her powerful sensuality.

"Detective James, I am so disturbed by the recent bad fortune of Thad Derrickson. Not that I was in any way a fan of his or of his boss, mind you. But I'm just shocked that Rachel Mooreshelton would be involved in such a horrible crime." Hurley spun her curvaceous body back around to face Mike and took a seat in the large, brown, soft-leather chair behind her wide glass-top desk.

"Well, Ms. Hurley, we really have no idea at this point whether Rachel Mooreshelton actually had anything to do with Derrickson's death. What we do know is that Ms. Mooreshelton fits the description of the young, black woman who the victim's neighbor witnessed fleeing Mr. Derrickson's apartment last night. We're hoping to bring her in for questioning and an APB has been put out. I was also informed just minutes ago that she has not shown up for work yet this morning. Not a good sign, but we have nothing concrete as of yet."

"Detective, I saw that woman with Thad Derrickson last night. And let me tell you that I would have never paired those two up in a million years, but they looked a little too cozy to me to merely be friends." Hurley pulled out a cigarette with slender, agile fingers, despite the "No Smoking" sign that sat on her desk, lit it up, inhaled slowly and blew the white puffs of smoke precisely in the young detective's direction. Mike watched her intently through the haze.

"Detective, I am in no position to tell you how to do your job, but let me tell you sister to brother, off the record, I think they had some type of squabble last night. Maybe a lover's quarrel. Who knows, maybe he was having second thoughts about dating a liberal-minded sister. Maybe she found out he was chasing some blond, blue-eyed, All-American with a similar love for the Republican Party. I've headed this organization for four years and ran a division of five thousand at the Justice Department for eight. I may not have birthed this baby, but I certainly raised it to the nationally-recognized advocacy institution that it is today. And one thing I have learned in all this time is how to read people. When I ran into them last night at Old Ebbitt Grill, it was obvious they were both tense and upset about something, and they ran out of there without eating their food. And I specifically remember

Miss Mooreshelton turning back to look at me before she ran out as if to see whether I might have noticed how fast they flew out of there. Well, I did. You find Rachel Mooreshelton, you'll find who killed that man, Detective."

The woman was smooth. And those eyes. Mike felt as if he were in a trance. Beneath the black Italian leather coat with the waist wrap, his groin stirred. He was embarrassed at the unconscious thrust of blood to the bulk of manhood inside his Hane's. At least she hadn't noticed. Mike blinked to shake the feeling and decided to concentrate on his reason for being there, and focused his keen, brown eyes on the notepad in his hand.

"With all due respect Ms. Hurley, I thank you for your comments. But what I'm going to need from you is a more detailed account of what you saw, the content of your conversation with Derrickson and Mooreshelton. And what you may have overheard, if anything of the discussion between the two. And also, um, but, by the way, how did you find out about the discovery of Derrickson's body? Had you heard it on the radio news? a TV news break? About what time did you hear about the man's death? I was told your call came in virtually just after the body was found."

"Ah, yes, well I was listening to WOL-AM this morning as I do every morning while I digest the morning papers from back to front. I'm always up by 5:30, and believe it or not, that's when calls start to come in from some of my field directors here on the east coast. You know Detective James, it's not all glory and glamour running an organization of this magnitude." Juditha Hurley rotated her chair to the right, recrossed her long, satiny brown legs under the desk, and inhaled on her cigarette again. The bright red nails of her left hand tapped rhythmically against the glass. "Anyway, I heard the first news bulletin at 6:15 this morning. I know because I wrote down the time. I immediately took notice when I heard Mr. Derrickson's name since I'd just seen him last night."

Mike was surprised at how quickly his spell was broken. He rubbed his coarse, rusty-brown goatee and sat straight up in his chair. News of Derrickson's body hadn't hit the airwaves until well after seven that morning, after the crime unit was already on the scene. Hurley was a knock out, but there was also more to this woman than met the eye.

*   *   *

"No, Daddy, I don't want Spagettios. Big Mama said I didn't have to eat 'um if I didn't want to." Marcus James sat at the little table in his nursery school class, frowning over a bowl of pasta in Italian sauce. His bright, deep almond eyes showed a child's strong indignation over being asked to eat something he hated. *Come on little man, this is not the time to work my nerves.*

"Boy, I'm your father. And you're gonna eat that food or you're not getting up from this table." Mike had decided to take an early lunch break and had driven up 16th Street to eat with Marcus. "Come on, Marcus, do it for Daddy. Remember how I told you about the children over at Martha's Table who don't always have enough to eat?"

"Yeah," said the 3-year-old, banging his plastic fork against the little wooden table. "Can we take it over there so *they* can eat it?" Mike couldn't help but smile. His son never skipped a beat. Sometimes Mike wondered who was raising who. The boy was growing up so fast. Before he knew it, these days of innocence would be gone and the temptations of the street would compete with Mike for his son's attention. His pager went off, causing a whole classroom of three-year-olds to stop their chewing, their food-stained faces curious about a sound that had become more familiar to children growing up in a city full of drug dealers than it should have been.

"Alright, Marcus, you got lucky this time. Daddy's gotta go," Mike said, pulling his large, six-foot-two frame out of a miniature chair next to his son. "Who's the man?"

"You the man, Daddy. You the man." Mike reached his big arms down and grabbed the little, brown-skinned child and gave him a big kiss. "I'll see you later, all right? Don't you give Miss Jones any mouth."

On his way out of the tidy brick school building, Mike stopped to use the phone in the director's office. After a brief conversation with Lieutenant Gravino, Mike jumped back into his truck, put the siren light in the window, made a U-turn, cut across Missouri Avenue and sped back toward Capitol Hill. Raheed Stinson had been formally charged with the murder of Persy Pritchard. Rachel Mooreshelton still hadn't turned up for work. Juditha Hurley seemed to be playing out an agenda beyond that at the PPF. And his boss had already gotten some unofficial news about the cause of death in the Derrickson case.

Aw, not more snow. Mike looked through his windshield at the dark gray clouds hovering over the city, pushing the morning sun from view. Dark skies like this had always spelled trouble for him. Renata had left him on a day like this. His oldest sister Marva had died of breast cancer on a day like this. His last partner, before he made detective—a brother who grew up with him in Shaw off Florida Avenue, and one of the best cops he'd ever known—had been shot to death three years ago on a day like this. And he had a bad feeling that the major blizzard predicted to hit the mid-Atlantic later that day would bring with it something else he'd end up mourning. The gods were angry.

*   *   *

"JAMES! TAKE THIS CALL, WOULD YOU? VENABLE AIN'T HERE. Line two," shouted Alphonso Garner from the front desk at the headquarters. "It's some woman saying she knows something about the Pritchard case." Mike threw down Venable's notes from the Derrickson crime scene and grabbed the phone.

"Yeah, Detective James, how can I help you?" Mike paused at what sounded like crying on the other end. Maybe it was just the background noise of the busy station.

"Detective James. My…name is…Rachel. Rachel Mooreshelton. I haven't killed anyone…but I think maybe I know who has."

22

The space inside the telephone booth was close. Rachel could smell the wool of her coat and the scent of hunger on her breath inside its small confines. Again, a line of anxious Hill busy-bodies stood on the other side of the glass doors, rolling their eyes and clearing their throats. Washingtonians were the most stressed-out, anxiety-ridden, worka-holics Rachel had ever encountered. They'd just have to wait.

The detective on the other end was doing his best to persuade her to come in to the station for questioning. He swore that if she was inno-cent, that he would personally do everything he could to make sure she was never charged. His deep, soothing voice almost made her believe him. Rachel wanted to believe him. She'd already told him about the late-night crank calls she'd gotten the night before Persy died and wanted to tell him more. She was almost convinced that the care and concern in his tone was sincere. He had asked for her trust.

Trust. Black people had trusted in the American legal system and had been kicked in the ass by it time after time. As a wide-eyed college stu-dent, Rachel had trusted in the institution of politics, but since had watched Senators and House Members, Jew and Gentile, black and white, southerner and northerner, Republican and Democrat cheat the nation's taxpayers with their padded campaign coffers, cavorting with high-paid special interest lobbyists, sexual romps with under-age cam-paign aides, expensive overseas vacation junkets, vote intimidation and downright bribery. And now, she suspected her own boss, one of the most powerful black elected officials in the country, of getting away with *murder*. Before all this shit had hit the fan, she would have never doubted her trust in him. *Trust*. She had run out of that rare commodity in a world where trusting the wrong people could ensure career suicide or that one's body could wash up along the shores of the Potomac. But who were the wrong people? She was finding out that those who were trusted to represent and protect were sometimes those from whom they should be running.

"*Trust* you, Detective? Less than a week ago, I was just another sister making a living as a public servant. I've been trying to do the right thing with my life. If you knew what the last four days have been like, you'd know why the last thing I can do is trust you. The cops are looking for me because too many people trusted folks they *thought* they knew. So do you think I'm crazy?" Rachel regained some sense of composure. Her outburst had somehow steeled her against the sadness, suspicion and fear she had been up against all week.

"Detective James, I think somebody killed Thad because they thought he knew who killed my colleague, Persy Pritchard. And I think maybe Persy died Tuesday because he knew something that had been buried for a long time. But, see, I'm not coming in there so the police can have an easy target. I've seen on TV what happens to people who turn themselves in to prove their innocence. I watch 'COPS.'"

"Well, Rachel, why don't you let me come to you," Mike offered. "If those two murders are connected, we need to talk. We have to talk. I swear I'll come by myself. You'll be safe."

Thad thought he was safe. Persy probably thought he was safe too. And look at them. Hell no.

"I can't."

"Rachel, I know you're upset and you're scared, but if you're telling me the truth, there's nothing you can do by yourself. And to be perfectly honest, the longer you stay away, the worse things are gonna be for you when you're eventually brought in, in hand cuffs. I know all about not trusting people. You know what I'm saying…I know what it's like to lose trust in people, but you've gotta let me do my job. Look, I also know that only a person with an extensive medical background could have made such a precise laceration on Derrickson's neck, so I'm inclined to believe you. What if I tell you there was a note the coroner's office found on Derrickson's body." There was silence. She hadn't seen any note. But then she had been to overwhelmed to look.

"What do you mean a note?"

"A note, stuffed in his pants pocket. Hold on, I'll read it to you." Rachel could hear shuffling in the background. At the same time, one of the waiting Library patrons, an older white woman who reminded her of the last President's silver-haired matriarch of a wife, knocked on the door of the booth.

"Young lady, you respect that others also need to use the telephone." Rachel ignored her and turned back around to face the wall. *You're not running for your life lady, so chill out.*

"Hello, Miss Mooreshelton, the note says, 'If you love life, remember that some things are better left alone.' Does that mean anything to you? Miss Mooreshelton—" She could feel the blood rising to her head and the air in the telephone booth suddenly grow thin, making the little room spin.

"I, I have to go. People are waiting to use the phone. I just want you to know that I, I loved Thad. He was my boyfriend, and I didn't do anything to hurt him. I just need you to believe me. You and your colleagues are looking way to low." Click. In all the confusion, she had forgotten to tell him who she suspected. It was still too soon, anyway. She still wasn't even sure if her suspicions were right. She wasn't sure what was right at all anymore.

Rachel breathed deeply in and out, and in and out, to steady herself as she exited the booth, trying to head off another panic attack. She had to get to the main hall of the Library to meet Phyllis by 12:15. A long line of businesspeople stood watching as a nervous-looking young black woman with braids and a bright red coat ran down the vaulted hallway. She didn't want to see another phone booth for a long time. Rachel just wanted everything to go back to the way it was. When being a black woman Democrat on the Hill with a white Republican boyfriend had been her greatest dilemma. Fate had taken care of *that* and now it was her life she was worried about.

*   *   *

THE MAIN HALL OF THE LIBRARY OF CONGRESS ECHOED WITH quiet. The sound of silence actually bounced off the walls and became in itself something to hear. The circular ceiling looked as if it touched the sky and was etched with neo-classical designs that made America's European beginnings evident. The nation's largest library held within its walls the speeches of every president of the United States, and hundreds of thousands of periodicals, books and volumes of scholarly work dating back several centuries. Rachel and Phyllis walked in during the hall's busy lunch time hours, mixed in with hundreds of others, looking to the outsider like two busy Congressional staffers sent on a typical fact-finding mission by their boss. Except that they were paranoid. Scared to death was a better way to put it. Rachel wasn't looking forward to seeing the inside of a jail cell and Phyllis wasn't trying to join her.

Rachel retreated back to the spot back in the stacks she'd found hours ago while Phyllis scrolled through computerized reference records. With the information Rachel had slipped to her on the sly on their way in, she wrote down several newspaper file codes, legislation docket numbers and anything else she thought might be important. She wrote fast. Uncle Jet was on her mind. She had to go. She had to find him. Uncle Jet was like the old sweater in the back of your closet that you never wore, but never threw away because it had sentimental value. No matter that the man talked nonsense and spit and cussed like a wino out of food stamps. Despite her complaints, she loved him and his presence. For a long time, he had been the man of the house, whether he was capable of running it or not. If anything bad ever happened to him she would lose it.

Rachel and Phyllis huddled in a numbered corner cubicle in the farthest crevices of the stacks and filtered through the material that the Library's staff brought to them bit by bit. Rachel examined copies of House legislation according to the docket numbers Persy had scrawled in the note that had arrived in the Speaker's office. The two bills pertained to handgun sales legislation. Rachel's eyes didn't have to skim far to see that Bill Blasingame had introduced bills in the previous session to counter legislation requiring a waiting period prior to allowing the sale of handguns and limiting the sale of assault weapons. This had bothered her from the beginning. Why on earth would Persy send the material to Blasingame's office, addressed to a man who was no favorite to any of the House Democrats? She hadn't heard that duplicate packages had been sent to other Members of the Congress, so why the Bible-toting Blasingame?

For the first time, Rachel spread all the little bits and pieces of information out in front of them. She and Phyllis looked at it all, trying to think of what to do next. The two cassette tapes—one found in Persy's office, the other provided by Thad; the photos; the two notes in Persy's handwriting; the photo clipping from *The San Francisco Chronicle*; and the manila envelope that had arrived in the Speaker's office. The postmark stamp showed that the package to Blasingame had been processed through a D.C. post office on December 20, the day Persy wound up dead. So Persy had probably sent it the day before he died, Rachel reasoned.

Rachel filled Phyllis in on the contents of the two tapes after which they both looked at each other in disbelief. Persy had definitely been on to something. There was too much in front of them to deny that.

"Phyllis, this old Panther stuff is not what we need. These books and magazine headlines aren't gonna tell us anything," Rachel said, shaking her head in frustration. Most of the material consisted of autobiographical memoirs and pages of clippings lists highlighting the group's free breakfast programs, street protests, S.W.A.T. team arrests of members for various challenges to the American legal system, and the group's weapons stockpile. "I definitely didn't learn about all of this in the schools that I went to. We need to see FBI records from the Cointelpro investigations into the Panther Party, but we don't have any time to be filing Freedom of Information Act requests for de-classified material."

"Sorry to break up this party Rachel, but I hafta get outta here. I've stayed long enough. You're gonna hafta sort this all out yourself. I met you like you asked, but my uncle is missin' and I need to help my Mama find him. You'd just better hope nobody sees you back here."

"Your uncle's missing? Oh, I'm sorry Phyllis, but can you just help me copy some of this before you leave? Please Phyllis. You know I wouldn't ask if it wasn't this important. I can't stay here. Capitol Hill cops all over the place."

"Oh, you need me now. After all these years, now you need me. You can come down off your high horse to ask me to do something for you. You even sound like you're begging."

Rachel put her hands over her eyes and counted to ten. "Phyllis, I've never understood why we don't get along better. Maybe you just don't really like me, and maybe you're not one of my favorite people either, but right now we need each other, and we don't really have time to fight. Can we please work together for what it's worth? Can we put this bitchiness aside for right now?" Phyllis rolled her doe eyes and sat down. She pulled at the pile of papers and grabbed her purse.

"Fine, but we gotta copy this stuff now. I have to get home. My family needs me too. You're gonna be on your own. Well, are you coming?"

Rachel grasped a clipping in one hand and put her other hand to her mouth. For five seconds the earth stood still.

"Phyllis, look at this," she said, holding a copy of an old news clipping.

"What, I don't see anything. It's just a picture of a crowd standing outside a fire at a house. What?" Impatience and Phyllis were joining forces yet again. She looked at Rachel as if she wanted to slap her for wasting her time and getting her into a lot of potential trouble.

"Phyllis, *look*. You see this man standing here behind these people in the picture? Who is that? Who does that look like to you?" Phyllis grabbed the clipping and stared intently. Recognition smacked her square in the face.

"Oh my God, Rachel, that looks like Congressman Jackson. But so what?"

"Phyllis, this a photo of a crowd scene at the house fire that reportedly *killed* Anthony Ford. Now if Anthony Ford died in that fire like this other clipping that was sent to Blasingame's office said, how could he be standing *right there* watching the firemen put it out? The authorities must have never noticed…" Both of them stood in disbelief, still trying to absorb the bits and pieces of information that were all leading them to same ugly, unbelievable conclusion.

"Rachel, all I know is we gone have to talk to somebody else about this shit. I don't believe it for a minute myself. Maybe Anthony Ford was the other man, the one who's face somebody ripped off that picture. I can't explain these pictures and notes, but it's all bullshit. There's no way in hell that a man can run for Congress, stay in office for twenty years, in the public eye and get away with something *this* damn bad. Just no way. And the man we know would never do these things. *Never*. But you need to go on and talk to the police. You gon' get yo'self killed runnin' around like this. Look, you gon' copy this stuff or not? I have to go find Uncle Jet."

"Phyllis, I know how you feel. I've been through denial myself. I thought I was crazy even thinking anything this bad. But Phyllis, Persy is dead. My…my boyfriend is dead," whimpered Rachel, reaching for the photos and clippings. "How else do you explain all the crazy shit that's been happening all week? I don't have time for denial anymore. I think Jackson, or whoever the hell he really is, killed those people twenty years ago and might have murdered two more this week. I hate to think of this being true, but I'm almost positive now that it is. I don't even know why this is all happening now. This shit is bad. And I'm scared to death. I haven't slept well since Monday and I just....I just...just..." Rachel fell apart in the midst of her hysterical mumbling. Phyllis reached out and embraced Rachel closely and, for the first time in four years felt pity for a woman who she'd envied for her sheltered, well-to-do upbringing, her education, her effortless, brilliant writing skills and the classy, sophistication and poise that Phyllis wanted to have so badly.

Rachel wiped her eyes while she and Phyllis headed toward a row of copiers near the entrance of the main hall. Phyllis felt someone brush against her and looked to her side.

"Oh, excuse me. I left a book behind on this machine," said a tall, burnt-red-haired woman with a Mediterranean complexion in an elegant pants suit and a long string of gold baubles hanging around her slender neck. Phyllis immediately recognized Speaker Blasingame's wife from seeing her face on Fox-broadcast public service announcements encouraging the viewing audience to take in foster children. Phyllis handed the woman a thick book, the title of which she recognized— "Ten Years Under the Pig: The Truth Behind the FBI's Cointelpro Investigation of the Black Panther Party 1967-1977"—which caused her to take a second look at the sophisticated olive-skinned wife of the Republicans' most outspoken maverick.

"Thank you. Please forgive me for bumping into you. Have a good day." The woman turned and disappeared behind a shelf of reference books. Phyllis turned to her left to mention the encounter to Rachel only to see Rachel standing like a deer caught in headlights and Sergeant Filipidis standing in the main entrance only thirty feet away, their eyes locked on each other.

23

With the throbbing in her chest racing so fast that she thought her heart would leap right through her throat, Phyllis grabbed Rachel's arm and pulled her toward one of two additional entrances that led into the underground walking tunnels that connected Capitol Hill's primary office buildings, the Library of Congress and the Capitol. With a shot of adrenaline racing through her body and a piercing pain in her stomach, Phyllis led Rachel, while pushing and shoving people blocking their path, through a maze of poorly-lit tunnels with Filipidis on their heels. Phyllis knew the tunnels like the back of her hand from running errands for the Congressman for six years. She knew all the short cuts as well as the storage rooms and underground administrative offices for the maintenance staff. On many days, she would stop and trade gossip with women in the janitorial crew or flirt with some of the well-built, shit-talking men pushing brooms through the walkways.

They ran down a long corridor, made a sharp left and then a sharp right down another. Even though Phyllis was out of shape and over-weight for her medium-build frame, she and Rachel ran like trained athletes running for the gold. With the police coming at them from both directions, Phyllis and Rachel ducked down a third hallway and into a back room full of old bookshelves, typewriters and desks. Phyllis pulled her colleague through two additional rooms, their breathing hard and their chests burning from exhaustion.

"Mr. Darnell! Mr. Darnell! You gotta get us outta here!" Phyllis yelled to an elderly black man who stood with a clipboard in his wrinkled hands. Darnell Green had worked maintenance on the Hill for nearly forty years until forced retirement. His old boss had let him come back as a volunteer just to keep the old man busy. For the past eight years, he had helped classify used furniture from the Rayburn, Dirksen, Longworth and Russell Congressional buildings to prepare it for public auction. His sight was failing but his mind was sharp as a tack. He'd lived a quiet, non-descript life with just enough to eek out a meager existence. He stood staring at Phyllis and Rachel with cloudy, glaucoma-filled eyes while chewing on his gums.

"Miss Phyllis, what can I do for you?"

"Mr. Darnell, please, you gotta show us a way to get out of here. Please, we haven't done nothin' wrong, but they after us anyway. Where should we go?" Darnell stood a moment and tapped his worn, but neat brown loafer against the cement floor of his dusty, windowless office. Phyllis could hear a parade of heavy shoes running past the little office.

"Alright, Miss Phyllis, why don't you girls come this way. Baby, I don't know whatchu done gone and got yo'self mixed up in, but you been good to me bringin' me them lunches once a month, so I ain't got no complaints whicha. Come on here this way."

The frail little man led them through a series of dark, cluttered rooms and through another narrow hallway to a door at the end. He opened the door and held it to allow the two to pass. Weak daylight shone from above.

"Don't nobody ever use this entrance no more after they closed down these offices down here. Y'all girls be careful now." Phyllis hugged the man and she and Rachel ran up the steps and looked around to find themselves on the southern end of the Capitol Building where they could just barely see fringes of the crowd of furloughed federal workers demonstrating on the Capitol's front steps. Police were out in full force already, just minutes after their encounter with Filipidis.

"Phyllis, don't run," Rachel panted, pulling Phyllis back. "Don't run and maybe they won't notice us." They walked steadily toward the street beyond the Capitol with the wind at their backs and scarves wrapped tightly around their necks and faces to insulate them from the intensity of its sting. They walked past Channel Two and Channel Nine news vans and equipment crews, onlookers and busy Congressional aides running errands. Rachel put her right hand up to hail a cab already blocking traffic to watch the frenetic scene in front of the Capitol. The cabbie slid up to the curb, unaware of the role he was about to play in outwitting the Capitol Hill Police.

*　　　*　　　*

MIKE STOOD IN THE CROWD OF FRUSTRATED FEDERAL EMPLOYEES, many two weeks away from eviction or borrowing money to make Christmas special for their children. The wind stung his uncovered ears as big flakes of snow started to fall. He looked to see that the snow was sticking just like the all-weather channel had predicted. Twenty to twenty-four inches by Saturday morning. He had interviewed dozens of protesters and had been harassed by half a dozen news reporters already on the scene to cover the demonstration. No one had seen Rachel Mooreshelton and an unidentified woman racing away from the Capitol Building after eluding the police sergeant and his pack of uniformed officers. She had to know this was a no-win situation. There was no out. They'd catch up to her and there'd be nothing Mike could do then. She had his pager number and she'd have to use it, and tell him what she knew, for her to stand a chance of getting out of this mess.

At moments like these, it would hit Mike that his job called for him to hunt down people who in some cases he felt were innocent of all alleged wrongdoing. And Rachel Mooreshelton was one of them. He'd never even thought he'd make detective. But even though the job could be a bitch at times, it was a real thinking man's work and it allowed him to delve deeper into the criminal mind. Many of the other brothers on the force were content to run their careers out as unis rather than pick up a book to grasp at the gold shield. But Mike wanted to go as high as he could go—even all the way up to the Chief's slot. He'd probably do a better job than Ham Draper, the current chief, who'd promoted all his old cronies before he'd even had a chance to warm the big vinyl chair in his office. But here he was, rookie detective Mike James, standing in the cold, freezing his ass off searching for an educated legislative aide from a good family, running from him and his kind. She probably had never thought she'd be where she was either. He could feel for the sister, but would do his job first.

Mike's pager vibrated under his coat. He spotted a gorgeous black news correspondent for ABC with a flip phone in her hand, chatting it up with several enraged Treasury Department employees holding placards and bullhorns. He pulled out his badge and headed in her direction.

With the tiny phone in his hand, Mike dialed an unfamiliar number to hear a familiar and chillingly sensuous voice pick up.

"Hello. Detective James, I see you know how to get right back to a woman. I like that."

"This is Detective James. Can I help you?"

"Well, actually Detective, I thought that I might help you. This is Juditha Hurley."

"Yes, Ms. Hurley, do you have additional information that could assist us in Thad Derrickson's murder?" The wind howled behind Mike. He pulled up the collar of his coat around his neck and stuffed his left, gloved finger into his ear in an attempt to drown out the noise of the throng of people who surrounded him.

"Yes, I think I might have more that I can share with you. How about a light dinner at B. Smith's at Union Station tonight at eight sharp?" For a question, the tone on Hurley's determined voice sounded as if she gave Mike no choice in the matter. A chill went through Mike's body that was clearly stimulated by more than the bluster of cold and the falling snow.

"Ms. Hurley, with all due respect I don't believe that would be entirely appropriate under the circumstances. Could we possibly meet at the headquarters or again at your office?"

"Detective James, I don't believe there's anything wrong with business talk over a little dinner, do you? We're two mature, professional adults. Dinner at B. Smith's would give us a comfortable place to talk and sip a bit of wine at the same time. Why not kill two birds with one stone?" The shouts of the protesters grew louder as camera crews zoomed in for one final shot before packing up to escape the oncoming blizzard. Mike strained even harder to hear the somewhat husky-smooth voice of one of Washington's most powerful black women.

Since his divorce, Mike had sworn to himself to keep business and pleasure at arms length from each other, which wasn't always an easy thing to do in his line of work. His buddies at the gym ribbed him regularly about how many lovely ladies he encountered on his job, brilliant and sexy attorneys at court hearings, witnesses he interviewed from crime scenes whose eyes would linger a little too long, seductive hospital nurses who would escort him to the bedside of attempted homicide victims. He had been tempted by a few but until now had managed to restrain himself. But Juditha Hurley was like a powerful magnet and he could feel the force of her pull. How bad could it be to hear the woman out over some upscale cornbread, collard greens and catfish? He might be able to uncover the discrepancy in the time Hurley had told him she heard about the murder on the radio. Just this once couldn't hurt. But he'd give himself an escape route.

"Ms. Hurley, I'll meet you at eight, but only for an hour. I'll have to pick my son up from my parents' house after that. And no alcohol for me while I'm on the clock." Even though he'd be off-duty, this was business and, besides, he didn't need anything fucking with his common sense with a woman like Hurley around.

"Very good, Detective James. I'll look forward to it. I'll call to make reservations." Click. Mike had been living life a little dangerously all week. A major fall-out with his partner, an unauthorized interrogation of a suspect, sleuthing through Pritchard and Derrickson's case files without his partner's knowledge, an undisclosed phone conversation with a wanted suspect and dinner with a woman he had interviewed in connection with an ongoing murder investigation. Damn, he might just need that drink after all.

Mike spoke with Sergeant Filipidis, a still disgruntled Rick Venable and a handful of other uniformed officers, all miffed and frostbitten, and then headed back to headquarters to sign out for the day. Rachel Mooreshelton had disappeared through the tumultuous crowd without a trace.

24

Rachel and Phyllis emerged from a cab on Missouri Avenue and stood in the middle of a snow-covered sidewalk. Rachel placed her arm around Phyllis as they walked the four blocks down 8th Street to Phyllis' house. They had switched cabs three times on the way, hoping to elude the police in the event that the cabbies were ever questioned as to their final destination. Phyllis' stomach pains had worsened and she moaned loudly beneath her long, brown wool coat, hat, gloves and scarf. They walked through the back alleys behind row houses that were fast being buried under tufts of fluffy white flakes of snow. Phyllis unlocked the basement door of the little house at 8109 and she and Rachel hurried into its warmth and refuge.

The door to the basement opened into the kitchen and startled Phyllis' already nerve-wracked mother, who stood in the middle of the kitchen floor in tears, holding a stack of papers.

"Oh, Lord Jesus, Phyllis, what on earth are you doing sneaking in through the basement? You 'bout gave me a heart attack, Child!" The soft features of her mother's caramel-colored skin were twisted in worry. She had tried her best to give Phyllis a good life after her husband had skipped out on them seventeen years ago. Pearline Roberson had worked two jobs for most of the last fifteen years to keep up the mortgage payments on the row house and pay off the debt her absentee husband had mired them in. When it finally looked as if things were looking up for them—she could quit her night job now that she was only two months away from paying the house off and Phyllis was saving in the hopes of taking classes at Howard in the fall—Jet's disappearance had pierced her heart.

"Mama, have the police been here 'bout Uncle Jet? They still here?" Phyllis asked in a whisper peeking into the living room. "They found Uncle Jet yet?"

"No, baby. They sent over two of them officers from the Third District station over on Upshur. They asked me all these questions, and they said they gon' send a squad car around to talk to the neighbors. But Phyllis, baby, I'm scared. You know Jet ain't done nothin' like this before. I got a bad feelin' in my bones." The fifty-year old woman looked nearly ten years older from the worry and stress of living life month-to-month with little joy to ease the strain. She sat her short, cherubic body into a metal kitchen chair and stared at the floor. "Phyllis, I just don't feel good about this baby."

Pearline finally looked up at the stranger in her home and then back at her daughter. Phyllis sensed her mother's next question.

"Mama, this is Rachel from work. You remember me mentionin' her before," she said, and continued before her mother could wonder why on earth the two of them would be together in the middle of an oncoming blizzard. Phyllis explained their troubles to her mother while holding her stomach. In her frazzled state, Pearline just nodded and attempted a weak smile of sympathy for the young woman before her, who was much prettier and much more delicate than she had imagined her to be.

"Mama, Rachel's gonna stay here for a couple of days."

"I know what it's like to be in trouble and not have nowhere to go. Y'all go on upstairs and get outta them wet clothes. I'll put some tea on."

In the background, the TV blared a breaking news report and broadcast photos of the wanted woman that went unseen in the Roberson household.

"Police are still searching for a young woman in connection with the death of Thad Derrickson, a Republican Congressional aide to Speaker of

House Bill Blasingame. Rachel Mooreshelton and an unidentified woman eluded Capitol Hill police earlier today after an onfoot chase through the maze of tunnels beneath the Capitol. Derrickson's is the second murder of a Hill staffer in less than a week and colleagues and interns are alarmed at these unexpected losses. Chuck, is it true that the suspect, Rachel Mooreshelton was a close colleague of Persy Pritchard, Congressman Jackson's chief of staff, who was shot to death near the Capitol earlier this week?" Pearline Roberson stood over a kettle on the stove shaking her head. Life would never give her a goddammed break.

A blue and white squad car with the image of a golden shield affixed to its side panel, pulled up outside of 8109, throwing snow up onto the broken cement of the sidewalk. Two black officers exited the car and walked quickly up the three steps to the dead-bolted door of the house where the three scared and exhausted women sought comfort.

*　　　　*　　　　*

MIKE'S LEATHER BOOTS AMBLED ACROSS THE LARGE BLACK, gold and white-marbled tiles on the floor of Union Station as he headed in the direction of one of Washington's trendiest new restaurants. With an elaborate plaster ceiling above him and the bustle of the station's 50,000-odd daily visitors around him, he approached the fifty-foot columned entrance to B. Smith's, a popular eatery owned by black New York socialite and former model Beverly Smith.

Mike had driven home an hour earlier to change into black slacks and a dark green silk button-down shirt over a black wool turtleneck that accentuated his small, tight waist, washboard stomach and massive line-backer shoulders. He had tossed on Calvin Klein's hottest-selling cologne and had shaved the stubble on his face to give him the smooth, baby-soft appearance that always drew stares from the ladies.

"Good evening sir, do you have a reservation?" asked a chipper young blond.

"Yes, I believe they're under the name Hurley." Breathing in the cold wind outside had given Mike's voice a deeper, huskier bass than usual that had surprised him and had even forced the hostess to look up at him and smile. The woman escorted him back through several empty tables toward an intimate booth near the rear. The worsening weather had kept many away who would have otherwise dined on the chic café's highly-praised okra gumbo and southern-style ratatouille. Mike took a seat at the table and awaited Juditha's entrance.

He found himself jittery and nervous, far unlike his usual cool and calm. The woman rattled his nerves. Under the dimmed recessed lighting, complemented by skirted, candle-lit tables and contemporary, but appropriately understated art, Mike could feel his cold gun pressing his flesh, sending light spasms through his lower body as he waited for the woman with the figure that just wouldn't quit.

The feel of his gun also forced his mind to recap the crazy week he'd had. He had checked with the Property Division to see if the gun had ever come through their warehouse at some point over the past two years, and had found out that Dr. Salvi's stolen gun had turned up missing in the warehouse over three weeks ago, along with half a dozen other firearms and twenty-five thousand dollars in confiscated drug money. The officer at the warehouse said he was under strict orders not to provide any other details about the missing property, especially to his colleagues on the force. *Why was top brass trying so hard to keep info from members of the force?* Mike asked himself. *Must be some inside scam goin' on. Someone had needed Salvi's gun for something. They hadn't wanted him to have it back. And now Persy Pritchard was dead, shot with a gun that the police had had in their possession – stolen from right under their noses. This shit was major. Somebody with a shield to protect and defend was playin' some kinda crazy game with peoples' lives.*

After visiting Hurley's office late that morning, Mike had walked in on his partner in a hush-toned chat with Lieutenant Gravino and two other detectives in Gravino's office when he'd knocked to alert the Lieutenant of the chase at the Capitol. A glowering Venable had been holding a copy of what looked like that day's edition of the *Washington Post*, pointing to something in the headlines that seemed to have disturbed him. Mike had given Gravino the news and half the squad had dashed out to the Capitol, but not before Mike had had a chance to scan the front page of the *Post* lying on the front desk at the station. Pritchard's death had already been shifted back to the paper's Metro section and Derrickson's had been discovered after the presses had been run for the morning edition. Aside from stories on the drop in holiday sales from the year before, the never-ending struggle over the federal budget, the woes of furloughed workers, and the appointment of a special prosecutor to investigate the Speaker's campaign finances, a small piece in the bottom right-hand corner had caught his eye and had left him numb with anxiety. *Internal Affairs Seeks Information in Case of Missing Guns and Money at D.C. Police Warehouse,* the headline read. *Shit.*

Raheed Stinson had been formally arraigned that morning and sent, without bail to a holding prison within the District to await trial. Mike had gone through the painstaking effort of requesting phone records without authorization from the past week for his district's police head-quarters, Congressman Jackson's office and Persy's apartment, in the hopes that something would lead him in the right direction. The records would be available tomorrow afternoon. He'd also brought home a list of the names of Pritchard's colleagues at the Congressman's office, close friends and next of kin, that he'd copied from the case file, though he hadn't yet decided what to do with it. He was about *this* far from losing his job if anyone found out about his unsanctioned actions on either Pritchard's or Derrickson's cases. But something wasn't fucking right and he wasn't about to risk ratting out fellow officers to IAB without some solid-ass proof.

"Good evening Detective James," uttered the silky voice of the woman moving toward him. Juditha Hurley gracefully walked past tables and white columns, dressed in a silk-wool blend pantsuit the color of red wine with a neckline that dipped low to reveal buxom cleavage two shades deeper than brown sugar. Her jet-black shoulder-length hair was swept up into a dazzling, sleek French twist and her bewitching eyes had been sharpened with thick, black mascara and a thin glimpse of eyeliner. Hurley's million-dollar smile glowed in unison with rich, burgundy lip color. Mike stood to greet her. She shook his hand tightly and took a seat across from him.

"I'm so glad you agreed to join me, Detective. This is my favorite restaurant," she said, placing her matching tipped nails on the table before her. "It's been quite a day at the office. Our legal aide division is fighting an affirmative action case in Houston so I've been on the phone with the state field director down there all day. Do you mind if I smoke?" He couldn't believe she'd actually asked this time. Mike nodded. Juditha gently pulled a Virginia Slim Lite from its dainty package and wrapped her painted lips thoughtfully around the stem. They ordered a bottle of wine and a dinner of smothered fried chicken, zesty kale greens and sweetbread.

"So, Ms. Hurley—"

"Please, call me Juditha. I have enough folk calling me 'Ms. Hurley' everyday. It makes me feel old sometimes. And at my age old is not what I want to feel."

"Ms. Hur—Juditha, if I may say so, you don't look a day over thirty-five."

"Oh, a man after my own heart. Don't you know how to put on the charm?" Juditha peered at him over her sparkling wine glass.

"No, I just believe in telling the truth, Juditha. Speaking of which, wasn't there something you wanted to share with me this evening? More information about what you may have observed last night between Rachel Moorshelton and Thad Derrickson?"

"Oh, Detective James, just when we were beginning to enjoy the evening. I hate to ask, but can we push business talk back a bit? Let's get to that later okay? I'm much more interested in you." Those eyes were at it again. And Mike couldn't help but drink in Juditha's cleavage, flung right in his face as if to say, "Look, and become rock hard."

They talked over dinner and even laughed a bit. The conversation helped take Mike's mind off of the troubling thoughts about internal affairs at the station house. Juditha filled him in on her impressive legal career and her passion for community improvement and he spoke candidly to her about his divorce and the son who he cherished more than his own life. Mike checked his watch after they ate the last morsels of Mississippi mudcake. *Nine-thirty-five.* It was time to wind things up and pick Marcus up before his parents' fell asleep by ten o'clock. Now late into their fifties, Elroy and Jonnetta James awoke at dawn and were back in bed before the ten o'clock evening news. Juditha paid the bill with her corporate credit card and gave the perky waitress a healthy tip despite Mike's chivalrous attempt to foot the hefty dinner bill himself.

"Sweetheart, let me handle this one. You pick up the tab next time." Mike caught the glimmer in her eye as the last word rolled off of her tongue. "Detective, do you mind dropping me home? I have a brownstone on O Street near Dupont Circle. Would you be a dear and save a lady from standing in the cold for a cab?" Against his better judgement, Mike made a quick call to his parents' home to tell them he'd be a little late picking Marcus up. Johnnetta James promptly told her son that she was not about to wake her sleeping grandson at that time of night so that Mike could drag the poor boy out into a blizzard.

Outside, the snow had already left Mike's Navigator half buried. Mike opened the passenger door to let Juditha Hurley in and wiped the soft snow from the truck's windows. The bottle of wine, which he'd helped put away despite his initial misgivings, had him feeling warm and horny. And Juditha Hurley's stare was equally as warm and inviting. *Fuck the rules tonight*, he thought. He wasn't about to kiss and tell. A solid, rock hard mass grew in his slacks as he wondered what it would be like to fuck with power. The black truck sped off with its off-road tires into the night toward the city's eclectic Dupont Circle. *1GoodCop* was about to make a personal house arrest.

25

Phyllis curled up in her grandmother's old quilt and tried to ignore the pain that burned in her lower abdomen. She had hoped she could wish it away but it was only getting worse. Rachel sat on the floor of Phyllis' bedroom up against the side of the bed with a pillow between her knees and papers and cassette tapes spread out on discolored carpet that had been trampled across one time too many. They had eaten a light meal in near silence with Phyllis' mother and had made their way back up to the sanctuary of Phyllis' tired-looking but cozy second-floor bedroom to recoup from the horrors of the day. Both women had cried enough tears to last a lifetime and were now drained and scared but determined to dig themselves out of the onslaught of insanity that had wreaked havoc on their lives. Rachel looked over and noticed a dog-eared copy of a familiar book and picked it off the floor.

"Phyllis, I didn't know you had read 'Waiting to Exhale.' This told it like it is, huh?"

"Girl, what black woman in America hasn't read that book or at least seen the movie if she was too lazy to put her eyes to paper? That book is the story of my life. I've probably been through all that and more with these dumb-ass negroes I've messed with. But I guess you wouldn't know nothin' about that being with Mr. Blue-Eyed-All-American, huh?" Phyllis caught herself and suddenly felt sorry for what she'd said. The pain in her stomach having subsided a little, she sat up and looked at Rachel, whose eyes were full of tears again.

"Rachel, look, girl, I'm sorry. I can be a real bitch sometimes, but that was just mean. I know you cared about that man and I'm sorry about what happened to him. Really, I'm sorry." Phyllis patted Rachel's braids, wishing she could take it back. She held the long, thick braids in her hands and knew what they needed to do next.

"Rachel, you gone hafta take these braids out. The police are looking for a woman with braids. It'll be easier for you without these. We're lucky that those cops that came to the house a few hours ago were lookin' for Uncle Jet and not you. Let me take 'em out and do your hair. I have a relaxer kit in the hall closet. We might as well do somethin' besides cry all night. That ain't gon' bring nobody back." Rachel agreed. She needed to do something to move forward. Phyllis got up and brought a comb and a spray bottle of detangler back from the bathroom and together they began to unravel Rachel's hair and the problems in each other's lives—like two close sisters with nothing better to do.

Rachel talked about her anxiety over her relationship with Thad, how she wanted her father's constant approval and how she wished she could do something to save her brother Yarrick's life. Phyllis broke down and told Rachel about her pregnancy and the pains she'd been suffering from in the last few stress-filled days, her relationship with Brian, her desire to go to Howard and get out of a neighborhood that had sank over the years from working-class to drug-infested. They wrenched out the bitterness of the past four years with candor and empathy and connected in ways they never thought possible between two girls from opposite sides of the track. But the two matters that weighed on their minds most was the shocking mystery behind a man for whom they'd worked for years, with whom they'd laughed and in whom they'd believed. And the lingering question mark of the missing face in the photo. They both held out hope that the man behind the missing face would turn out to somehow be the Anthony Ford who'd committed murder then and perhaps again that week. They prayed that their long-held admiration in Congressman Jackson would then somehow be sustained.

After they finished undoing Rachel's braids, Phyllis massaged and moisturized her scalp and combed gently again through each section of hair. They decided to put off completing Rachel's hair for the morning to get down to the ugly business of sorting through the information Rachel had unintentionally removed from the Library of Congress in their race away from the police. It was impossible to link Persy's talk of a little white girl from Tennessee to the House of Representatives' hand-gun legislation, to Persy's note to the Speaker about how none of them were innocent of wrongdoing, to Thad's death, to the address on Bladensburg, to the missing piece of the photo, to the Rosewood & Hall lobbying firm, to the series of numbers on the back of the note. What was the connection?

"Phyllis, we've been over all this for hours. Even if Congressman Jackson was involved in the murders of those people in Oakland, there's nothing here but suspicion to tie him to Persy's murder or Thad's. Filipidis told us that Persy's time of death was around 5:45 a.m. Tuesday morning, but the Congressman has a live-in housekeeper. You remember Romelda Alvarez from the birthday party at his house back in August? She would have known if Jackson had been out early that morning, wouldn't she? The police questioned all of us right? The Congressman must have been at home or she would have mentioned his absence. And last night, Jackson attended that White House dinner and a late private reception in the residential wing with President Gray, Secretary Wilder and the Vice President to discuss strategy for next year's presidential election. He was no where near Capitol Hill when Thad was killed."

"Umm hm," Phyllis replied. "But what about the mayor? He's been hanging around the office and calling like crazy all week, even stopped by again today. He knew Persy, but it's not like he woulda been all that upset about his death enough to practically *live* at the office. And we know there ain't no bills pending right now that involve the District government, so what kind of bug is up his ass? I thought Mayor Grace was outta his goddam mind grabbing my arm like he did." Rachel's eyes lit up for the first time in what seemed like months.

"Phyl, don't Grace and Jackson go way back? They served in Vietnam together right? And doesn't he know Juditha Hurley from his Atlanta days when he was running that community center? You think they know about what he did and have been holding it all these years? Or maybe one of them, or *both* of them are somehow involved too…"

"Yeah, but Juditha Hurley would never be a part of that kind of scandal. She's got too much class."

"Phyllis, how well do we really know Ms. Hurley? Except for the political events she's attended with the Congressman and stories in *Jet* about the PPF's legal victories and that piece in *Essence* last spring about her wonderful career after she received an Essence Award, what else do we really know about her on a personal level? Honestly, something about her has always given me the creeps. And the Congressman has been dodging her like a bullet all week. I could swear that was her on the phone with him when I walked in on phone conversation yesterday. It sounded to me like whoever it was threatening him. You should have *seen* his face, Phyllis."

"She wouldn't be part of—"

"Phyllis, black folk in high places can do wrong just like white people. Even when we know they're doing wrong, we dare anyone to bring it to light because of the bad press that'll hit the majority media. Nothing makes our leaders any less susceptible to corruption and wrongdoing than white leaders, and no less accountable for their actions. You and me Phyllis. We don't have a choice but to expose this information so shit'll end. I'm not trying to get myself killed holding out on something somebody else did."

"Without that job, I ain't got shit. I gotta a baby on the way and won't have no job." Phyllis stood in the window, watching the snow collect on the sill and looking out into a street blanketed in white flakes. "I don't have nothing without Congressman Jackson."

Rachel peered at her sympathetically. "We gotta find the missing piece of that picture. *Someone* didn't want anybody to know they were mixed up in this mess. Someone has gotten away with murder all this time. And they'll keep killing to keep the cat in the bag. And we're holding the bag…"

*   *   *

JUDITHA HURLEY SLID HER FEET OUT OF SUEDE BURGUNDY pumps and walked along the bleached wood panels of the first floor of her pricey brownstone to a combination bar and entertainment center. Mike watched her as she stood under strategically placed track lights, pulled a CD from a glass cabinet and slipped it into a CD player mounted on the wall above bottles of cognac and brandy.

"Mike, why don't you have a seat? Please make yourself at home," she mouthed just barely over the sensuous croon of Teddy Pendergrass' "Looks Like Another Love TKO."

"You've got a real nice place here. It's been renovated?" he asked taking a seat on the plush brown leather couch below a large Jacob Lawrence original. "I certainly couldn't afford anything like this on my cop's salary." Mike rubbed at his sandy-colored goatee, a habit he had developed in college when he was agitated or nervous. Juditha brought him a drink and settled down next to him on the couch.

"Yes, I bought this place five years ago and had it completely redone to fit my taste. In my position, it's important to have a home where one can entertain, suitable for a guest list of a hundred or *just one*." The glint of her hazel eyes shone like tiger eye under the light. She moved closer. Feeling himself having second thoughts, Mike hesitantly shifted his weight away.

"Juditha, I just don't think—"

"No, Mike, don't think. From the time I saw you standing in the lobby this morning, I knew I wanted you right where you are. I believe in protecting my special interests and for tonight, you're the only interest I want to protect." Juditha leaned in and kissed him on the neck and then ran her soft lips along his jaw line leaving a trail of red-wine lipstick to his mouth. No longer resisting, Mike wrapped his muscular left arm around her and gently pressed her down into the supple couch, balancing his 220-pounds of dusky brown brawn effortlessly on top of her.

Mike ran his hand along the curves of Juditha's hips to the crest of erect nipples that poked proudly through her thin silk, double-breasted blazer. Teddy Pendergrass's sexual desire turned up a notch as he belted out the first lines of "Turn Out the Lights." Mike dipped his tongue into Juditha's luscious mouth and tasted the sweet of her tongue dancing erotically around his. He began a slow, rhythmic grind, pumping his groin against the inside of her thighs as he pulled skillfully at the buttons of her blazer. Goddam, she felt so good, *he thought*. Listening to the slow, low moan emerging from her lips, he pulled the blazer away and molded his honey-colored hand around her ample, pointed breasts, glistening from the building perspiration. He buried his face in her chest, licking and teasing her nipples and the round of her breasts and running his tongue along the valley of milk chocolate skin between delicious, dark fudge-toned mountain peaks.

Juditha unzipped his cotton slacks, slid them down and over his tight, smooth behind, grabbed his hardness and caressed it aggressively in her hands. Mike let out a groan of pleasure that hastened their pace.

"Let's take this upstairs, baby," Juditha whispered in between heavy breaths. She grabbed his hand and led him up a winding staircase to the master bedroom at the end of the hall. Teddy Pendergrass floated upstairs with them, piped in on speakers placed on either side of the king-sized bed.

With a crease of subtle light etching its way through a crack in the door, Mike watched in anticipation as Juditha removed her suit and panties piece by piece and knelt down before him. In a single swift movement, Juditha had both removed his silk briefs and enveloped his large erection with her smooth hands, letting out an arousing sigh of pleasure at the treasure she'd discovered. Without a word, she took him into her mouth and fondled his extended stiffness with her tongue and the forceful muscles in her throat. *Awww.* Life on Homicide seemed a million miles away. Mike's doubts about the evening's turn of events evaporated without a trace. For a few minutes, Persy Pritchard, Thad Derrickson and Rachel Mooreshelton had dissolved into figments of his imagination.

Juditha released him after several moments of indescribable indulgence and laid her lithe body across the wide wooden sleigh bed. Mike dipped his mouth between her thighs and didn't emerge until she had grabbed his tuft of curly hair in ecstasy. Mike shifted Juditha's body toward the headboard, peeled away the wrapper of the condom he had placed on the nightstand and rolled it gently down manhood that burned with wanting. He licked hungrily at her left nipple as she grasped his lower back and pulled him into her, hard and strong in a single thrust. Mike felt the power of her pull. Juditha Hurley was used to power, to getting what she wanted and being on top of her game. He was fucking with power, but she was fucking with fate.

26

"Phyllis! Phyllis! Oh, Jesus help us! Phyllis!" Pearline Roberson ripped up the stairs of the row house in a frenzy of screams and moans. She tore open the door of her daughter's bedroom and shook her frantically. "Phyllis, wake up baby! Oh, God!"

Pearline ran toward the black-and-white TV on the dresser and pulled at the on-switch. She stood and wept as Phyllis and Rachel sat up abruptly.

"*...and in an unfortunate discovery two days before Christmas, the body of a man identified as Leroi Strong III of northwest Washington was found this morning in snow along the banks of the Potomac near the Lincoln Memorial. Police are looking for leads in what they believe to be the suffocation death of the 48-year old Vietnam veteran and are working to contact the victim's next of kin. Anyone with information in connection with this homicide should call Crime Watchers at 800-555-1111. And in other news this morning...*"

Phyllis and Pearline Roberson huddled together and cried aloud as the voice of the news anchor mumbled on. "*Mary Ann Friedrich, wife of Rosewood & Hall vice president Gary Friedrich, whose body was found in his Bethesda home almost two years ago, has filed a suit against her husband's firm for withholding evidence believed to be key in the unsolved strangulation murder. Four in the Morning correspondent Maureen Butler-Wilson interviewed Mrs. Friedrich—*"

Rachel sat in silence knowing that things couldn't possibly get any worse. She reached for a piece of paper on the dresser with one hand and grabbed the phone with the other. It was time for this mess to end.

*   *   *

BEEP! BEEP! BEEP! BEEP! BEEP!

Mike smacked his head on the wooden headboard in Juditha Hurley's bedroom, awakened rudely from sleep by the irritating sound of his blaring pager. *BEEP! BE—Click.* Feeling somewhat disoriented, Mike looked around the room to see that Juditha had already arisen and disappeared elsewhere in the brownstone. Mike rubbed the sore spot on the side of his head and wiped the sleep from his eyes. He looked down at the digital display of his pager at the number that popped up. It wasn't familiar.

He got up, still nude from the night before, stretched his muscular physique, flipped on the huge TV, increased the volume and headed to the bathroom off the master suite to empty his bladder. He returned from the bathroom, sat on the edge of the bed and pulled up his briefs to help defend his skin from a slight draft seeping in from the window by the television. He flipped nonchalantly through the channels, landing on Channel Nine and an unexpected update to an early morning news report. A photo of a middle-aged man with unkempt hair and two women appeared on the screen as the anchor described victim Leroi Strong II and the photo found with his other possessions in a small plastic sandwich bag. Mike had interviewed one of the women in the photo on Tuesday in Congressman Jackson's office.

Mike picked up the phone, checked the number on his pager again and dialed it.

"Hello."

"Detective James. I was paged."

"Mike James?"

"Yes, Detective Mike James. Homicide." Somehow he knew who it was before she uttered another word.

"Detective James, this is…Rachel Mooreshelton."

"I know all about that body found over near the Lincoln Memorial and I already know the man is a friend or relative of Phyllis Roberson's. Are you ready to talk?" A ten-second pause made him wonder if the woman was still on the line.

"Yes, I'll meet you, but not at the station. There's still too much I don't understand but I just don't want anybody else to die."

"It's probably only a matter of hours or maybe a day before the force'll track you down, so there isn't much time. Look, I can meet you anywhere you want. Just name the place. I'll come alone."

"I, I don't know. Just somewhere where nobody'll know me."

"How about Ben's Chili Bowl over on U? We could sit at a booth in the back."

"What about the police?"

"Miss Mooreshelton, I *am* the police. You'll be safe. I promise." Mike checked his watch, lying on the night table along with his keys and the wedding band he'd had remolded and embedded with an eye-catching black onyx. It was just eight-thirty in the morning.

"Okay. Seven-thirty. I'll be wearing a brown wool coat."

"And braids?"

"No, no braids. I'll probably be wearing a hat. And you?"

"Uh, I'm a big guy, brown-skinned, black leather coat. I'll have my gold shield attached to my belt. You'll see it when I take the coat off. Are you alright?"

"No. I haven't been alright since…since Tuesday, but I'm safe."

"Have you contacted your family at all?"

"No. No, not even my brother. I haven't talked to anyone but—I haven't talked to anyone. Detective James?"

"Yeah?"

"I hope you have an open mind. I have some information that might be hard to swallow."

"This week, my mind is about as open as it's gonna get. Page me again if you have any problems…before seven-thirty." Mike heard a noise on the line and paused briefly. Was probably nothing.

"Thank you Detective. I know you shouldn't be doing this."

"Hey, you're a sister in trouble. I'm just trying to get to the bottom of some questions I have myself. I don't think you've hurt anybody. Look, you be careful." Click.

Mike threw on his slacks and turtleneck and wandered downstairs to tell Juditha he'd have to cut out without breakfast. He had to get through over a foot of snow to give Marcus his daily good morning hug and make his way over to headquarters to check out the phone records he'd requested. Where had the woman gone? The house was quiet.

He walked toward an open door from which he heard the murmur of a woman's voice.

"Why? You didn't have to do it. We've made it too long to get sloppy now goddammit." Mike turned on his heels and headed back up the stairs to retrieve the rest of his clothing. He didn't believe in eavesdropping on other people's conversations. Juditha's business was her own whether they'd slept together or not. He'd call her later. He dressed quickly and wrote a note for Juditha which he propped up against a pillow on the unmade bed.

Outside, the black of the Navigator could just barely be seen under a mound of snow that had eaten smaller vehicles whole. Mike chipped through ice to open the hatch, grabbed his small snow shovel and dug out the truck at a speed only a big man could muster and pulled off like a bulldozer through the blinding whiteness. His hands gripped the steering wheel as awareness of the reality of work crept back into his conscience. As he had feared, the blizzard had brought with it another death. He had to do what he could to prevent yet another that might even be remotely connected to Persy Pritchard. No more bullshitting.

Mike's black Navigator wound its way around Dupont Circle, paused at a traffic light, turned right onto Massachusetts Avenue and two blocks down, made a left onto 16th Street. Several cars behind, a metallic gray Trooper also spun its way around the Circle, turned quickly onto Massachusetts and followed with a left onto 16th, carefully keeping just enough distance to remain undetected. Wearing a black knit hat and sunglasses Rick Venable grinned. That black bastard was about to wish he'd never joined the force. He'd waited long enough to shut him up.

*   *   *

MIKE TIED UP THE IDLE CHIT-CHAT HE'D HAD WITH THE officer standing guard at the apartment on 12th Street where Persy Pritchard had lived. He pushed past the yellow tape across the door warning against entry, and entered the apartment, now silent following a police search by Mike's partner and a few uniformed officers. *He'd been paged late on that one too.* He walked to the small kitchen and noticed that the trash had been rifled through, but had not been removed. The odor permeated the entire apartment. Mike made his way through the living room, stepping over files and assorted papers tossed across the floor. He made a mental note to read through the material on the floor later and continued back toward the bedroom.

Upon entering the bedroom, Mike spotted bottles of alcohol on the bed, but looked around to see an otherwise meticulously well-kept room. Everything seemed to have its place. The neatness of the clothes in the closet resembled a department store display and the shoes were lined up military fashion according to color and type. *Damn, this brother was a neat-ass dude,* Mike thought, shaking his head in subtle amusement. *This shit is almost too orderly.* The closet continued to draw his attention. It hadn't been tampered with. All the suits were still hung carefully on hangers with precise spacing between each one.

Mike searched between the suits, knocking a few pairs of shoes out of place. His eyes leapt to several brown taped boxes on the shelf above the clothes. *Apparently, Venable hadn't deemed the closet too key to his search of the apartment,* Mike thought, as he pulled two of the boxes down for further examination. He paused, hearing the familiar voice of his partner in the hall just outside the apartment. *Damn.* He hurried his search of the first box. He didn't need long. Photos with familiar faces, a journal referencing key names along with major criminal allegations and a couple of newspaper articles grabbed his attention immediately.

Mike picked up the box as he heard the voices drift off into the distance. He peeked through a crack in the window blind just long enough to see Venable pacing angrily on the sidewalk below. His partner whipped out his cell phone and began to walk back toward the apartment building's entrance.

Mike darted to the door, peered out into an empty hallway and made a quick run for the stairwell in the hopes that Venable would choose the elevator. He ran down the steps hoping to God that he'd taken the right route to get out of the building without confronting his partner.

"Hey, Detective James, you can't take that!" yelled the uniformed officer as Mike pushed his way past in the lobby. He made a bee-line to his truck. He pulled out his keys with one hand while balancing the box with the other. He cursed, fighting with the key in the lock, throwing off his grasp of the box. The key clicked in the lock just as a newspaper photo slid out of the box and onto the ground. He threw open the door and grabbed the photo to throw it inside. For a second that seemed like an eternity he froze and stared at it. *Blasingame. You goddam twisted sonuvabitch!*

27

Ben's Chili Bowl was an institution on U Street in the heart of Washington's "black Broadway." The intersection at 14th and U Streets had served as the heart of Washington's black renaissance in the arts for decades in the early part of the century, had fallen victim to the angry riots of the 1960s and had lain dormant for years, a broken and bitter memory of the fires that had ripped through its core. Prostitutes and drug dealers had ruled the alleyways and sidewalks of the neighborhood. In the late eighties, the city began bringing life back to the area with the construction of the Reeves Municipal Center and a slow resurgence in new enterprise. Now, funky dance clubs, black-owned bookstores, and chic little restaurants of every flavor and fortune lined the main streets of what was fast becoming a popular district for both business and pleasure.

Rachel loved hanging out at the U Street clubs and never thought she'd find herself back here as a frightened suspect in a homicide case. Dancing to the pulsating rhythms at Zora's had helped her to release the tensions of long, hard days at work that seemed as if they'd never end. Rachel stood across the street from Zora's on 14th Street, dressed in a pair of Phyllis' Timberland boots, a brown wool coat, knitted black hat and patterned scarf, holding her shoulder bag and staring longingly at the bright white neon sign that hung in the window of her favorite haunt. She wanted to mix in with the rest of the buppie crowd paying ten dollars and showing IDs to have a chance to get their groove on.

She stepped away from the bus stop and walked carefully over the snow in the direction of Ben's Chili Bowl. A twinge of anxiety tore through her as a squad car drove past slowly and disappeared down U Street. She hurried her pace and stared straight ahead. She had spent the day tucked away in the upstairs bedroom while Phyllis and her mother dealt with the authorities, went down to the morgue to identify her uncle's body and tried to begin making arrangements for a burial of some sort. Phyllis hadn't been in any shape to come with her on the Metro bus ride.

Rachel looked up at the worn red sign that had marked Ben Ali's famous house of chili for nearly thirty years. She stepped inside, bumped hastily by Mayor Grace, who, though he knew Rachel from his visits to the Congressman's office, didn't appear to recognize the woman as he rushed past on his way out of one of his favorite eating spots to a waiting black, Lincoln Towncar. Rachel was relieved to be ignored by other patrons, mostly older men loud talking about politics and sports, and walked to a crooked booth near the back where she hastily took a seat facing the front door. She looked around at the faces at other tables and at the bar. The detective hadn't arrived.

"Hey there, young lady, you gone order something?" A bald-headed, dark-skinned man with a moustache like twisted barbed wire looked over at her from behind the counter. "You gon' need to order somethin,' sweetheart, if you gon' stay." Rachel stared up at the wall menu and ordered a chili dog and a Coke. The strong smell of barbecued pork, chili and hot grease wafted through the overheated air. She removed her hat and entangled her fingers in the knitting while nervously waiting for Detective James to show.

"Well, hello there." A voice from behind startled her. A football-player sized man walked around and sat down across from her and pulled at his belt. He lifted up a gold shield and placed it on the table in front of her. He smiled, more to allay his own anxiety than to ease hers.

"Detective Mike James. Let me guess. You must be Rachel." She took a glance around the eatery, expecting what she didn't know.

"Yeah…that's me. I wouldn't mind being somebody else right about now though." Detective James was starkly different from what she'd imagined. He was much better looking and had gentle dark brown eyes. She had made him out to be a middle-aged man with a beer belly, bad skin and dark wrinkles around his eyes. Too much TV, she thought. He seemed nice enough.

"Are you ready to tell to me about the connection between Pritchard and Derrickson? I'm all ears." Rachel let go of the knit cap, reached into her shoulder bag, pulled out a thick manilla envelope and handed it across the table to Mike.

"Open it. I've written down everything I know and some stuff that I'm just guessing about for lack of further information. None of it is pretty." Mike pulled out Rachel's handwritten note, skimmed it quickly, grasped at his goatee and looked up at the attractive woman. She wore no make up and had her wavy black hair pulled back into a bun at the nape of neck.

"You can't be serious…Congressman Ray Jackson, Jr.?"

"Um hmm, take a look at the rest of it. The only thing missing is the face in this photo here," Rachel mentioned, pointing at the hole one of the photos. "You've got to find out whose face is missing. He could be the link to tie it all together. He could be the one responsible for Persy and Thad being dead." Mike examined the notes, photos, news clippings and Congressional bill copies. Rachel handed him a hand-held cassette player she'd borrowed from Phyllis and pointed at the tapes. Rachel got up and walked to the counter to pick up her chili dog and canned soda. She had no appetite and set the food aside. "Oh, shit," he uttered after fifteen minutes of reading, listening and silent contemplation. "Oh, shit."

"Now do you see why I couldn't just stroll in to talk to the police? There's no way in hell I wanted to say anything bad about my boss unless I knew for sure it was all true."

"Yeah, I'll be goddammed if I don't know exactly how you feel," Mike offered, thinking about the uninviting stares he had gotten from Venable and Gravino when he'd walked in on them Friday morning. His mind was spinning with the revelations. Some of the information Rachel had given him answered questions that had worked him into a frazzle all day. "But there's more to this than you think. I don't think Jackson was responsible for those deaths, at least not the ones that have occurred this week. But…I…damn, I'm gonna hafta get you outta here. I need to take a quick leak and we're out, okay? Don't worry, this is gonna all be over soon." Something in his eyes let her know it would. He placed his enormous hand on her small one, hesitated slightly at the soft touch of her skin and got up and retreated into the dingy men's room. Her heart rate slowed a bit. She gathered the papers and cassettes and stuffed everything back into the envelope and put it back into her bag. Rachel picked up the gold shield, rubbed her fingers over the texture of the badge and checked the name on the inside. Michael Walter James— Homicide Division. The man had three first names. She took a deep breath and waited for him to return.

A white cop walked in through the glass door, nodded at the man behind the counter and took a seat on a stool at the bar. Rachel's pulse ricocheted through her body. She picked up the chili dog, looked down at the table and prayed. The officer traded barbs with the man on the grill, spun on the stool and walked directly toward Rachel in well-paced, premeditated steps. He drew a gun before she could take another breath.

"Rachel Mooreshelton, I want you to stand slowly and come with me."

*   *   *

MIKE DROPPED AN ASPIRIN IN AN ATTEMPT TO STAVE off a migraine that was coming at him fast. The left side of his head throbbed and the contents in his stomach had begun to sway. He had joined the force to put the bad guys away, but damn, he wasn't prepared for this shit. He had a sudden urge to call Marcus. He had left him at his parents' house for the second night in a row, something he very rarely did. He missed his son. They had missed their Saturday morning ritual of cartoons and Fruit Loops. And Marcus' Friday night superbath—a full hour of suds, plastic space ships, Power Ranger dolls and water guns in which Mike sometimes got as wet as Marcus. Instinctively, he clutched at his belt for his shield, only to remember he'd left on the table near Rachel's arm. *I'm gonna have to bring the Feds in on this. I can't protect this woman by myself. No heroics, man. Just do whatchu got to do to keep her safe.*

Mike opened the door to the men's room. The cop held a gun to Rachel's head as she stood and stepped away from the booth. The restaurant's six other patrons had all stopped eating and talking to hold their breaths. Mike, with fury in his eyes, moved toward the cop who turned the gun on him and held it steady. The cop's lip twitched as he sneered at Mike.

"You had to keep digging into shit that was none of your *goddam* concern. I tried to tell you to let me do my fucking job, but you had to try to play hero to the people. Don't you take another step!" Mike's heart stopped and blind impulse took hold of him.

"Rick, man, don't do this! Let her go!"

"You had to be a nosey-ass-black-motherfuckin' rookie who didn't know how to look the other way!" Mike charged forward like a bull with a spur dug into his side.

"Ven, don't—" An explosion of gunpower erupted and tore into the left side of Mike's upper abdomen. His brain fought to comprehend what had happened as his huge body was thrown cattycorner by the impact. He lay semi-conscious on the dusty floor. With his right eye, he could just barely make out the image of Rachel fleeing the restaurant with Rick Venable on her heels. Everything grew cloudy. The last thing his mind could grip was the image of Marcus at daycare, his big eyes lit up like Christmas lights. *"You the man, Daddy. You the man."*

28

Rachel's first reaction was to run like hell as soon as the shot was fired. She knew the crazy cop would probably pull the gun on her next. The Timberland boots thumped through the snow as she brushed past those who had been bold enough to brave the bad weather. The snow was slippery, even under the thick mountain-ready boots she'd borrowed, and hindered her speed. If she fell, she was dead.

Rachel hit the corner of U and 13th Streets, darted to the right down 13th and fled down an alley where the trash from McDonald's and several bars had awaited pick-up for two weeks due to the latest city budget crisis. Looking behind her, she coughed and sputtered with exhaustion and fear as she scrambled down the alley. She could hear police sirens growing closer and what she believed to be the footsteps of the officer behind her in the dim light. She caught her breath and made a sharp turn down a narrow back access street, where stray cars were parked illegally and uncleared snow made her attempt at escape arduous. She ran for what seemed like an eternity, gasping for air in the cold.

The end of the access street opened back out into what she guessed was 14th Street. She ran toward the light and the passing four-by-fours she could see several feet ahead. Looking straight ahead, she made one leap to race across the street to a cab idling in front of the community theatre. Somewhere from the side, someone grabbed her arm and yanked her back into the alley. She screamed out at the force of the pull, knowing she was about to come face to face with the cop who would put a bullet in her head. She thought she recognized the sleek black,

Lincoln Towncar sitting at the curb, its engine still idling. Was it Mayor Grace's car? Or maybe—?

She looked back to see a face that, from her childhood in Baltimore, had symbolized integrity and trust and strength and courage. She whimpered, helpless against his grip and cowered as shock and sadness overtook her.

"Congressman Jackson, please, I didn't—" The raisin-brown face of the man portrayed a combination of disappointment and sorrow. His large body overwhelmed her tiny frame. A small gun barrel was aimed straight between her eyes as the Congressman backed her into the darkened back entry of a building off the alley.

"Rachel, you should have just let sleeping dogs lie. It would have all come apart sooner or later, but you should have never pried into this kind of thing. You have no idea what a horrible secret this has been to keep, the years I've spent wondering when all of this was going to end, not knowing—" The Congressman jerked to look behind him at the sound of a homeless man struggling past. He shoved Rachel inside the building and partially closed the door. Still scrambling to make sense of the past few hectic moments, Rachel edged backward with her hands stiffly at her side, her eyes darting around the dully lit storage room.

"Why are you doing this Congressman? Why come after *me*? I'm not the one who shot three people trying to rob a bank," Rachel cried, her voice stinging with accusation. "I had nothing to do with that! Why are you coming after me?" Her teary eyes searched his face for understanding. The wail of the police sirens grew louder as the seconds ticked by.

The Congressman's voice lowered to a tentative whisper. His words came quickly. His tone was desperate. "You'll never understand what it's been like hiding from what I did. I never meant to hurt anyone—never. It was never supposed to happen like that. All I wanted to do was get some money, money that white people owed us for everything they'd put us through. I just wanted money that would help keep the Panthers' school and free breakfast programs going. That's all I wanted to do. We were on the verge of having to shut them both down 'cause we were runnin' out of money. I never wanted to kill those people. It just went down the wrong way, and I couldn't seem to—to—stop it. I was so angry. And it all happened so fast. And then, they were just dead. I have relived that day in my mind almost every waking moment for over twenty years. It never should have gone down that way."

"But Congressman, why are you holding a gun to my head? I've been there for you for the past four years. I supported you. I admired you. I looked up to you just like thousands of other people have. I *believed* in you. Are you going to kill me too?" Rachel dropped to her knees, not to plead for her life, but from sheer panic and fatigue and disappointment.

"I never wanted anybody to be afraid of me, Rachel," the Congressman whispered, a look of longing in his eyes, now as teary as his captive's. "This is not how I wanted things to be. I convinced a group of people, a group of friends, to rob that bank, and they believed in me enough to think we could pull it off. I have begged for forgiveness for what I did, and I'll keep begging God to forgive me. But, Rachel, those times were different. I did a lot of foolish things, some brave things, some cowardly things. Black people didn't have nothing back then— '*nothin*'," he exclaimed, waving the barrel of the gun randomly.

"That black beret and that leather jacket and those guns made me feel like I was on top of the world—like I was a *man*." Rachel could feel his hot breath on her face as he moved closer to her. "Like I could be one of those who could force change—could make white people treat us the way we *deserved*. Things were crazy then. I was a hot head, always mad at the world, always with a chip on my shoulder. We all felt like we'd been dealt a bad deck, and just wanted to do something, sometimes anything to make it better." He paused, listening once again over his shoulder.

Rachel stared at the floor, refusing to feel sorry for him, refusing to look him in the face. She hated him suddenly. He had the nerve to want to make her understand why he'd killed those people. There were no excuses good enough, nothing he could say that would allow her to pity him, or feel guilty for the betrayal she felt. Her stomach churned with dread over what he would do next.

"Look at me!" The Congressman breathed. Rachel jerked at the abrupt words. Overwhelmed, she started to cry.

"Look at me!" he said again. Rachel's eyes peered upward. The sirens screamed in her ears. "I can't live this lie anymore," Congressman Jackson cried out. His hands shook as his left hand wiped the tears away from his face. "I can't face all those people who'll look at me on TV tomorrow. Tonight, I wanted to stop you from, from telling them about me. I didn't think I could let you do it, but, I, I, I can't hurt you." A look of relief washed suddenly over his face. He grabbed her arm with one hand and reached toward her slowly, gun in in the other. "It's all finally over. I—" *Click, click!*

The barrel of a large gun, thrust from behind, touched Ray Jackson's temple. Rachel could hear rough coughing as a familiar face appeared just to the side of the Congressman's right shoulder.

"Drop it now!" The Congressman released the weapon. It landed heavily on the concrete floor. "Congressman, you're under arrest for the 1972 murders of Janet Polasky, Russell Williams and Queenie Wasserman," Mike shouted in a gravelly voice filled with exhaustion. Mike limped around the man, holding his side with one hand and the gun in the other. "Let go of her arm and step away! Turn and walk forward. You have the right to remain silent. Anything you say—" As the three exited the doorway, shots rang out nearby. Rachel could hear several sets of feet racing toward them and shouting voices from the dark reaches of the alley.

"Stop right there, Detective Venable! Drop it!" Three uniformed officers surrounded Rick Venable in a matter of seconds. Rachel heard a gun clank against a clearing in the snow. "Don't move!" Eight squad cars descended upon the scene in mere moments while Rachel stood shaking, clasping her shoulder bag in shock.

After several minutes spun by, two officers escorted Rachel to the open passenger side door of a squad car and helped into the seat. She couldn't keep her hands from shaking. Blinking red and blue lights created a dreamlike scene as she watched an injured Mike James lead the Congressman, his hands cuffed behind his back, to a white District police cruiser. A confused crowd gathered behind a human barrier of cops, witnessing one of Washington's most recognizable faces being led away, his head hung low. Rick Venable stewed in the rear seat of a squad car, surrounded by members of the force.

The man who'd been a role model to her and thousands of other Americans had finally been brought to justice after twenty-five years above suspicion. Rachel rested her head against the seat and closed her eyes. There were no more tears to shed.

*   *   *

MIKE HELD HIS SIDE. THE DAMN BASTARD. HE WANTED TO RIP Venable's heart from his chest and set it on fire. He was lightheaded from the pain of the slug that had ripped partially through his bullet-proof vest, leaving his body excruciatingly sore. Despite his colleagues' assurances that they'd handle things from there and stern promptings to let the medics take him to the hospital, Mike refused to sit or rest while men in blue questioned witnesses and collected the weapons for evidence.

Mike willfully declined to offer any information to the lieutenant on the scene until Geoffrey Moyer, assistant director of the FBI, arrived. Mike had summoned the FBI because he knew Chief Draper would try his best to sabotage the impending investigation into crimes that had only begun to be unearthed.

Mike made a call to his mother to let her know he was alright and not to be alarmed by news reports that would hit the airwaves within a matter of minutes.

The curbside throng of mostly black onlookers shouted angry epithets at the cops, some throwing bottles and debris at the sight of one of their heroes being detained in the cruiser. Reinforcements were brought in to secure the area. Mike limped as he walked to the black-and-white where Rachel sat and placed his hand on hers. The warmth of his hand gave her a sense of security.

"Are you okay?" he asked, his breath growing shallower.

"Yeah, I'll be okay. Jackson's going to jail, isn't he?"

"Yep, I think it would be safe to say that our mighty Congressman will be lucky if he doesn't get the death penalty. Goddam waste of admiration been spent on that man. But Rachel, it's not over. We're gonna need you to work with the FBI over the next couple of days to pull together the rest of what we'll need for the grand jury indictments." Rachel turned to stare at the detective who'd saved her life and whose hand was warm and soft and comforting.

"What do you mean *indictments*?"

"You wouldn't believe me if I told you."

"Detective James, a respected black Congressman is responsible for the deaths of three people. My boss *killed* people and lied to people all over this country. I think I'd believe anything you told me."

29

The clinking of tableware and the busy chatter of voices resonated throughout the intimate executive diningroom at the Mayflower Hotel. A brightly-lit, huge, spruce pine Christmas tree, decorated with delicate antique porcelain ornaments of angels and choirboys, golden satin bows, garland and strings of red thistleberries stood proudly near the lectern as the trademark of the Heritage Council's exclusive annual Christmas Day brunch. While families around the Washington Beltway scuttled in fuzzy slippers through houses smelling of ginger and cinnamon, opened Christmas gifts around a tree with excitable children, and treasured a day of quality time to reconnect with their loved ones, a select group of conservatives from across the city left that all behind to politick and close ranks at Lindy Hobbson's Heritage Brunch.

The mistress of ceremonies cleared her throat ceremoniously to lower the cheerful dialogue. She looked out and smiled at the sea of important pale, rosy-cheeked faces. Senators, House Members, business tycoons, lobbyists, lawyers, and executive directors of other conservative think tanks interrupted talk about the federal budget, the election year ahead and the shocking arrest of long-time Democratic stalwart, Ray Jackson, Jr.

Certainly, many of them had dipped into annuity funds and charitable contributions, falsified with staff budgets and accepted an illegal thousand dollars in PAC monies here and there to line their pockets over the years. Some of their colleagues had even seen a little white-collar jail time for falsifying financial disclosure statements, tax evasion, racketeering and even bribery. But no one in recent memory from amongst their ranks of power had ever taken a fall for murder. They rejoiced privately, of course, that the Democrats would suffer clearly one of the worst scandals in American political history and were giddy thinking about the certainty of victory in November.

The dainty MC tapped a sterling silver spoon against a crystal goblet and cleared her throat once more. Waiters with foreign accents, crisp white tuxedo jackets and starched black pants took care to quietly cater to the elite group.

"Good afternoon Heritage friends. For those of you who haven't had the opportunity to join us in past years, my name is Lindy Dale Hobbson. My husband is retired Senator Carlisle Hobbson, Chairman of the Heritage Council," Lindy Hobbson said gesturing to a gray-haired gentleman seated next to the podium. "and we are so happy that you have taken time away from family and friends to join us this Christmas Day for a little food and frolic."

"On Christmas Day every year for the past fifteen years we have rec-ognized colleagues who inspire trust and who aspire to guide a shared agenda. We are so delighted to have with us this afternoon a man who has led the conservative revolution in the Congress with strength of conviction and a love for his God and his country. Speaker of the House William Thurston Blasingame who we all know as just Bill. Bill, why don't you come on up here and let me give you a hug?" Lindy Hobbson's thin, sun-spotted arms patted Bill Blasingame on the shoul-ders in a hearty half hug. She stepped to the side and took a seat next to her aging husband, whose bristly arched brows showed his pleasure at seeing his old friend at the podium.

"Well, Merry Christmas!" trumpeted a chipper Bill Blasingame with the glowing charisma that had propelled him to party leadership. His straight white teeth gleamed as he broke out into a proud grin at the sight of cronies from past and present in the seventy-odd guest audi-ence. Senator Jim McAllister, Chairman of the Senate Banking

Committee, Jay Arnold Rorbacher, president of Virginia's largest firearm manufacturer, Glen Redding, the Majority Leader of the House, Harvey Silowicz, former President Rowland's White House Budget Director, Sally Renoit, his tireless legislative director and the rest of his loyal staff smiled back. He did miss the presence of Thaddeus Derrickson, one of his trusted aides. *Poor boy, such a misfortune,* he'd uttered to several colleagues over the days since the young man's untimely death. But it was Christmas, time to look forward to the good times ahead for the Party. At sixty-two, the man reigned over the Congressional House agenda, was envied by others and admired by right-wing masses across the country.

Blasingame introduced his lovely bride Allison, sitting to his left, and enjoyed the several seconds of attention that her unique beauty always commanded. In addressing his colleagues, Blasingame rejoiced in the resurgence of the right-wing agenda and pledged his continued devotion to the ultra conservative blue-print to recapture the White House. At the end of his remarks, Blasingame raised his crystal water goblet, in unison with those sitting before him. Christmas Day sunlight shone through the curtained windows, and bounced off the dozens of air-bound crystal goblets, creating dancing sun shadows on the ceiling, floor and surrounding walls. The room broke out into enthusiastic chit-chat once again.

Five stern-looking men pushed their way through the double doors and into the dining room, causing everyone present to spin around, wondering what on earth was going on. Detective Mike James stood alongside one of the men as the three others made their way to the podium and surrounded the Speaker, whose stunned face reflected confusion and arrogant disbelief.

FBI Assistant Director Geoffrey Moyer handed bound papers to the Speaker and motioned for the deputies to move in closer.

"William Thurston Blasingame, under federal authority, you are charged with ten counts of bribery in connection with confiscated monies under the custody of the D.C. Metro Police Department and the Police Department of the Commonwealth of Virginia; two counts of conspiracy; five counts of illegal campaign reporting; one count of accessory to murder for the death of Gary Friedrich, and two counts of first degree murder in the deaths of Persuvius Pritchard and Thaddeus Derrickson."

The whole room let out a loud solitary gasp, followed by whispers and coughs. Lindy Hobbson fainted, Senator McAllister's walking cane dropped to the floor and Allison Blasingame stared at the floor. All eyes fell on the Speaker of the House.

"This is preposterous!" thundered Blasingame, gritting his teeth and daring the deputies to touch him. "What in hell's name is this about? I'll sue the whole goddam Bureau for this, you idiot!"

"Mr. Blasingame, I must advise you that you have the right to remain silent. You may forfeit that right at your own—"

"Preposterous!" he yelled again, struggling against the grip of the deputies. "You can't touch me! You can't do this to me! You bastard!" Blasingame turned on his heels and directed fiery eyes at the woman at his side. He nearly choked on the venom in his throat.

"You deceitful bitch!" he hissed. All eyes shifted to the woman who was the object of his ugly words.

Mike walked around the dais in response to the bewildered look on Allison Blasingame's cafe au lait face. He grabbed her arm and began to lead her out of the room behind her husband. He stared at the shock in her maple-syrup brown eyes, and almost felt sorry for the woman for all she'd been through in the last two and a half decades. And the revenge she'd wanted so badly to get by marrying her father's biggest political enemy.

"Gail Allison Ford Blasingame," he uttered softly. The young woman looked up at Mike, for several seconds, before her eyes fell back to the floor in defeat. Tragedy had come full circle.

30

Ray Jackson Jr. held his solid brown hands firmly together and stared out the black bars of the window of a private six-by-eight foot cell at the D.C. jail. He'd been informed by his attorney that he'd be extradited that afternoon to San Francisco to await a trial that had been a long time in coming. The FBI had been abuzz all week with activity, putting all the pieces of the puzzle together.

Jackson's face, known and cheered by black people in South Central, Philly, Brooklyn, New Orleans, Miami and Atlanta, was pained. Black parents, from poor to rich taught their babies that they could grow up to be like Congressman Raymond Jackson, Jr. Held him up as a shining example of what a black man could do with his life. "Baby, you shake that man's hand. Maybe it'll rub off on you." But they didn't really want their babies to be like Ray Jackson. Not like the man under the stolen name.

The force of the falling wind chill forced the stars and stripes of the flag out in the front courtyard to snap at him violently as if the American flag itself was mocking a man who had sold his soul to the devil himself to redeem himself in the eyes of his people. Even if they had never known why he needed their redemption. His people meant everything to him and always had. From his days as a freedom fighter in southern Georgia and his more militant years as one in an ultra radical sub-set of the Black Panther in California, to more sober days as a community activist in the angry city streets of poor Atlanta, his love for his people had driven his actions, good *and* bad.

He'd hated their system. The white man had built up his political institutions to keep the black man out. Gave him the vote, but tried to keep him from using it. So he'd joined their system with hate in his heart and blood on his hands, to do his work from the inside. Over the years, though, something in him had changed. They'd accepted him. Gave him a home in their hallowed halls, in their legislative chamber, and in their back rooms. And the hate had dissolved. And the hunger had disappeared. And now, only guilt consumed him. Guilt that all the ballot boxes, PAC donations, standing ovations and award ceremonies in the world couldn't wash away.

The strong-willed man closed his eyes in meditation and rested his head against the back of the unforgiving concrete wall. Campaign after campaign, poll after poll and through one reporter's indepth story after another, he had waited. In the beginning he had been so afraid of being caught that he didn't sleep nights, for months at a time. Then he had been wary. But in the past several years, he had just waited. It would all somehow come to an end. He'd hidden so long from the truth that sometimes he actually believed that the horrified screams and the ear-splitting gunshots and the look in Queenie's eyes when she took her last breath were figments of a faltering imagination.

Persy Pritchard's death had been his fault. Thad Derrickson's death had been his fault. Whether he had actually pulled the trigger or not, more innocent people had died because of the wrong he'd done as an arrogant, hate-filled young brother who acted way outside of anything the Panthers would have sanctioned.

They had watched Persy for months. Ray/Anthony had tried to convince Cleavon and Juditha that Persy was harmless. He had entrusted his old friends with his secret many years ago and they had protected him at all costs. A paranoid Cleavon Grace had quieted Jet Strong, the only surviving gunman, for fear he'd eventually open his mouth. Grace had even cut his own face off an old photo of Jackson with him and Queenie Wasserman as insurance against Jackson's secret ever being traced back to him in any way. And a power-hungry Juditha had stood by and watched the two men die. Though she never saw the face of the man who had snuffed out Thad Derrickson, she'd witnessed a man *and* a woman fleeing the apartment at different times, as she sat in her car surveilling the building. Getting into Jackson's office the night before Persy had been killed hadn't been any easy feat either, and Jackson had cursed her for sneaking in. Out of fear, they'd all gotten sloppy. But felt they were above all suspicion. Too high to be reached.

They'd blamed each other for Persy's murder, only to find out that Blasingame had taken him out. Blasingame, *of all people*. And Gail. He'd thought of his little girl often but had known early on after the shooting that he could never risk contacting her. The poor girl's bitterness had eaten at her from the time she was a tiny child. He had taken her mama away, and with her any chance at a normal life. He'd destroyed so many people's lives under his own twisted guise of helping others.

"All right, Congressman, time to go," shouted a burly, blue-black prison guard. The man pushed a button at the end of a short hallway and a thick metal door with a bullet-proof glass window slid open. The guard sauntered through the door and down the short corridor to the cell housing Jackson/Ford. A powerful sense of relief washed over him. It was all over. Time to face the fat lady, who was singing louder than she had in over twenty years.

"I'll never believe what they pinnin' on you, Congressman," offered the guard loudly, leading his prisoner through the hallway. "You know they always got some conspiracy against the black man. They gone always bring the black man down. I know it was a set up, man. But brother, I'll be prayin' for you." The Congressman stared at the man and stopped walking.

"There's no conspiracy here, my brother. Don't waste your prayer on me," he articulated sternly. "God doesn't want to hear my name." Stunned, the guard hung his head low and shook it from side-to-side with skepticism.

Epilogue

"Catch, little man!"

Mike wiped sweat from the back of his neck and lightly tossed his old high school football a few feet away into Marcus' open arms. It fell through the boy's chubby brown arms. His small hands picked up the ball and threw it back in the air. But instead of his Dad catching it, the worn football flipped behind the little boy and rolled down the hill adjacent to the Washington Monument. Father and son chased after it and landed in a human ball at the bottom of the hill, laughing as the hot August sunshine and famous Washington humidity brought beads of perspiration to their faces. Mike held the boy in his arms and looked up to the sky, the Monument bouncing recklessly in the background. He winced for a moment, having rolled onto the tender spot where the bullet had nearly pierced through his bullet proof vest after being shot at point-blank range. Though he hadn't sustained any permanent damage the soreness still woke him up at night if he rolled in his sleep.

After the trials, Mike had been offered a big-money investigative position with the FBI, as well as partnerships with private investigation agencies in L.A. and Boston. The FBI had liked his attitude, his honesty and his courage in breaking the secrets behind the police department thefts and guns-for-money scam that put Venable, Gravino and Draper behind bars. He'd lain awake nights thinking of what he could do with the extra money. Buy a big house out in the suburbs. Take a big vacation every year to some tropical paradise hand-in-hand with a beautiful woman the color of the darkest sand. Buy his mother the new car she'd wanted for years. But the new job would have also required him to be away for weeks at a time, trailing suspects and evidence, and missing too much time with his son. The District was his home and it was that city he wanted to police. He was gonna take care of home. So, he'd turned it down. He'd turned them all down for a not-so-shabby promotion in D.C. Metro.

The FBI had overlooked his indiscretion with Juditha Hurley, who kissed and told about their evening together, hoping to bring him down with her. Her eyes had burned holes through him while he sat in the witness stand, their night of steamy passion long behind. They'd arrested her and Mayor Grace, her on accessory to murder charges and him on one count of murder in the first degree for choking a delirious Jet Strong to death. In a thorough search of Strong's basement apartment, the FBI uncovered documents and old photos that brought enough to light, in combination with Persy's box of goodies, to bring in guilty verdicts in Hurley's and Grace's trials by juries weighted heavily with black jurors. Their peers had delivered justice.

The spotlight of his role in exposing the widespread scandal involving the Congressman, the Speaker and the Mayor gave Mike his fifteen minutes of celebrity that brought with it movie and book offers and fine women knocking at his door. The attention was okay for the months before the trials but he tired of it rather quickly, choosing to decline additional talk show interviews to get back to a private life with his family.

He and Rachel had both testified in the five-month trial of Anthony Leon Ford aka Ray Jackson, Jr. and the three-month trial of dethroned Mayor Cleavon Grace. Though the Blasingame murder trial was still ongoing after four months, Mike had finally completed his time on the stand. With so many counts against him, the Blasingame prosecution had to dig through a tangled web of crime that would reportedly go on for as long as another year. Blasingame and several high-ranking police officials in D.C. and Virginia, conspiring also with two major Virginia-based gun magnates, had traded legislation that would help keep guns on the streets for campaign contributions and bribes from profits of sales of guns stolen from the property division. Thousands of dollars stolen from the property division had also been laundered and donated to Blasingame's campaign coffers. Monies had been wired into several bank accounts under the name of a Blasingame political action committee handled by an executive at Rosewood & Hall. When Gary Friedrich had decided two years before that he wanted nothing more to do with the scam, he'd been promptly eliminated. With the lists that the telephone company had provided, Mike had seen four calls from Blasingame's office in the Capitol Building to Jackson's at the same time and on the same day Rachel had been there alone. Blasingame had behaved like the arrogant, self-consumed rogue Mike had always believed him to be, making childish crank calls to scare Persy. Mike figured that Blasingame had believed himself invincible, so high up nobody would ever point a finger at him, for the calls or for the guns-for-money scam. He'd had the thrill of a lifetime watching that bastard being carted out of that fancy hotel before all of his fancy friends—in hand cuffs. *Greedy bigot sonuvabitch.*

He'd tried to stay in touch with Rachel over the past several months. She was the kind of woman he wanted to get to know better. She had the kind of integrity and gorgeous good looks he wanted to slide a wedding ring on one day. But they'd both been jostled around so much in the past nine months that he understood if she needed some time to herself. He could wait. He had all the time in the world.

*　　　*　　　*

HER ARMS LOADED DOWN WITH BRAND NEW TEXTBOOKS, Phyllis stood up from her spot on the concrete steps of Founder's Library and walked across the yard toward Blackburn Center. Classes at Howard had begun the day before and she still had an extra twenty minutes to kill before her Constitutional Law class. A bustle of students of every shade of brown walked, strolled, strutted and ran back and forth in all directions, talking, shouting, laughing and meditating quietly. Dressed in a denim skirt, white sleeveless cotton blouse and leather sandals, and sporting a new short bob of a cut that lingered behind her ears, Phyllis groped at her book bag to hold it steady on her back and checked her change for the call she wanted to make to Rachel.

She and Rachel had tried to stay as closely in touch as possible since the Congressman's arrest. The office staff had scattered to new jobs, some in Washington and some not. And Phyllis found herself caught in the middle, trying to figure out what to do next and how to pay the bills. One week to the day after Congressman Jackson had been indicted, Phyllis had suffered a painful miscarriage that had added to the confusion she'd already felt. She and her mother Pearl continued to grieve for Uncle Jet, but the days were becoming easier to get through without his cussing, spitting and Bible-quoting.

They learned a lot about the mysterious man who'd returned from California in '73. As the FBI soon uncovered, Jet had served as one of four gunmen and had witnessed the unintended murders. The jungles of Vietnam had already done a number on his sanity and the guilt of watching two innocent people die seemed to have been the last straw. His mind had snapped. To prevent Jet from ever going to the police, Cleavon Grace had forwarded any incriminating documents to Jet, in whose room they were discovered later by the FBI. Through intimidation, Grace had kept the man quiet.

When an NBC producer approached Phyllis about a made-for-TV movie deal in early summer, she and her mother had agreed to it for an undisclosed sum that would guarantee her education at Howard and give her and Pearl enough money to buy a bigger house closer to Rock Creek Park. Hell, Jackson had sold his soul for power and influence. She had sold a story to guarantee her future. Not a bad deal, she figured. *Who the hell wouldn't have?*

"Hey pretty lady," whispered a tall glass of water walking her way. "How you doin'?" Pleasantly surprised by the attention and drawn in by his admiring gaze, Phyllis paused for a moment to talk, but then thought better of it. She had plenty of time to have a man. It was time for Phyllis to concentrate on *Phyllis* and a degree in pre-law. The past year had changed her mind about communications. She wanted to work for people like Jet who couldn't help themselves. In her mind's eye, she could see the drug corners of Kennedy Street, her young friends with two and three babies and eviction notices evaporate into little particles of dust that she could place in her hand and blow away. Things were lookin' up and God was on her side.

*   *   *

RACHEL STARED AT THE HEADLINES ON THE POST'S FRONT PAGE. *Blasingame Declines to Testify in Second Most Watched Murder Trial of the Century, Interim D.C. Police Chief Steps Aside for New Head—Harris, PPF Suffers Under Factional Infighting over Appointment of New Executive Director, Former Black Panthers Sue Post for False Reporting in Jackson Case.* Related stories had consumed the headlines all year, nearly surpassing the O.J. trial in number of headlines around the country. Rachel crossed her bare cocoa-brown legs and threw the paper on the large bleached maple desk of her office. The air conditioner kept the stifling late summer heat on the other side of the windows. She'd asked the receptionist, Tanya, to hold her calls for the next few minutes so she could return some important calls of her own.

She'd replaced her long braids with bold Senegalese twists that gave her an unabashedly regal look. Policy briefings were scattered across her desk in a fashion that she'd become accustomed to in her first two months as Congresswoman Paulette Freeman's legislative director. In

the months after Jackson's indictment, Rachel had floundered personally, no longer sure of what she wanted to do with her life. Politics made
her sick. Literally sick to her stomach at the mere thought of another
election or voter or piece of legislation.

Aside from the time spent with the authorities and involved in the
trials, she had burrowed herself in her apartment with the shades closed
and the phone ringer off. The memory of Congressman Jackson, cowed
at the defense table, had haunted her. She couldn't understand how
Anthony Ford could have been so full of hate as to have gone against the
Panthers' own rules of using weapons only to defend themselves, not
for killing innocent people, and not for robbing banks. The man had
had it all. The power. The admiration. The respect—all right in his
hands. She never wanted to hear his name again.

And Persy. Poor Persy. A tear still fell whenever Rachel thought of
how Persy must have felt when he realized that the man who was more
to him than just a boss had betrayed him. All he had wanted to do was
serve the people the best he could. When the police finally did do a
thorough sweep through his apartment, they found a sealed box that
contained his notes, more news clips and taped phone conversations
between him and Allison Blasingame. Apparently after coming across
some old photos in the Congressman's office, Persy's curiosity had been
piqued. The more he had dug into the Congressman's past, the more he
had found that didn't fit. And the more he had found that didn't fit, the
more obsessed he'd become with the whole mystery. According to the
materials in the box, Persy made a number of phone calls and even a
brief trip to Oakland, secured FBI files through a Freedom of
Information Act request and had checked birth records and talked to
high school teachers of the man named Anthony Ford to confirm that
he was indeed the man who had called himself Ray Jackson, Jr. for
nearly twenty-five years.

Persy had tracked Anthony Ford's daughter, who had been turned
over to child welfare, shuffled to relatives in Jackson, Tennessee, and

again dumped into the foster care system where she remained until the age of eighteen. Persy had apparently tracked her whereabouts to Washington all the way to the Speaker's house. Though somewhat unclear in Persy's notes, somehow the two had struck a deal that in exchange for Persy's silence about her father, Gail Allison would ferret damaging information about her husband's dirty campaign contributions to Persy, who then began to anonymously forward the information to the *Post*. And the expose on campaign corruption had been born. Venable's testimony has shed some light on what must have happened next. The Speaker discovered his wife's little ruse and set up a meeting with Persy in Folger Park on the pre-dawn morning of December nineteenth to discuss an end to the press leaks. Blasingame had shot Persy that morning because he couldn't intimidate him into keeping quiet and had given Venable the gun and the two incriminating envelopes Persy had carried to get rid of. Dorothy Huddle had also testified to seeing the Speaker in the lobby of Rachel's building the night Thad was killed. It had all finally come out. And Rachel shook her head at the thought of such arrogant crime, and how Blasingame had proceeded like business as usual through all of it.

The only other thing Rachel had managed to do while awaiting the trials was to visit her brother Yarrick in his hospital room, where the two grew closer. He had encouraged her to forgive their father for his control-driven style of loving and the cold shoulder he had turned to Yarrick in his time of need. He had learned forgiveness to gain peace of mind in the last few years of his life and shared his thoughts with Rachel. Rachel picked up the phone and paused before dialing an old familiar number—Thad's. She had finally come to grips with his death, but still forgot at times about the whole nightmare, dialing his number only to hear a Bell Atlantic recording. *Damn.*

In May, with Yarrick's encouragement and Phyllis' healthy nudge, Rachel had agreed to meet with Congresswoman Freeman about her desire to bring on a woman with conviction and honesty to direct her legislative agenda. She felt an immediate bond with the tiny four-foot-eleven giant from Los Angeles. Paulette Freeman was gutsy, direct and warm, traits that had catapulted her into office at the young age of thirty with very little money. After having Mike James do a thorough check of the woman's background, Rachel was satisfied that Paulette Freeman was just who she said she was—all ninety-eight feisty pounds of her. Rachel realized during her talk with Congresswoman Freeman that she couldn't just high-tail it and run away from politics because of the bad apples, some of them rotten to the core. The fresh, sweet green apples had to hang on to their branches long enough to push off the old and the worm-infested. She would stay and do what she did best. And try to get over the rest.

The trials had been sensational to say the least. The arrests of so many so high up and for such appalling crimes had sent tremors through local and national politics and had quickly altered voters expectations and perceptions of those who stood before them for reelection in the fall. Rachel and those involved, on both sides, had become the center of a feeding frenzy in the media, from New York to London to Tokyo. Rachel still had problems crossing the street without a microphone shoved in her face or a TV camera jockeying for a good angle. She'd hated the attention from the beginning and had tried to patiently await the hoopla to die down. She'd granted only one interview to Barbara Walters and one to Oprah, who had devoted an entire spring segment to Rachel's nightmare. The rest she turned down and prayed they'd go away. She had agreed also to an upper six-figure book deal with a major publisher only to defray the expenses of her brother's medical care.

With the phone still in hand, Rachel dialed and waited for an answer. A voice mail picked up. The man's voice was deep and soothing and stirred her heart at the thought of the feel of his warm hand on hers on that freezing night in December. Rachel left a brief message and put the phone down. She'd catch up with Mike sooner or later.

They'd joked a few times that they'd make a good pair. She was watching the law and he was watching her back. And there was still plenty of watching that needed to be done to build the people's trust back up in a system that still had too many loopholes and safeguards for those who dared to trespass.

Rachel flipped on the computer as rays of sun bounced off the top of her monitor and pulled up an important file. Congresswoman Freeman was delivering a Labor Day speech before members of the PPF and Rachel had penned it. She took one more look at her draft, printed it out and smiled. The words had come easily.

About the Author

Washington, DC native Gretchen Cook-Anderson is a public affairs professional and former Capitol Hill lobbyist who has written freelance for several magazines and teaches Japanese at Howard University. She and her husband Thomas, a high school vice principal, live in Silver Spring, Maryland. This is her first novel.

9 780595 096596